Darcy looked into Toni's eyes as another flash of lightning lit up the room. As Toni softly kissed the tears away from Darcy's eyes and cheeks, her fingertips caressed the outline of Darcy's lovely face.

Then Toni pulled her close once more. She could feel the firm fullness of Darcy's breasts against her own. Their hearts seemed to beat in rhythm as one.

They lay this way for a long time. Not moving, not speaking, drinking in the warmth between them. Then, slowly Toni raised her head. She cupped Darcy's chin in her hand and pressed her soft full mouth against Darcy's. The kiss became deeper as Darcy rose to meet Toni's lips.

ALSO BY DIANE DAVIDSON

Deadly Rendezvous

Deadly Gamble

DEADLY
Butterfly

Diane Davidson

RISING TIDE PRESS

Rising Tide Press
PO BOX 30457
Tucson, AZ 85751
520-888-1140

Printed in the United States on acid-free paper.

Publisher's note:
All characters, places, and situations in this book are fictitious, or
used fictitiously, and any resemblance to persons (living or dead) is
purely coincidental.

Cover art by Jude Ockenfels

First Printing: May 2001

Davidson, Diane
Deadly Butterfly/Diane Davidson

ISBN 1-883061-34-2

Library of Congress Control Number: 2001 088881

DEDICATION

To those who simply turned and walked away.
To true friends that never stray.
To the lover who returned to stay.
To the family so good and strong.
To time so swiftly gone.
I thank you all.

Chapter One

"I can't breathe," she gasped. "Where's mommy?"

Swallowing hard to hold back the deep sob filling her throat, Darcy pulled herself into a tight ball. Her knees pressed hard against her small chest as she slid deeper into the dark corner.

Her curly red hair lay matted and wet against her forehead and neck. Dust filled Darcy's nostrils, and the oppressive heat made her feel sick to her stomach.

"Why doesn't mommy come? I've waited so long," she whispered.

Mother had put her in the air duct outlet over half an hour ago, now all she could do was sit and peer through the metal grill that covered the entrance to her cramped prison.

With shaking hands and tear filled eyes, her mother had hurriedly removed the metal cover and gently urged Darcy to crawl inside the air duct.

She had whispered to Darcy not to move until she returned. Darcy knew something very serious was happening and this was not a game.

"Promise me you won't come out until I return." Her mother had said as she replaced the grill.

Darcy nodded yes as a whimper escaped her lips.

"Don't make a sound no matter what happens. I love you." Then her mother was gone.

A scream caught in Darcy's throat as she heard the footsteps approaching. A floorboard creaked and she held her breath. *Can't make a sound; mommy said not to make a sound.*

The steps were heavy and slow as they neared Darcy's hiding place. A huge bare foot came down inches from where she hid and paused for a moment; then, turning away, the feet moved slowly toward the bed.

The four poster feather bed sat across the room directly within Darcy's line of sight. A giant of a man was bending over it with his back toward her, as he dropped something onto the bed.

Tears began running down Darcy's small round face as she put both hands over her mouth to stop the scream before it escaped.

The man was bare from the waist up. His back was hairy and thick. Her small heart was beating so hard it felt as though it would burst through her chest, and her body was frozen with fear.

Slowly, the man straightened up. He stood motionless, his back still toward her.

At first the blur of color didn't register. Then, Darcy blinked her tear filled eyes as the blaze of bright colors began to clear and take shape. Her mouth fell open in disbelief. A bright butterfly was sitting on the man's bare shoulder.

The beauty of the butterfly startled her. It was purple, and pink, and blue, and green. It seemed to be all colors gathered into one glorious creature. It sat calmly perched on his shoulder.

She was mesmerized by the beautiful array of colors wavering in the bright light streaming in through the bedroom window. It gave Darcy a feeling of serenity. Maybe everything was going to be all right after all. *The butterfly man wouldn't hurt me,* she thought. Her eyes drank in the wonder of it as a slight smile crossed her lips.

With a sudden movement, the man turned. Darcy gasped in horror. He had no eyes! Two pieces of black coal were where his eyes should be. He cocked his head to one side, and then the other, listening. His coal eyes scanned the room, darting from corner to corner. His chest was covered with a big red circle that had long fingers running down to his waist.

He heard me. Oh mama, where are you? He heard me!

Now he was walking straight toward her. She tried to pull further back, but there was nowhere to go. Each slow, menacing step brought him closer. She was suffocating. The blood drained from her face and Darcy's body shook uncontrollably. Just inches from her the feet suddenly stopped. Darcy opened her mouth to scream, but nothing came out.

A hairy hand appeared at the grill. The long thick fingers began pulling at the thin lines of metal. Darcy's head was splitting and her breath came in short pants. The sound of her pounding heart was breaking her eardrums. She was going to die!

Screaming her way back to consciousness, Darcy fought with every fiber of her being to free herself.

The covers were wrapped around her in a tight knot. Ripping at them, she rolled from one side of the bed to the other until the sheets and blankets fell to the floor.

Sitting straight up, she began gasping for air. Her eyes were glazed and wide open. She began shivering as she slowly realized where she was. Wrapping her arms around her cold, naked body, she began rocking back and forth. With every uncontrollable sob, her head felt as though it would burst.

"Oh God, why is this happening to me?" she cried out.

The first rays of a gray dawn had just begun breaking through the window as she continued rocking back and forth in the middle of her bed.

After several long minutes, Darcy attempted to get to her feet, but her legs were like rubber. Falling back onto the edge of the bed, she felt weak and drained.

Taking deep breaths, she tried once more to stand.

Getting to her feet, Darcy took one unsteady step after the other until she reached the bathroom door. While leaning against the door jam, she continued breathing deeply. Then, as if moving in slow motion, she made it into the bathroom.

She felt sick, and bitter bile filled her mouth. As Darcy sank to her knees the room began spinning and blackness bore in around her. Holding on with every bit of strength she had left, she vomited into the toilet. Her body wretched until there was nothing left in her to come up.

Once more Darcy pulled herself up. Leaning over the sink she turned on the cold water. Using the edge of the basin as a brace, she splashed the icy water over her face.

Darcy's red hair was wild and tangled. Her eyes were red and swollen, her skin was ashen in color. Tears rolled down her face as she stood staring into the mirror. She couldn't stop shaking.

Grabbing on to the shower door Darcy steadied herself. Then, carefully, she stepped inside the stall and turned the shower on full blast.

Almost immediately, the hot water began to splash against her skin. Steam filled the enclosure while she stood, eyes closed, allowing the warmth to fill her. The hot water beat on her aching head, and ran down her body warming her feet.

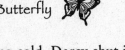

After the water began turning cold, Darcy shut it off and reached for a towel. Drying off quickly, she put on her long fleece robe and furry slippers. She still had a slight chill, but hoped some fresh hot coffee would warm her.

In the kitchen she quickly prepared a pot of coffee. Pouring a large mug full, she sat down wearily at her kitchen table. The dark hot liquid felt good as it worked its way down to her empty stomach.

She had managed to compose herself somewhat, and slowly rose from her chair and walked to the cabinet. Darcy's hand shook as she reached for the bottle of aspirin. Taking out four, she downed them with one gulp of coffee. Pouring another cup, she returned to the table.

The bright light above the kitchen table seemed to be boring through her head. Reaching up, Darcy pulled the cord and turned it off, allowing the room to settle into a soft grayness.

It was October, and in Seattle, the sun was rarely seen. The days remained, for the most part, gray and colorless. The sun had become a mere shadow. Covered by thick dark clouds, it seemed to slowly drift across the sky behind them. The sun's warmth would be hidden by the relentless winter until late June.

Rising from her chair, she walked to the living room and stared out the window at the dark choppy waters of Puget Sound. The gloominess of the sky only added to her feelings of confusion and depression.

With a pained expression, she turned and walked to her soft recliner chair and sat down, leaning back. The once soft morning rain began to intensify and the freezing wind beat the heavy drops against her window as though thousands of fingertips were tapping against it, trying to get in.

The minute Darcy closed her eyes, the horrible vision of her dream flooded back into her mind. Forcing her eyes to open, she got up quickly from her chair, and walked to the window again. Her insides were churning, and she couldn't seem to settle down.

"Why am I going through this again after all these years?" she said aloud. "This is the third dream within a month. I thought I'd out grown this. A child's nightmare shouldn't haunt an adult. I've got to talk to someone, I can't go on like this. If I do, I'll lose my mind for sure." Darcy reached for the phone.

"Hello?" The husky voice on the other end of the phone whispered.

"Frankie, is that you?"

"Who the hell do ya think it is?" The voice was not friendly.

"I'm sorry. Did I wake you?" Darcy replied, with an apologetic tone.

"Do you know what the fuck time it is?" the voice snarled.

Darcy glanced at the clock on the mantel. "Oh god Frankie, it's only 7:30 a.m." Darcy felt like a complete fool. "I'm really sorry."

"Darcy, is that you?" Frankie was alert now, and a little more like herself.

"Go back to sleep. I'll call you later. Please, forgive me." Darcy hung up as her green eyes filled with tears. "This is ridiculous, I've got to get a hold of myself. I'm thirty years old, and acting like some frightened teenager. Damn it, Darcy, you're a bright woman, start thinking like one." She continued mumbling to herself as she got dressed.

Suddenly the phone rang. She picked it up on the second ring. "Hello."

"Why the hell did ya hang up on me?" Frankie's tone was angry.

"Frankie? I'm sorry, I didn't realize what time it was when I called. I know how you like to sleep in on the weekends, and I thought maybe you could go back to sleep."

"My, *EX*- best friend," Frankie growled jokingly, "calls me in the middle of the night, voice shaking, and then hangs up on me, and I'm suppose ta go back to sleep?" Frankie's voice softened. "Now tell me what the hell's goin' on?"

Darcy laughed. "First of all, it wasn't the middle of the night, and second of all, what do you want to do, sleep your life away?"

"Okay, okay, so I exaggerate a little. So, what's up?"

"No big deal, just had the wee-bee gee-bee's over a bad dream, that's all." Darcy tried to make light of her call. "Guess I needed *Big Daddy* to make it all better."

"Okay, my little cherub, what can I do?" Frankie barked back.

Darcy laughed again. "You always make me feel better, you old dyke."

"Stop! I can't take anymore of this praise," Frankie laughingly replied. "So, anyway, what time is everyone gonna to be at your place tonight?"

"Oh my god, I almost forgot. I'm having a party aren't I?"

"God damn *girl*, that really must have been some dream you had. You've been planning this thing for over three weeks, remember? Shit, it's Saturday night, time to let our hair down. Have you even bought the food yet?"

"Yes, I've got everything. Don't make fun of me, I've had a rough morning. Everyone should be here by eight o'clock. Think you can get your act together by that time, you old fart?"

"Don't old fart me. Remember I'm only fifteen years older than you and twice as cute. Do ya need me to bring anything? A new brain for you maybe?"

"No, just you, Beth and that friend of yours who's visiting from California. You know, the *sharp* one you've been raving about. Someday, you've got to quit playing matchmaker. Haven't you learned yet, I'm just not ready to meet anyone new."

"Well, you know how we *daddys* are. See ya later kid."

Darcy could still hear Frankie chuckling to herself as she hung up. Darcy loved Frankie. Her quick wit and caring nature had endeared Frankie to her almost immediately. She had met Frankie two years ago. A chance meeting in the super market had begun, what was now, a very close friendship.

While at the supermarket picking out some fresh fruit for her lunches, Darcy had bumped into Frankie and Beth. Darcy knew Beth from work, and although they were not close socially, their working relationship was cordial.

Beth was extremely feminine. She was pleasingly plump. Her nails were finely manicured, and of course, the color always matched her lipstick. She had been married twice, and from her actions and conversation at work, she still projected the straight world image.

Beth became more open and friendly with Darcy after the chance meeting in the market. After seeing Beth and Frankie together, there was no doubt in Darcy's mind that Beth was a lesbian.

Frankie was short and stocky. Her hair was a salt and pepper gray and cut like a man's, and she was masculine in her dress and manner. Darcy wasn't one to judge people on face value. Just because she wasn't into the butch/femme attitude didn't mean she wouldn't accept those who were. Roll playing wasn't Darcy's cup of tea, but Frankie was her friend and it just didn't matter.

Under Frankie's rough exterior beat a big heart, and she made Darcy laugh. Darcy had just gone through a bad breakup and Frankie took her under her wing immediately. She had truly become a dear and trusted friend.

It concerned Darcy that Frankie worshiped the ground Beth walked on. She never felt quite sure of Beth's commitment to lesbian life, and in the back of her mind, worried that at sometime in the future Frankie's heart could be broken. *I'll be there for her, if that time ever comes.* Darcy had thought.

Darcy busied herself all day cleaning the apartment, cooking, and preparing dips. It helped keep her mind off of her dreams, and it lifted her spirits to know the place would soon be filled with laughing, friendly faces.

At 4:15 p.m. Darcy's phone rang. It was Carol Masters.

"Hi Carol, what's up?" Darcy asked in a warm tone.

"Hi Darcy. Are Taylor and I suppose to bring anything else besides our booze? You know how I am. I can't remember my name unless someone reminds me." Carol joked.

"Not a thing Carol. Everything's taken care of. I'm just excited about seeing your smiling faces, so you'd better be here on time."

"Okay, if you're sure, then we'll see you around 7:30 p.m.. It's casual right?"

"Yes Carol it's casual. See you soon." Darcy chuckled.

Carol Masters also worked for The Great Northwestern Bank. She was Vice President of the Loan Administration Office. Carol was forty-eight. She had been with the bank twenty years and had fought her way up the corporate ladder.

Darcy and Carol had gotten to know each other two years before Carol moved to the corporate headquarters in Everett, Washington and she hadn't seen much of Carol since that time. They spoke on the phone from time to time, always promising to get together soon, but somehow never did.

Darcy had met Taylor Austin, Carol's lover, only twice. The first time was right after Taylor and Carol had gotten together. Carol had stopped by to introduce Taylor to her.

They had had a quick lunch, during which Taylor had said very little. Carol on the other hand, had been beaming and couldn't seem to stop talking. It was as if she had finally caught the brass ring.

The second time she had met Taylor was at Carol and Taylor's house warming party. Taylor was a tall dark haired woman. Both times Darcy had seen her, her long hair was pulled straight back away from her face. Taylor's hazel eyes and olive complexion were accentuated by her finely chiseled features. She was elegant and striking. There was, however a distance about her which kept her apart from everyone else. She was a gracious host, yet she seemed to look through you instead of at you.

Taylor owned her own travel agency in Seattle, and she was fifteen years younger than Carol. They were both tall and made a striking couple. The blondness of Carol and the almost Indian look of Taylor played well together.

Carol Masters had always been a friendly person, but a very ambitious one. Even though everyone at work liked her, she had no close friends except for Darcy. Darcy was the only person Carol seemed to be relaxed with.

Three weeks ago Carol had come into Seattle for a business meeting and they'd had lunch together. That's when Darcy had invited her and Taylor to the party.

Carol had hesitated at first, but then said, yes, after Darcy reminded her of how long it had been since they had seen each other socially. Carol seemed uptight and nervous at the time, and Darcy kidded her about taking time to smell the roses.

She sensed all things might not be quite right in Carol's life, but couldn't tell if it was a personal problem, or

just the stress of work. Since Carol hadn't mentioned anything being wrong, Darcy didn't pry. *She'll let me know
what's up when she's ready.* Darcy had thought.

By 6:30 p.m., Darcy was showered and dressed. She
had decided to wear a blue sweatshirt and white sweat pants.
Comfort and relaxation was the theme of the party. Just
friends sitting around having drinks, discussing the problems
of the world, and coming up with wonderful solutions for
everything. *The world isn't such a bad place after all,* Darcy
thought, smiling to herself.

Just as she finished laying out the last of the dip and
chips, the doorbell rang. "Hum, someone's early," she said
out loud as she opened the door and was greeted by Frankie's
round smiling face.

"Hi kid," Frankie said, wrapping her arms around
Darcy.

Beth was right behind her. "Hi Darcy. It's really great
to see you." Beth kissed Darcy on the cheek and hugged her.

"Oh Darcy," Frankie motioned, as she and Beth stepped
inside. "This is my old and dear friend, Toni Underwood."

Toni stepped forward, and extended her hand to
Darcy. "It's nice to finally meet you. Frankie's told me a lot
about you ever since I arrived. All good things, I might add."
Toni said, smiling at Darcy.

Darcy's face flushed for a moment as she returned the
smile. "Thanks Toni, I hope I live up to them. Welcome to
my home. Come on in, and fix yourselves a drink. The food's
on the table, and all my CD's are over by the stereo. You
know better then to expect me to treat you like guests."
Darcy's manner was easy and warm. Toni liked that.

"Why don't you come over here, and help me pick
out some music? I'm sure Frankie can make you a drink."
Darcy said turning to Toni.

"Sounds good, lets see what you've got." Toni answered, giving Darcy another big smile.

In the kitchen, Frankie proceeded to mix the drinks. "Whatta ya think?" She whispered to Beth.

"Think about what?" Beth replied, with a puzzled expression.

"About Darcy and Toni. Looks like they hit it off right away, huh?" Frankie motioned toward the living room with her head.

"You're such a romantic; they just met. Give them at least an hour before you have them running off together, okay?" Beth laughed softly, and kissed Frankie on the cheek. Then, they returned to the living room with the cocktails.

"What's up you two? You both look like the cat that swallowed the canary!" Toni said, as she took her drink from Frankie.

They didn't answer, but Frankie winked at Toni. Toni scowled at Frankie, and shook her head.

"Excuse me, there's the door again," Darcy said as she rushed to answer it. "Carol, Taylor, welcome, welcome."

Darcy hugged them as they entered. She introduced Carol and Taylor to Toni, explaining that Toni was a close friend of Frankie's, from California. This seemed to interest Taylor and she immediately engaged in conversation with Toni. Drinks were poured all around and the group settled into light conversation.

Without warning, Darcy's front door suddenly flew open.

"Ta-Da!" Mary Ann Clayton shouted, taking a cheerleaders pose.

Everyone turned abruptly.

"Mary Ann! My god, you just gave us all a heart attack. I'm going to take that key away from you yet." Darcy huffed getting to her feet.

Posed in the doorway stood Mary Ann Clayton, behind her were Jo Madira, and two women Darcy didn't recognize. Mary Ann had a wide grin on her face while Jo just stood there shaking her head.

"Bet you didn't think we were going to make it, did you?" Mary Ann chirped sarcastically.

"Well, the thought did cross my mind. But then knowing you, what else could I expect? You'll be late for your own funeral." Darcy smiled, and hugged Mary Ann and Jo.

Darcy had known Mary Ann for years. They both started working for the bank at the same time. Mary Ann was fun and always lived life a day at a time. She had transferred to the Bellevue branch a year ago, but she and Darcy had stayed close.

Hanging on to money was not one of Mary Ann's strong points. She loved to go shopping and would drag Darcy through the mall for hours. Jo was the sensible one and tried the best she could to keep Mary Ann on a budget. It was futile. Mary Ann knew just how to get around Jo, and in most cases got her way, and Mary Ann's way was to spend and then spend some more. She and Jo had been together six years.

Jo worked for the Boeing Airplane Company as a mechanic. She was always harping on Mary Ann about her lack of responsibly when it came to money, and how they were going to end up in the poor house if she didn't learn to save. Mary Ann would give Jo a big kiss and tell her *mama* would make everything all right.

Mary Ann worked in the loan department at the bank. She would wink at Darcy and say all she had to do was transfer some of the loan funds to her own account, and then she could go shopping again. As always, Jo just shook her head and mumbled to herself. They made a great couple. The tall skinny hyper blonde, Mary Ann and the short chunky brown haired, Jo.

"I hope you don't mind, but we brought a couple of friends with us. They called this morning. They're only going to be in town three days and I couldn't just leave them out. Is it okay Darcy?" Mary Ann whispered with a pleading look on her face.

"Of course it's alright. You know me, the more the merrier. Please introduce me to your friends."

Darla Owens and Viola Henderson thanked Darcy for not being angry with their party crashing. Since Darcy was never surprised at what might crop up when Mary Ann was involved, she took the arrival of the extra couple in good spirits. Darcy always had plenty of food and would never make anyone feel uncomfortable.

While Darcy was busy introducing Darla and Viola to everyone, Toni made mental notes on each woman. Height, weight, body language and names. Old habits were hard to break.

As the evening progressed, Toni stayed close to Frankie. She tried to act interested in the minor chit-chat between the old friends, and she even joined in the conversation now and then, but her real interest was elsewhere.

Her eyes continually sought out Darcy. Observing her easy manner and quick warm smile, Toni couldn't help but notice how Darcy's whole face seemed to light up when she laughed or smiled.

Their eyes met several times across the room, and each time it happened, a warm flush rushed to Toni's cheeks. She would have preferred to just stand and talk with Darcy the entire evening. There was something below the surface of this well packaged redhead that Toni felt drawn to; a sadness, perhaps, that even her closest friends seemed to miss.

Still feeling a little uncomfortable with all these new people, Toni remained her reserved self. Her years as a police officer had conditioned her to be cautious of new relationships. *Look beyond the eyes and smiles. Knowing the heart takes effort and time,* her mother had always said.

After Megan's death almost two years ago, it took all she had to rejoin the human race or even talk to anyone. If it hadn't been for her Aunt Vera's pleading letter a year ago, Toni would probably still be living a solitary life. She would have never gotten to know her aunt, or become the wealthy woman she was today.

Now, somehow, Darcy had touched the cold, empty place where Toni's heart lie idle and still. She wanted to know more about this woman, but this was not the time.

Walking to the window, Walking to the window, Toni stared out at the rain soaked street. The murmuring sounds of conversation and music faded into the background as her thoughts drifted back in time.

Chapter Two

Toni had spent almost a year in Las Vegas after the murder of her aunt. She had much to learn about being a multimillionaire and the responsibility it carried with it. Gloria Miller, her Aunt Vera's attorney had gone out of her way to assist Toni in mastering the ins and outs of managing the vast holdings, but Toni remained uncomfortable and off balance.

Gloria had suggested Toni find a reliable assistant with a solid business background to work with her. Someone she could trust. That had been a tall order, and one not easily filled. Toni knew many people, but for the most part their backgrounds were in law enforcement not finance.

Royce was a true and trusted friend, but had no talent for managing business affairs. At this point in time, Toni remained without a good right hand, and was still searching. Gloria had volunteered to keep things running smoothly, but this was only temporary and Toni knew she had to find someone on a permanent basis.

Smiling, she remembered her conversation with Frankie last month. "You're coming up to Seattle? Well goddamn, I can't believe it. I haven't seen that ugly face of yours in four years." Frankie's gruff manner couldn't hide her excitement at the prospect of seeing her old friend again. "Ya gotta stay with Beth and me. Don't even suggest stayin' in a motel, or I'll break your neck."

So, that was that. Toni knew better than to argue with Frankie, and in her heart, staying with her old buddy was just what she had been hoping for. The point of the trip was to look over the estate in Washington that Vera had left her, and to decide whether to sell or hang on to it.

The estate was breathtaking. It sat on the edge of a private lake surrounded by thick lush woods and gentle rolling pastures. Eight other homes were scattered here and there around the large lake. The eight bedroom single story home had been closed up for several years, with only a care-taker and his wife looking after the place.

The stone and brick L-Shaped house was built to afford each room a view of the lake and surrounding trees. The entire front portion was all windows. A winding gravel driveway led up to the front entrance. Green shrubs and plants of every shape and size filled the gardens. A cobble stone path led from the main house down to the lake and boathouse.

Frankie had let out a long slow whistle as she approached the front door. Beth followed Toni and Frankie inside with her mouth hanging open as if she had suddenly been struck dumb. None of them said a word until they had wandered through the entire house.

Once again, Toni smiled to herself as she remembered Frankie's comments. "Damn, have we all just died and gone to heaven? I've never seen anything like this. You mean ya own it outright?" Frankie had looked at Toni wide eyed, in disbelief.

"Oh Toni, you can't even consider getting rid of this wonderful place," Beth chimed in breathlessly.

"I guess not," was all Toni had managed to say at the time.

"A penny for your thoughts."

Toni jumped at the sound of Darcy's voice.

"What? Oh hi." Toni's voice was a whisper as she shook herself back from her daydream.

"Where were you?" Darcy asked softly.

Toni took a deep breath. "It's a long story Darcy. I'll tell you about it someday. Come on, I need another drink."

As they made their way through the living room to the kitchen. Toni remarked, "Great party. Really seem to be a nice bunch of people."

"Well, I hadn't expected so many, but what can you do when friends bring friends?"

Toni must have looked confused, because Darcy glanced up at her immediately and said, "Oh, I didn't mean you. I was expecting you. Oh damn, I'm goofing this up aren't I?" Darcy's face turned beet red.

"I understand what you mean." Toni broke into a wide grin. "I'm very happy to be here, and no offense taken."

"Thanks," Darcy's responded. "Sometimes, I just can't seem to keep my foot out of my mouth."

An awkward silence fell between them as Toni mixed the drinks. It was as if they had suddenly become two shy teenagers that didn't know what to say next.

"How do I go about seeing you again? I mean, I'd like to take you to dinner." Toni suddenly blurted out. "You can show me the high-spots of Seattle, and we can get to know each other better. Would that be acceptable to you, or am I being too pushy?"

Darcy smiled. "That would be perfectly fine with me.

Just call tomorrow, and we'll make a date for your *tour*."

Darcy slipped her hand into Toni's as they returned to the living room.

Frankie spied them as they entered and poked Beth with her elbow. "What did I tell ya, just look at 'em."

Beth just smiled and kept eating dip and chips.

By 2:30 A.M., everyone had left except Frankie, Beth and Toni. They all joined in helping Darcy clean up the mess.

"Good party kiddo," Frankie commented with a smile.

"Yes, Darcy, we had a lovely time," Beth added in her ultra feminine manner.

Darcy looked at Toni and raised her eyebrows. Toni winked at her and laughed.

After hugs and kisses, Frankie and Beth walked down the hall ahead of Toni and waited for her by the elevator. Toni had lagged behind so she could have a private word with Darcy.

"Thanks again, I'll call you around one o'clock tomorrow afternoon." Bending over, she gave Darcy a soft kiss on the cheek.

Darcy stood in the hallway, and waved as they all entered the elevator. Touching her fingertips to her cheek, she wished the kiss had been more.

As the elevator doors slowly slid shut, Toni smiled broadly, and mouthed, tomorrow. Darcy's cheeks flushed. The smell of Toni's Armani cologne still lingered in her nostrils.

Smiling, she stepped back inside her apartment and closed the door. She could still feel Toni's soft full lips on her cheek. Humming to herself she checked the windows, made sure her door was locked, and turned out the lights. After undressing, she crawled into bed. For the first time in months, she felt warm and happy inside.

"Please God, no dreams tonight, please . . ." Darcy whispered as her eyelids slowly closed.

Darcy would dream this night, not of the man with coal eyes, but of a childhood spent growing up on Whidbey Island, and of her Aunt Mae and Uncle Fred. The two most important people in her life.

Chapter Three

Darcy's dreams and remembrances of her childhood and young adult life on Whidbey Island seemed to fill her thoughts more and more of late. She moaned slightly as the vision of her Aunt Mae flashed in her dream. She was seven again, and holding on tightly to Aunt Mae's warm hand.

Aunt Mae and Uncle Fred had become her legal guardians after the death of her mother and father in a plane crash. Darcy was only six at the time, and had very little memory of her parents. Aunt Mae would show her pictures and tell her of the fun filled times they all spent together, and of how much her mother and father had loved her.

"Our island is one of the hundreds of islands which make up the San Juan Islands chain, and we're the second largest island in the continental United States. We are known as the garden spot of all the islands," Aunt Mae would proudly repeat to Darcy each time they returned from a mainland shopping trip into Seattle.

She held Darcy tightly as she sat her on the railing of the ferry boat. Darcy always listened intently as though hearing the words for the first time.

Darcy's eyelids moved and fluttered as she dreamed of the spray from the freezing waters of Puget Sound sticking to and glistening on her round rosy cheeks. She strained her eyes to get a glimpse of the island as the ferry boat moved slowly through to water.

Whidbey Island had been a wonderful place to grow up. The small quaint town of Coupeville bustled with tourists during the summer months and its authentic false front buildings and hundred year old homes projected the feeling of a time long since past.

The shoreline was indented by many coves and inlets, which over the centuries had been carved by the sea and weather. Back from the shore were gently rolling hills and slopes dotted by patches of woodland and lush meadows. The soil on Whidbey Island was rich, and orchards and wheat and dairy farms flourished here. Cows could be seen from the main road grazing in the wooded pastures that swept back from the highway.

Darcy had always remembered the excitement she felt when she and Aunt Mae would catch the ferry from Columbia Beach on Whidbey to Mukilteo and go into Seattle for lunch and shopping.

The crowds and busyness of Seattle intrigued Darcy. She knew she would live there one day, but there would always be Whidbey Island when the pressures of everyday life caused her to seek a quiet haven all her own to escape to.

She loved her Aunt Mae and Uncle Fred very much. They were the only mother and father she had ever really known.

Her uncle Fred had died two years ago and Darcy begged her aunt to move in with her, but Mae was set in her ways, and remained on the island, living alone in the two story farmhouse Uncle Fred had built for her.

The house sat in the middle of a meadow, surrounded by a lovely grove of trees. A small natural lake was near the back of the estate while a lazy stream wove its way through the grounds.

In all, Aunt Mae owned fifty-four acres of land on the island. None of it had been disturbed, except for where Aunt Mae's house was built, and of course, where the *old house* still stood.

Darcy got a weird feeling in her stomach every time she caught sight of the old house. It stood alone, deeper into the thick woods. Yet, it could still be seen from Aunt Mae's kitchen window when the wind caught the branches of the trees just right.

The old driveway was still visible even though over the years weeds and dirt had covered most of it.

As Darcy's dream continued, she heard her young voice calling out. "Aunt Mae, why are you here? I've been looking all over for you." This had been the first time she found her aunt standing in front of the old house, just staring. Darcy was seven.

A slight frown crept across Darcy's forehead as her dream pulled her back to that day. Aunt Mae's words had been clear and sharp.

"Oh my God, child, you scared the life out of me. What are you doing out here? I've told you never to wander off into these woods." She grabbed Darcy by the hand, and hurried away from the house.

She knew her aunt was very upset, and by the time they reached home Darcy was crying. Aunt Mae sat her down at the kitchen table. Then she sat across from Darcy.

Aunt Mae had beautiful blue eyes, and a complexion like a fresh ripe peach. This day, however, her face was flushed and stern. Her forehead was wrinkled, and her mouth tight. Mae took Darcy's small hands in hers.

"My sweet child, I'm sorry if I frightened you," she began, "but I want you to listen very carefully to me." Aunt Mae spoke quietly. "I want your promise that you will never go near that house again. There are open wells scattered throughout the area, and the house is very old. It's not a safe place for a little girl. Do you understand?"

Darcy's lower lip was quivering. She nodded her head up and down in answer to her aunt's instructions.

Mae pulled Darcy up on her lap, and held her tight for a long time. "Now," she finally said. "Lets you and me have some cookies and milk. What do you say?"

Darcy smiled up at her aunt as the last teardrop ran down her cheek. Mae kissed her, and hugged her tight.

Afterwards Darcy knew that whenever she couldn't find her aunt, she would be at the old house quietly staring at the decaying gray structure which seemed so cold and alone.

Darcy stirred slightly in the bed and a soft smiled formed on her mouth as her dream took her ahead in time to the warm summer morning, she and Uncle Fred headed for the lake.

It was her eleventh birthday. He had bought her a new fishing pole, and she was anxious to use it. They did this often during the summer months. Both loved fishing, and Darcy enjoyed these special times with her uncle. Fred would tell her stories about her mother and father, and how much fun they had all had together.

Darcy never grew tired of listening, even though she heard the same tales many times over. While relating these stories, Uncle Fred would always get a sad faraway, look in his eyes, shake his head, and heave a deep sigh as he finished. Then he would give Darcy a big hug and a kiss.

On this particular day, they had taken the shortcut to the lake. This pathway took them close to the old house. She

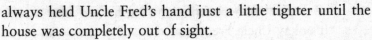

always held Uncle Fred's hand just a little tighter until the house was completely out of sight.

"Uncle Fred." Darcy said looking up at him. "Why doesn't anyone live in the old house?"

Fred stopped dead in his tracks. "Why would you ask me a question like that, honey?"

"Oh, I don't know Uncle Fred, I guess because it just sits there empty and cold. Maybe the house wouldn't seem so scary if someone lived in it."

"Well, honey, it would just cost too much for your aunt and me to fix it up. So, we just leave it alone. Maybe someday, but not now." Fred began walking once more.

"How come you don't tear it down then?" Darcy asked innocently. Her Uncle Fred did not respond. "How come Uncle Fred?" she repeated.

By this time, they had reached the lake. Fred sat down, and proceeded to get their poles ready.

"Uncle Fred," Darcy began once more. She was standing very close to him.

Suddenly, Darcy whined and threw her covers off. Again a frown covered her sleeping face.

Fred grabbed Darcy by her arm. "Look Darcy, forget about that old house. It's just there, okay?"

Fred looked angry, and was hurting Darcy's arm. She pulled free, and began to whimper, rubbing at the red marks left by his fingers.

Then, Uncle Fred's expression changed as he realized what he'd done. He had never laid a hand on Darcy in anger before, and it frightened her.

"Oh, my God, Darcy. I'm so sorry, please forgive me." Fred hugged her to him. Darcy began crying softly. "I promise you, I will never scare you this way again. Please forgive this old fool." Tears were in his eyes.

Darcy pulled back from him. She looked deep into his eyes. "It's okay Uncle Fred, sometimes, I get in a bad mood too." She kissed him on the cheek and smiled.

The fishing was good, and she and her uncle laughed all the way home with their catch. Aunt Mae was waiting for them at the back door, beckoning them to hurry before the chocolate chip cookies got cold. Darcy rolled over, nestling her head deep into her pillow, a sweet smile on her sleeping face. When she awoke on Sunday morning, somehow she could almost smell the warm scent of cookies in the air.

She had been plagued with the nightmares most of her childhood. Aunt Mae and Uncle Fred would comfort her each time one occurred, but nothing they said or did made them go away.

By the time she reached her teens, they became less frequent, and during her twenties, they were gone.

Then why now, why now were they returning when her life was just getting back on track after the breakup with Lisa? This question, would in time, challenge Darcy's emotional strength and take her to the darkest recesses of an insane mind.

Chapter Four

The nurse's rubber soled shoes squeaked against the shiny tile floor; the sound echoing down the long sterile hall. It was 2:00 a.m., and all was quiet. The humming of the computer at the nurse's station was the only other sound in the east wing.

The halls were dark except for a small light over each doorway. It had rained most of the day, and a relentless chill seemed to fill the air inside the main building.

"Hi Sam, how's tricks?" Nurse Fletcher asked the husky security guard, as they passed in the hallway.

"Everything seems to be nice and quiet Mary," he answered.

Mary Fletcher made her way to the door leading to the main lobby. The door was always locked, and could only be opened by a switch controlled from the other side. Wire crisscrossed the unbreakable glass window in the center of the heavy door.

Mary spoke through the microphone on her side, "Hey George." As usual George Hudson was dozing off at his desk. "George!" she shouted.

He jumped, coughed, and looked at Mary.

George pushed the button on the desk. Mary waited for the click signaling the door was unlocked, and then, stepped through.

"George, you know you're suppose to make me show my I.D. badge before you unlock this door and let me out of the ward. One of these days you're going to get in trouble for not following the rules around here."

"Calm down my fair beauty." George smiled. "I knew it was you. After all you're the prettiest woman around this place."

"I'm the only woman around this place you mean."

Mary couldn't stay mad at George. He was such a kidder. He always had a new joke for her, and it brightened up an otherwise dreary night.

"So, just makin' your rounds Mary, or couldn't you stay away from me?" George asked smiling.

"You're so full of it George. I'm old enough to be your mother. Don't think all this flattery will get you any-where with me." Mary shook her finger at him in mock anger. "I'm going to the cafeteria and see what I can find to eat. Do you want anything?"

"No thanks, *honey*, I brought a lunch," he answered.

The cafeteria was to the left of the main desk, it was illuminated by the lights of the vending machines and service counter.

She opened the refrigerator and smiled, *Good old Sonja, she always makes sure to leave me something.*

Sonja, the head cook, had made her a large shrimp and crab salad. Mary picked up a fork, a few packs of salad dressing, some crackers, and headed back to the ward.

"See ya later, Mary my girl." George smiled and pushed the button, allowing Mary to re-enter the east wing.

Mary checked the medication chart before sitting down. "Good," she said aloud. "No medication due for an hour."

Settling into her chair at the nurses desk, she slowly ate while reading her Reader's Digest. It was 2:30 a.m..

He lay on the bed looking straight up at the ceiling. Not blinking, his black eyes stared into the darkness. The side of his mouth twitched. It was his only movement.

Aaron Blake had come to the Washington State Mental Institution twenty-five years ago. He was only sixteen at the time, but the nature and viciousness of his crimes warranted lifetime confinement in the maximum security wing of the facility. There was no doubt Aaron Blake would remain here until his death.

Mary Fletcher was hired on the same day Aaron arrived. She had just turned twenty eight years old, and this would be her first experience working in a mental hospital. Mary was nervous and apprehensive at the prospect, but the pay was good and she needed a job. It took six months before she completely understood the system and rules of operation at the institution.

All nurses were instructed to have an attendant with them at all times when administering to the inmates. Sometimes, it would require the assistance of two attendants just to take a patience's blood-pressure. The inmates doors were always kept locked and doubled checked before shift changes every evening.

Mary had worked the night shift for ten years. There was less stress, and the inmates were usually medicated before she came on duty, so she didn't have to deal with them on a personal level. They became just names on a list, *except* for Aaron Blake.

Over the years, Aaron had developed a resistance to just about all the tranquilizers available. The effects would last for only a few hours at a time. Each night, Mary was required to medicate him every four hours during her ten hour shift.

If the medication was late, Aaron became almost impossible to handle. He would begin pacing back and forth, then without warning he would hurl himself against the padded walls, pounding his fists against them as though attacking some unseen foe.

It took four large men to subdue him, and even then he fought like a wild beast. Only after a powerful dose of medication was injected could the guards release him.

He was a hulk of a man. Six foot four and two hundred and eighty-five pounds of pure evil. He hadn't spoken a word in twenty-five years; his eyes spoke for him. When he looked at you, you could feel a black, deadly hate radiating from deep inside him.

After Doctor Hull's brush with death at the hands of Aaron Blake fifteen years ago, Aaron was never permitted to exit his room without first being shackled.

When out of his room, Aaron's legs were chained together so he could only take small steps. His hands were cuffed behind his back. This sight would cause an unknowing person to feel pity for him, but for those who dealt with Aaron, these chains represented the difference between life and death.

Mary always made sure Aaron's medication was given on time. She dreaded going into his bare room each night. The hairs on her neck stood up every time she looked into those black, staring eyes.

The guards on her shift were strong, big, and trained in the art of self-defense. Sam not only carried a nightstick; he had a stun gun as well.

Sam would always enter Aaron's room first. The light

switch was outside the door, so they never entered in the dark. Aaron's bed was bolted to the floor.

It was 3:15 a.m., when Mary began preparing Aaron's medication. She unlocked the drug cabinet and reached in, but as she did, the cuff of her blouse caught on a large bottle. The bottle teetered for a moment, and then fell. As Mary reached out in an effort to grab it, her hand hit the shelf breaking the glass. Blood began running almost immediately from a deep cut on her hand.

"Damn!" Mary muttered grabbing a towel to cover the wound. Going quickly to the nearby basin, she began washing the blood from her hand. After washing the jagged cut, she applied an antiseptic and three large gauze pads. She picked up a roll of tape, and taped the pads securely to her hand.

"That should do for now. I'll have the doctor look at it in the morning," she said as she began sweeping up the glass.

"Hey Mary, a little late with Aaron's shot tonight aren't we?" Sam asked, as he peered down at her from above the counter.

"Oh my god!" Mary responded with a shocked expression.

She looked at her watch. It was 3:40 a.m. Quickly, she filled the hypodermic needle.

"I'm over ten minutes late with his shot. Come on Sam, and watch yourself when we open the door."

Sam reached over and flipped on the light switch next to Aaron's door and the room was flooded with bright light. Arron was still laying on his bed staring at the ceiling, motionless.

"Everything seems to be okay Mary. Take a look."

Sam stepped aside, away from the unbreakable glass window in the door.

Mary studied Aaron through the glass for a few

minutes. He didn't move. He appeared to be as one would in a trance.

"I guess it's all right," Mary said half heartedly. "If he makes just one move though, we get out. Is that understood?"

"Don't worry Mary, I won't let anything happen to you. I can handle this nut." Sam smiled at her.

Mary's hand was throbbing, and her head hurt as she quietly unlocked, and opened the door. Sam stepped inside the room, and took a position by the door, his baton in hand.

Mary entered cautiously. She took one slow careful step after the other, until she was standing next to Aaron's bed. She looked down at him. He didn't move. His coal like eyes were still staring blankly at the ceiling. Her heart pounded hard against her chest and a chill ran down her spine.

After quietly setting the tray down next to the bed, she picked up the hypodermic needle. Then, holding it up, she pushed the plunger. Tranquilizing fluid spurt from the hole.

Out of the corner of her eye, she looked down at Aaron once more. His eyes were looking directly into hers!

She started to turn and call for Sam, but before she even moved, the huge hands were on both sides of her head. With one quick flick of his wrists, Aaron Blake snapped Mary's neck.

It took a moment before Sam realized what had happened. He took one step forward before Mary's limp body hit him squarely in the chest, knocking the wind out of his body. He went down hard. Sam's baton flew from his hand as he hit the ground. Aaron moved like a flash of lighting. Grabbing the nightstick; with one blow Sam's skull was shattered.

Aaron stood over his latest victims. A cruel smile crossed his distorted mouth. Carefully opening the door, Aaron flipped the light off. Then, he closed the door. Bending down, he picked Mary up, and threw her body onto the bed.

It had taken Aaron Blake less than thirty seconds to snuff out two lives.

Sweat began pouring down his pock marked face. He felt alive again; power surged through his muscles. Quickly, he covered the body of Mary Fletcher, and then walked to where Sam still lay. A large pool of blood now covered the floor under his crushed skull. Aaron undressed Sam's limp body and placed the uniform on himself. Then he pulled Sam across the floor and pushed him under the bed.

Aaron stuffed his wild unkept hair underneath the cap and pulled the bill down as far as possible to cover his face. His eyes scanned the room for a moment, and then he stepped out into the corridor.

All was quiet. Everything had happened so fast, none of the other inmates were even disturbed. Taking a quick glance up and down the hall, he turned and headed for the lobby door.

Flattening his body against the door, carefully, he moved his head so he could see George through the thick wired glass.

George was bent over the desk. His head was resting on his arms, and he was breathing heavily. Aaron tapped at the glass. George didn't move. He knocked harder. George twitched, and slowly raised his head.

Still not sure of what woke him, George stretched and yawned. Aaron stood in front of the glass peering out at George. He held his head down slightly so George couldn't see his face. Then he tapped on the glass once more. This time George looked at him. Aaron waved as if to say, "Hi," and pointed to the door.

Rubbing his eyes, George spoke into the microphone on his desk. "Hey, Sam, what's up?"

Aaron didn't answer.

"Okay, okay, I know you're a man of few words. Guess you want out huh?" George smiled sleepily.

Aaron returned the smile, and nodded his head. His body was wet with perspiration, his hands shook as they tightened into fists.

Slowly, George's hand reached toward the button. Aaron's eyes grew wide. At the sound of the first click, his hand pushed against the door. It swung open, and with one giant step, Aaron was out and standing over the stunned guard.

George's mouth dropped open as the realization of who was standing there hit him. Before he could reach for the alarm, Aaron struck him in the face with his fist. The back of George's head hit the wall as the chair fell from under him. Aaron was on top of him instantly, both hands around his throat.

George clawed frantically at Aaron Blake's arms. They were like rods of steel. His eyes were bulging out of his head, as Aaron's vice-like grip strangled the life from him. Even after George's dead body lay before him, Aaron continued squeezing.

Slamming the dead man's head against the floor, he rose to his feet. Rolling George over with his foot, Aaron bent down and went through his pockets.

Taking the wallet out, he found a hundred dollars inside. With what he'd gotten off of Sam, he had a total of one hundred and seventy-eight dollars. His eyes gleamed as he put the wallet in his back pocket, and crammed George under the desk.

Aaron went through the desk drawers. *Keys!* Keys to the hospital station wagon. He hadn't driven in years, but nothing that trivial would stop Aaron now. He grabbed the keys, took one last look around, and ran through the front doors.

A steady rain fell, and the wind was howling. Aaron stood beside the station wagon, head back, eyes closed. The rain ran down his face as he breathed in the icy, wind-swept air. His mouth opened, and from somewhere deep inside Aaron Blake's insane soul came just two words, "Darcy Bennett."

Chapter Five

It was 1:30 p.m., and still no call from Toni. Darcy began to wonder if Toni meant what she had said last night, or was she just trying to be polite.

Oh well, no biggie. After all, I don't even know the woman. Just because she's a friend of Frankie's doesn't mean I'd like her, Darcy thought as she walked to the living room window.

The rain had let up, but the grayness of the day held on. A light fog clung to the ground and streaks of water ran down the window pane. Darcy's mood matched the weather.

We had such a nice time last night; why wouldn't she call? She asked herself. *She didn't seem the type to play games.* Darcy jumped at the shrill ringing of her phone.

"Hello."

"Hi Darcy, it's me, Toni. I'm really sorry about calling so late, but that numb-nut Frankie ran out of gas on the way to the store, and I of course had to go save her. I just got back."

"I was wondering what happened." Darcy tried to sound casual.

"Believe me, I'm not a person who likes to be late, and I apologize. Now, if you forgive me, are we still on for dinner tonight?"

"Well, I guess I have to give you a chance to redeem yourself. After all, it wasn't your fault. Why don't you pick me up at 7:00 p.m.? I'll take you to a small place I know down by the waterfront. Does that sound okay?"

"Sounds great. I'll see you then."

Darcy hung up and smiled. "Boy it's really funny how one phone call can change a person's mood in the blink of an eye," she said smiling.

By the time seven o'clock rolled around Darcy had changed outfits six times. She didn't want to look too formal, yet she wanted to wow Toni in some small way. Finally settling on an emerald green soft knit sweater and black wool pants, she stood back and looked at herself in the full-length mirror.

"Hum, not too bad," she said aloud studying the fit of her sweater. "Clings to the boobs just enough. Now, high heeled black boots, black jacket, and I'm ready."

After putting on her hooped earrings and thin gold chain, she sprayed one more spurt of Opium under her chin and walked out to the living room. Just as she came out of the bedroom door the front door bell chimed. It was exactly 7:00 p.m.

"Toni, good to see you, come on in for a minute." Darcy said as she motioned for Toni to enter.

Toni handed Darcy a large bouquet of flowers, and kissed her on the cheek. "A peace offering," she said with a sheepish grin.

"Oh, how lovely. Let me get these in water. Sit down, I'll be right back."

Instead of sitting down, Toni walked slowly around the living room. *She has a good eye for decorating,* she thought. *Some good books here on the shelf too.*

Darcy returned almost immediately from the kitchen carrying a vase filled with the flowers and placed it on the mantel. The flowers brightened up the whole room, as did Darcy's smile.

"Would you care for a drink before we go?"

"No thanks. I'd just as soon get going. Maybe we can have one later." Toni replied as she got to her feet.

As Toni helped Darcy on with her jacket, her hand brushed across the back of Darcy's neck. Her neck length curly red hair was soft and thick. The feel of it against her skin caused Toni to flush suddenly.

All of a sudden, Toni's gray turtle neck sweater seemed too heavy and warm. Darcy turned to face her. They were standing very close together. Small beads of sweat broke out on Toni's upper lip as Darcy's green eyes locked in on hers.

"Is everything alright?" Darcy whispered, a concerned look on her face.

Taking a deep breath, Toni answered, "Oh, sure, everything's just fine. Guess this sweater is a tad too warm for me, that's all." She dabbed at the sweat with the back of her hand. "I'm sure I won't feel that way once we get outside."

"Well then, shall we?" She flashed Toni a wide grin, and stepped out the door.

It took thirty-five minutes to reach the restaurant. Their conversation was light during the ride, with Darcy pointing out places of interest as they went. Toni found it difficult to keep her mind on what Darcy was saying. The scent of Darcy and their closeness in the Mercedes seemed to be all Toni was aware of.

The restaurant was small, but quite nice. Netting and sea shells decorated the walls. Large fish tanks were scattered throughout the dark quiet cafe.

The waiter showed Darcy and Toni to a secluded

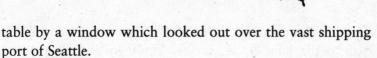

table by a window which looked out over the vast shipping port of Seattle.

"Would you care for something to drink before dinner?" the waiter asked quietly.

"Yes, I'll have a white wine please," Darcy answered.

"And, I'll have a tall Kesslers and soda," Toni added.

"So," Darcy began, "tell me something about yourself." She smiled across the table at Toni.

The candlelight from the small lamp on their table danced on Darcy's short red hair. The natural curls softly framed her oval face and high cheek bones. Her green eyes glistened in the light. Even in the pale candlelight, Toni could detect a smattering of freckles across Darcy's small nose.

"I suppose Frankie filled you in on most of what's happened in my life in the past two years," Toni answered.

"Yes, some of it, and I can't even begin to tell you how awful I feel for you. I know how hard it is to lose someone you love, but it's impossible to imagine the pain suffered by losing her the way you did." Darcy gently took Toni's hand in hers.

"Thanks, Darcy. I'm doing okay now. Just kinda taking things one day at a time, if you know what I mean." Toni squeezed Darcy's hand. There was a long silence between them as if time had suddenly stood still.

Toni cleared her throat. "Look, I'll tell you what, why don't we just have a nice dinner, enjoy each other's company, and then go back to your place and talk?"

"You got a deal." Darcy answered warmly.

"Now, tell me about Seattle, your job, and how long you've lived here." Toni asked as she motioned to the waiter.

For the next hour, Darcy told Toni of her life on Whidbey Island, the death of her parents, and her job as the loan manager for The Great Northwestern Bank. She did not mention the nightmares that were again plaguing her life.

"If the weather clears up for a couple of days I'll take you to the Pike Place Market. You'll love it. People rent booths and bring in their vegetables, fruits, canned goods, crafts . . . just about every kind of wonderful food you can think of is sold there. The fish market alone is one of the biggest in the world.

"We can go down to Lake Washington and see the houseboats and I'll take you across The Lake Washington Bridge. It's the largest pontoon bridge ever built. We can have dinner one night at the Space Needle. It revolves and gives you a beautiful view of all of Seattle. Oh yes, and Chinatown, you have to see Chinatown, and the Elliot Bay waterfront."

Darcy suddenly paused for a moment and blinked her eyes. "God I sound like a tourist guide don't I?"

Toni smiled, her blue eyes twinkling with humor. "I think you sound just great. There's more to Seattle then I thought, and I'd love to see everything . . . with you."

"But I don't even know how long you're planning on staying. It could take weeks to do all the things I just rattled off to you."

"Lets not worry about that. Like I said, one day at a time. There's no place I *have* to be."

As Toni listened intently to everything Darcy said, she still sensed a sadness in this woman. Something under the surface, something waiting to be discovered. It was the same feeling she had the first night they met. This made Darcy all the more interesting to her.

The drive back to Darcy's apartment was quiet, except for an occasional question from Toni regarding the area. By the time they reached Darcy's apartment house, the rain and wind were pelting the car.

Toni parked as close as she could to the entrance, and they made a mad dash for the doorway trying to keep as dry as possible. It did no good. By the time they reached the lobby they were both soaked through to the skin. Even the umbrella couldn't protect them from the onslaught of rain and wind. Laughing and dripping wet, they stood looking at each other.

"You look like a wet noodle," Darcy stated gasping for air.

"Well, I'd say, you're the soggiest date I've had in a long time," Toni answered, laughing.

Darcy unlocked her door, and they rushed inside. Puddles of water formed at their feet from their sopping wet clothes.

Out of breath, Darcy panted, "Come with me."

Toni followed her into the bedroom. Her boots made squishing sounds with each step she took.

"Here." Darcy handed Toni a towel and robe. "Go jump in a nice hot shower, and put this on. I'll throw your clothes in the dryer."

Toni smiled. "Thanks, I'll be out in a jiffy."

The bathroom door opened ten minutes later and Toni was followed out by billowing clouds of steam. Darcy had already slipped into a pair of sweats and shirt and had made a fresh pot of coffee.

"Feel better?" Darcy asked, as Toni entered the kitchen.

"That was great," she replied, running her hands through her dark, wavy, still wet hair.

"Can't have you catching a cold on your visit, now can we? Would you like a brandy, or some coffee?"

"Right now, a brandy sounds just *swell*," Toni quipped.

The two women walked into the living room and Darcy poured two brandies. Then she threw two large logs into the fireplace, and soon a warm fire was blazing. Toni sat down on the soft couch facing the fire, and Darcy settled into her recliner.

"Now," Darcy said. "Perhaps you'd like to tell me about yourself, since I've spent most of the evening blowing my own horn."

Toni smiled, leaned back against the couch, took a deep breath, and began the story of Toni Underwood. Her years as a police officer, and how finally the stress and tragedy connected with her career and the death of her lover, Megan, had almost destroyed her. She related briefly the adjustments she was dealing with as a result of her unexpected wealth.

She purposely left out her brief affair with Sally Murphy. Sally was still searching for her own sexuality and Toni had not been ready for a commitment. Hopefully, over time, their friendship would flourish again. Toni hated the thought of losing Sally as a friend. They had been through a lot together and Toni would do anything for Sally, but she wasn't in love with her.

Toni concluded her story by saying, "I'm not sure what I want to do with my life at this point. Most of my anger is gone now, and I know I'll always be committed to helping those who may be suffering some silent pain or anguish. But how I'm going to go about doing that is something I haven't figured out yet. So, right now I'm just plain old Toni Underwood, vacationer and tourist."

It was midnight by the time Toni finished. She was amazed she had been this open and candid with someone she had known for such a short time.

"I can't believe I've told you all these things. I never talk about myself this way. I hope I didn't bore you."

"Bore me? My god, I've never met anyone as complicated or interesting as you. The things you've done. The life you've led. To someone like me, you only come close to someone like you in a movie."

Toni laughed. "My life hasn't been that unusual. You've just never been close to a cop before, that's all."

"Well maybe so, but no matter what you say, you are different, and that's the truth."

Toni stared at Darcy for a long time without saying a word. The fire danced on Darcy's hair and face. Darcy silently sipped her brandy, returning Toni's stare over the rim of her glass.

"Do you mind if I ask you a question?" Toni finally broke the silence between them.

"Not at all," Darcy quietly answered.

"I know we don't know each other well, but since I've told you everything about myself, I thought maybe you wouldn't mind a very personal observation. I've never been one to beat around the bush, so if my bluntness offends you, please stop me, okay?"

"Yes, go on." Darcy urged, with a questioning look on her face.

"Is there something bothering you? Something you haven't, or can't mention? Something very frightening to you?" Toni's look was intense.

"Oh my god, how did you know?" Darcy's face suddenly turned pale.

"I was a policewoman for many years, Darcy; call it intuition, a gut feeling, or whatever. I sensed something last night, and again over dinner tonight. Something about the way you spoke, or held yourself, just *something*. If you don't want to tell me, it's okay, but if I can help, please, feel free to confide in me. It will go no further."

Darcy's eyes suddenly filled with tears. Toni knelt down in front of her, and took her hand. Leaning forward,

Darcy put her arms around Toni's neck. She was crying openly now.

"I want to be your friend," Toni whispered. "Come over here on the couch, and try and tell me what's wrong."

Toni put her hand around Darcy's waist, and helped her to sit down. Then, Toni poured two more brandies. Darcy sat staring at the fire. Finally, she turned her head, and looked into Toni's eyes.

"This may sound so farfetched you'll laugh, or think I'm insane," Darcy spoke quietly.

"If it's serious to you, then it's serious to me." Toni answered.

Darcy knew by the expression on Toni's face that she meant what she said. Hesitantly, she related the nightmares to Toni. The story of the old house, and how it frightened her as a child. How her aunt and uncle became very disturbed if she mentioned the old house to them. When she had finished the story, Darcy sighed deeply, leaned back, and closed her eyes.

The room was still and quiet except for the crackling of the fire. Then, without a warning, Darcy's eyes flew open and she sat straight up. "You think I'm crazy, don't you?" she blurted out.

"You're not crazy Darcy. Something happened to you when you were a child. You can't remember it, but it happened. The nightmares prove it. You've repressed whatever it is, and the subconscious mind is still trying to get through to you. Why these dreams have started again after all these years I don't know, but it means something."

"But my aunt and uncle never acted as though anything was wrong, or mentioned any dark past to me."

"Think Darcy why did your aunt find it necessary to return to the old house time after time, and just stand and stare at it? Why did your uncle become so upset when you tried to question him about it? Something was being covered up; something they were trying to protect you from."

"I never thought of that. But if it was so bad, how come I didn't sense it, or somehow find out about it?"

"Maybe you never really wanted to know. Now it's beginning to interfere with your adult life, and those questions need to be answered." Toni took Darcy's hands. "If you want me to help you solve this thing, and rid your life of these nightmares, I will."

"What do we do? Where do we start?" Darcy's voice was childlike and pleading.

"Well, the first thing we do is take a trip to Whidbey Island and visit your Aunt Mae. Just say I'm a friend from California, and you wanted to show me where you grew up. Let me handle the questions. We'd like to stay a couple of days and relax. From there, we play it by ear."

"When do we start?" Darcy asked. She felt a sudden excitement grip her.

"As soon as possible. I have no plans, and I'm at your disposal." Toni smiled.

"I have a week's vacation coming. I'll put in for it tomorrow. I'm sure there won't be a problem."

Darcy's excitement grew with each word. Finally, perhaps she could end these dreams, and return to a normal life.

"Now, where are my clothes? I'm going to get my butt outta here so you can get some sleep. I've got things to do, and plans to make." Toni said getting to her feet.

Her clothes were still damp, and she knew she'd better get home before the cold reached her bones. They held each other's hands tightly as Darcy walked Toni to the door.

"I'll see you day after tomorrow, *Red*," Toni whispered.

Then, she placed her hands gently on each side of Darcy's face and looked into her eyes. Bending down slowly, she kissed Darcy on the mouth. A warm, soft kiss, a kiss which held more then just friendship. Darcy returned the kiss as their lips melted together for a moment.

Toni drew back and smiled slightly. "Call ya tomorrow, sleep well." Then, she turned and walked to the elevator. Darcy watched until Toni entered the elevator and the doors shut. She felt wonderful and safe. No nightmares this night, only warm dreams of Toni's mouth on hers.

Chapter Six

Darcy walked briskly into work humming. As she passed several co-workers, she gave each one a warm smile, and a "Good morning, isn't it a lovely day."

Darcy had not been extremely happy and friendly of late, and this welcome change was a pleasant shock. After hanging up her coat and sitting down, she half-heartedly flipped through the stack of pending loan papers that covered one corner of her desk. Her mind was definitely not on work this Monday morning.

Glancing across the room to Mr. Rebal's office, she thought, *I wonder if he's in yet?*

Mr. Rebal was the branch manager, and he never arrived before 10:30 a.m. Darcy liked him, and felt he would grant her request for vacation without a hassle. She took a quick look at the clock on the wall, it was only 9:55 a.m. Giving out an impatient sigh she forced herself to concentrate on the work in front of her.

"Oh Darcy," Sue Olsen called out.

"Hi Sue. I didn't see you sitting there," Darcy answered

as she walked over to the desk where Sue was sitting. "What are you doing here? I haven't seen you in ages." Darcy flashed Sue a warm smile.

Sue Olsen was at the branch finishing up an audit. She worked out of corporate headquarters in Everett. She was head auditor, and knew the job better than anyone. Sue had recently married and lived in Edmonds, a small town on the Puget Sound.

People kidded Darcy and Sue on how much they looked alike. Both had red hair, green eyes, and a liberal amount of freckles. Sue was heavier than Darcy. Sue was five foot five inches and Darcy five-seven, but all in all, from a distance, it was easy to confuse the two.

Sue was an extremely serious person when it came to doing her job. She had worked for The Great Northwestern Bank for seven years and had a knack for catching errors with an ease that seemed uncanny to many.

Five years ago she had blocked an embezzlement scheme which helped make her a valued and respected employee. The chairman of the board allowed Sue a free hand in the company.

"Oh, I'm just here finishing up an audit. How have you been Darcy? God, I haven't seen you in months." Sue responded, returning the smile.

"Nothing much new Sue," Darcy lied. "You know me. I like a quiet, untangled existence. Congratulations on your marriage, I know Tom is a great guy. Listen, can we talk later? I've got to see Mr. Rebal about something really important." Darcy turned to leave.

Putting her hand on Darcy's arm Sue whispered, "Have lunch with me."

Sue's tone had changed and her facial expression had become quite serious. There seemed to be an urgency to her request.

"Sure Sue, I'll see you at one o'clock, how's that?"

"That's just fine . . . and thanks," Sue replied.

Darcy straightened her clothes and knocked on Mark Rebal's door.

"Come in." The deep voice boomed out.

"Good morning, Mr. Rebal. May I speak with you for a moment?" Darcy asked shyly.

"Sure Darcy, anytime, you know that," he replied with a smile. "Have a seat. Would you like some coffee?"

"No thanks, I'm coffee'd out."

"Well, what can I do for you then?"

"Something very important has just come up Mr. Rebal, and I was wondering if it would cause too big of a problem if I took my weeks vacation starting tomorrow?" Darcy held her breath waiting for an answer.

"Wow, that's pretty short notice," he paused for a moment. "But if it's that urgent, of course you can. Just make sure your work is covered by someone."

"Oh, I certainly will, and I can't thank you enough Mr. Rebal. I wouldn't have asked if it was something I felt could wait. I hope you know that."

"Of course I do Darcy. Don't give it another thought. Are you sure a week is enough time to handle whatever it is?"

"I hope so sir."

Darcy got up, shook his hand, and left the room. She appreciated the fact he had not pushed to find out what her reasons were for taking the time off.

Returning to her desk she dove into the mounds of paper work. She made sure notes were left on each file as to their status. Before she knew it, it was one o'clock, and Sue was standing by the desk waiting.

The lunchroom was still crowded, but slowly people began to filter out and return to work and a table opened up for them within five minutes.

They both ordered coffee, and looked at the menu. After ordering, a long uncomfortable silence settled in between them. Darcy had the feeling Sue had something to say, but couldn't quite find the words to begin.

"So Sue, how's married life? I hear the two of you bought a beautiful home in Edmonds," Darcy finally said, attempting to make small talk.

"I'm sorry, what did you say?" Sue had been miles away in thought.

"Oh, it wasn't important." Darcy shrugged her shoulders and took a bite of her salad.

Again, there was a long silence. Sue stared into her coffee cup as she continually stirred it with her spoon.

Darcy could stand it no longer and grabbed Sue's hand. "Look Sue, is something on your mind you want to talk to me about? You seem so preoccupied."

"God, Darcy, I thought I did, but now I don't know." Sue was clearly confused and disturbed.

"Well, I won't push you, but you'd better get whatever it is off your chest soon. You look like you're going to explode. You always know I'm here when you're ready to talk, okay?" Darcy squeezed Sue's hand.

"Thanks Darcy, you're a real pal. It was just something stupid, and after thinking about it, I may be jumping the gun if I discuss it now. Give me a few days, and then I'll try again, okay?" Sue raised her eyebrows apologetically and smiled slightly.

"No problem kiddo. Now, tell me all about what's been going on with you."

Their sandwiches arrived, and things seemed almost normal, they talked about work, and about Sue's new husband

and her new home in Edmonds. As soon as they got back to the bank Sue said a hurried goodbye, gave Darcy a big hug, and left.

Strange, very strange, Darcy said to herself. Then, once more she buried herself in the work on her desk.

As the afternoon wore on, she began feeling a nervousness in the pit of her stomach. Was she really going to find out about the nightmares once and for all? The prospect of what might happen in the week ahead caused her heartbeat to quicken. And Toni, was there a possibility of a relationship forming there? So many questions, and no answers. Darcy felt drained and frustrated by the end of the day.

Bending down, Darcy picked up the newspaper lying outside her front door. She stepped inside the apartment and flipped on a light. The apartment felt cold and damp. Quickly she adjusted the thermostat until she began to feel the warm air blowing through the vents. *That's better,* she thought.

Going into the bedroom, she slipped into some warm sweats and slippers. Then, heading back through the living room she grabbed the newspaper and entered the kitchen. Laying the paper down on the table, she continued to the refrigerator and opened the door.

"Hum, leftovers from the party. I'll just make a sandwich, and have vegetables with dip. Good healthy dinner if you ask me!" She said out loud.

After pouring herself a glass of wine, she sat down and opened the newspaper. "MAN ESCAPES FROM STATE ASYLUM, KILLS THREE!"

Darcy read on; "Aaron Blake, mass murderer, escaped the from maximum security ward at the Washington

State Mental Hospital. Blake killed three people, and stole the hospital station wagon. A nurse and two guards were his latest victims. No information has been released on Blake's background at this time. Police warn he is extremely dangerous. If seen, do not approach this man, but notify your local police immediately. Blake is six foot four, two hundred and eighty-five pounds. Muscular build, black hair, and dark eyes. His face, although covered by a heavy beard, is scarred by deep pock marks. He is forty one years old.

Above the article was a photo that had been taken of Aaron five years ago. Darcy continued reading. Police believe he is wearing a security guard's uniform and driving the hospital station wagon. A statewide manhunt was launched early this morning involving all local, state, and FBI agencies.

A shiver ran down Darcy's spine.

"God, how terrible." She whispered. She stared at Aaron Blake's picture, "Something about him, *something about the eyes.*"

Somehow, even though the newspaper picture was not clear, it seemed as if the black eyes were boring right through her.

Mae Harmon sat frozen in her chair. The blood had drained from her face, and her breathing was quick and hollow. She could not move her eyes from the newspaper lying in front of her.

Her lower lip quivered, and her hands shook. Fear consumed her very being.

"God in heaven, the Devil is lose among us!" she whispered in a hoarse voice.

Mae recognized the face staring back at her from the

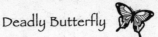

front page. Even after twenty-five years it still filled her with dread.

"What am I going to do? Darcy. Oh God!" Mae screamed as she threw the newspaper down.

She forced herself to stand. Then she began pacing back and forth across her kitchen wringing her hands as tears streamed down her face.

"Somehow I have to tell Darcy about Aaron Blake. I can't just let her go on not aware of the danger she's in. Why did this happen? We believed it was all over when they put him away, and she'd never have to know. We have to leave until he's caught. Leave the state. Yes, that's it. We'll go to Oregon and stay with Phil." With each step across the floor, Mae Harmon became more frantic.

Phil Harmon was Darcy's other uncle. He was her Uncle Fred's brother. No one had seen much of Phil since Darcy was five years old, but Mae kept in touch with him by letter. He lived alone, away from the city, and over the years had become a recluse. Mae knew Darcy probably didn't even remember him. It didn't matter. They'd be safe with Phil.

The wind was howling through the woods, and rattled the loose boards on the porch. The house was creaking, and rain was coming down in sheets, beating against the windows.

Suddenly, Mae stopped pacing. Her heart leapt into her throat. She realized she hadn't checked the doors and windows to be sure they were locked. Panic overtook her as she raced from room to room, checking all the locks and pulling down all the shades.

"What's that?" She stopped dead in her tracks as a loud banging coming from up- stairs startled her. Straining her ears, she listened. Barely breathing, she listened. A freezing gust of wind wound its way down the staircase and bit at her ankles.

Ever so carefully she approached the staircase, and placed her shaking hand on the banister. Again, she stopped to listen.

The relentless pounding was definitely coming from the second floor. As quietly as possible, she began ascending the staircase. By the time she reached the landing, she was gasping for air. Pausing, she closed her eyes for a moment. The constant pounding was definitely coming from Darcy's old room. The wind moaned as it blew out from under the closed bedroom door.

Holding onto the railing, Mae took one unsteady step after another until she stood in front of the door.

"Who's there?" she screamed. For a few seconds the banging stopped, and then began again, with even more intensity.

Mae's mouth was dry; she reached for the knob. Slowly, she pushed the door open. The wind and rain slapped her in the face taking her breath away as she stepped inside.

She held her hands up trying to block the torrent of water blurring her vision. Pushing her small frame against the wind, she finally reached the window sill. The window was wide open.

A shutter had been ripped loose, and was banging against the side of the house. As she reached for it, the shutter fell and shattered into pieces on the ground below. Then, with all the strength she had left, Mae pulled the window down. Standing alone in the dark room, she shook uncontrollably while warm tears streamed down her face.

After several minutes she turned and weakly made her way to her own room. She stripped off her wet clothes, towel dried her hair, and put on her robe and slippers.

Still shaking, she returned to the kitchen. She had not felt such terror in twenty-five years. Mae poured herself a stiff drink and downed it in one gulp. Pouring another, she sank into a kitchen chair and held her head in her hands. When the phone rang, her heart almost stopped beating.

"Yes, hello." Mae's voice was a whisper.

"Aunt Mae, is that you?" Darcy asked.

"Yes Darcy, it's me." Mae's voice was weak and low.

"What's wrong? You don't sound good. Are you alright Aunt Mae?"

Mae took a deep breath. "Oh sure honey, I'm okay. Must be a bad connection. There's really a bad storm outside tonight. In fact, I'm surprised you even got through. What time is it anyway?" She attempted to sound casual and reassuring.

"It's pretty bad here too. And, oh yes, it's 10:00 p.m. Am I calling too late?"

"Not at all sweetheart. It's so good to hear your voice honey. How have you been?" Mae took a large gulp of whiskey.

"Oh, I'm fine Aunt Mae. I thought I might come over and visit for a few days. A friend of mine is here on vacation, and I wanted to give her a tour of the island. Would that be all right with you?"

Mae hesitated. *What should I do? Bringing a friend. Should I tell her now? No, can't do this on the phone.*

"Aunt Mae, are you still there?" Darcy yelled into the mouthpiece.

"Oh, I'm sorry honey. I was just thinking that's all."

"Did you have other plans this week? If it's not convenient, we won't come." The tone of Darcy's voice was apprehensive.

"No honey that's fine. You bring your friend and come on over. We'll have a grand time." Tears filled Mae's eyes as she lied to her niece.

"See you tomorrow then. Sleep well." Darcy's voice was cheery once again as she hung up.

Mae sat staring blankly at the phone receiver she clutched in her quivering hand.

Darcy picked up her phone once more and dialed Frankie's number. Four rings, and then, "It's your dime, speak."

"Frankie, you're such a jerk." Darcy laughed. "I want to talk to Toni please."

"What's the matter, ain't I good enough for ya anymore?"

Darcy laughed again. "You know I love you the best of all, you old dyke. Now, get Toni on the phone before I come over there and break your neck."

"Now, that sounds more like the *sweet* Darcy we all know and love. Hold on a minute, *please*."

"Hi." Toni's soft low voice filled Darcy's ear.

"Everything is set for tomorrow. That's if you still feel like going through with this." Darcy said.

"I'll pick you up at 9:00 a.m., and yes, I still want to go through with this." Toni responded softly.

"Okay, don't forget to bring heavy clothes, rubber boots, and a rain jacket. The weather is really getting bad, and I want you to stay well."

"As long as I have you around to keep me warm, I'll stay *super* well." Toni replied, teasingly.

"I'll see you in the morning then; good night," Darcy answered smiling to herself.

A mixture of feelings poured through Darcy as she hung up. She was excited about spending time with Toni, and yet she was terrified by what she might find out about her past and her nightmares.

His coal black eyes scanned the shelves. The light from the refrigerator fell on his mask like face. Aaron's hair was still wet from the rain and stuck to his damp skin. The body lying on the floor at his feet was partially blocking the refrigerator door. Roughly, he shoved it aside with his foot as though it were a sack of potatoes.

Reaching in, Aaron grabbed the leg of lamb and the gallon of milk. He ripped at the meat with his teeth. Bits fell from his mouth and clung to his beard. He tipped the bottle of milk to his lips, streams of it ran out the corners of his mouth. Then he sat the milk down, got up, and began going through the cupboards.

Cookies. He liked cookies. After filling his belly with the lamb, he poured the box of cookies out onto the table. Taking a handful, he shoved them in his mouth. Crumbs and pieces fell all over. Tipping the carton once more, he finished off the milk, throwing the empty container on the floor. Aaron sat back with his eyes closed. Breathing deeply, he suddenly expelled a loud burp, patted his stomach and smiled.

A few minutes passed before he lifted his heavy body from the chair and stomped back toward the bedroom. Blood covered the walls and floor of the room.

The body of a woman lay on the floor under the window. Her nude body had been stabbed and ripped by multiple knife wounds.

Ignoring the lifeless body, Aaron opened the closet door. He yanked a wool shirt, pair of work pants, and heavy waterproof jacket from their hangers and threw them on the bed.

Entering the bathroom, he searched through the

drawers until he found a pair of scissors. The scissors clicked as he hurriedly cut his hair and beard. Then he grabbed a razor and shaved his face.

Returning to the bedroom, he quickly undressed and changed clothes, leaving the blood soaked guard's uniform in a heap on the floor. The dead man was closer to Aaron's size, and his clothes fit better than Sam's uniform.

Casually Aaron turned and walked back to the kitchen. Stepping over the man's body, he grabbed the car keys and wallet off the counter and went out the back door.

He stood motionless under the patio cover for a moment. The wind caught his hair and blew it back from his face. In the lightening flash, Aaron's black unblinking eyes gleamed.

Then, hurrying to the station wagon, he got in and pulled it behind the house. Jumping out of the wagon, he opened the garage door, got in the blue Toyota truck, and backed down the driveway.

Once more he returned to the station wagon and drove it into the garage. Aaron closed the door, got back in the truck, and headed for the freeway. The house filled with death lay silent and dark behind him.

Chapter Seven

Darcy had been up since dawn. She had packed Monday night, and was filled with an eagerness she hadn't felt for a long time. The morning had burst upon the scene with booms of thunder and an ever-growing wind. Even the threat of rain couldn't dampen her excitement and anticipation of what might lie ahead.

The hands on the kitchen clock moved to 9:00 a.m. At almost the same time, she heard the knocking on the door. Darcy's heartbeat quickened as she rushed to answer. A wide grin spread across her face as she opened the door.

There stood Toni looking like a misplaced Eskimo. Darcy's hand went over her mouth in an attempt to hide her laughter.

"What's so funny?" Toni said, with an extremely serious expression on her face. "The guy at the store told me this was what's in for winter wear in Washington."

Still trying to suppress her laughter, Darcy motioned Toni to enter.

"I didn't mean to laugh, but you look like you can barely move in all those clothes. I sure hope you don't have to go to the bathroom in a hurry." Darcy couldn't help herself, she laughed again.

"Look, Red, I'm from a very hot place in California, and I've got this real thin blood. You people who live up here are used to this weather. I've been freezing my ass off ever since I arrived. Believe it when I tell you, you <u>don't</u> want me to catch a cold. My sneezes are *deadly*. They've been compared to a sonic boom. Funny or not, this is the first time I've been warm, so the clothes stay. Got it?" Without warning, she grabbed Darcy and kissed her.

Darcy pulled back and gave Toni a seductive smile. "As long as you keep that up, you can wear moose skin, and it'll be just fine with me." Then, she put her arms around Toni's neck, and gave her a long deep kiss.

"Wow! Now I'm really warm. Maybe I won't need all these clothes after all." Toni said kiddingly. "Okay Red, lets hit it, or the boat's gonna leave without us."

"It's not a boat. It's a ferry, and they run every hour." Darcy chuckled and shook her head, as she locked the door behind them.

The wind was howling as Toni and Darcy sat in the car waiting for the slow moving ferry to dock. The black clouds on the horizon were moving quickly toward them.

The freezing waters of Puget Sound looked ominous and dark. White caps covered the choppy water, and the ferry rocked as the waves beat against its hull.

"Are you sure this is safe?" Toni asked, with a worried look.

"Well, I've made this trip hundreds of times in worse conditions then this, but then nothing in life is guaranteed."

Somehow, this answer didn't ease Toni's mind.

Once it was secured, the back of the ferry opened and the platform lowered to the dock. Toni started the car and followed a mini van onto the deck. Within ten minutes the ferry was loaded. The engines roared and the deck creaked under them as they slowly pulled away.

"Do you want to get out of the car and go upstairs for coffee?" Darcy asked casually.

Toni didn't answer. Her grip on the steering wheel tightened with each wave that hit the ferry. The boat dipped back and forth as the water battered itself against the immense hull.

"Toni, are you alright?" Darcy put her hand on Toni's.

"What? Oh, sure I'm okay. What makes you ask a question like that?"

"Well, maybe it's because you're crushing the steering wheel, or maybe because you look so green."

Toni blinked, and looked at her. "It shows doesn't it?"

"Yes, I'm afraid so." Darcy tried to keep a straight face. "Look Toni, there's nothing to be ashamed of. Lots of people get uptight about crossing the sound, even when the water is like glass. You'd have to be nuts if you didn't admit there are times when you're scared to death. That's only human." Darcy squeezed her hand.

Toni gave Darcy a weak smile. "Thanks," she whispered.

The twenty minute trip took over forty this day because of the wind and rough water. By the time they docked Toni was ready to throw up. She had fought back the overpowering sick feeling in the pit of her stomach, but she knew if they'd stayed on the water one more minute her breakfast would be decorating the deck. She drove the car off the ferry and pulled over to the side of the road.

"Do you want me to drive?" Darcy asked. She was concerned now, and could tell Toni was dizzy.

"Yeah, that might be a good idea," Toni answered. "But just let me stand outside by the car for a minute and get some fresh air first."

Darcy stood out in the wind with Toni holding on to her arm. Toni took one deep breath after another until a little color returned to her cheeks.

Finally leaning against the car, Toni sighed. "Man, if this is seasickness, they can have it. I'd rather face an angry mob then have this again."

"Are you ready?" Darcy asked softly.

"I'll be all right now . . . I think. I'm really sorry about this Darcy. I hope you don't think I'm some kind of boob."

"Get in. I think you're great." Darcy gave her a smile.

After driving for ten minutes, Darcy turned off the main highway and headed up the private road leading to her aunt's house.

Due to the storm the night before, the road was in bad shape. Large potholes had formed where the gravel had been washed away by the heavy rains. The dirt had turned to thick mud. This made the going slow and tedious. And now it was pouring again.

Neither Darcy nor Toni said a word as Toni's Mercedes slid and bumped its way down the damaged road. The woods grew thicker and deeper. The wind was reaching gale force and rain was hammering the car. Leaves and broken branches pounded against the windshield. Darcy could barely see where she was going.

Suddenly, the woods ended and they were out of the trees. An open meadow stretched before them.

"We're almost there." Darcy's voice was barely a whisper.

Ahead was a lovely two story farm house surrounded by trees and large bushes. A white picket fence ran around the outside of the house. Toni noticed some of the fence was missing.

Just then, Darcy jammed on the brake throwing them both forward unexpectedly. She had tried to avoid a large pothole, but the sudden stop caused the back end of the car to slide sideways. The left rear of the car dropped off the road with a loud thud into a mud filled ditch.

"Damn," Darcy sputtered. "Now we're stuck."

"Don't worry about it. Lets just get our stuff and make a run for the house. I'll take care of the car when the weather gets better." Toni was already out of the car and grabbing at the suitcases in the backseat.

The wind took their breath away as they ran toward the house. Rain soaked their outer clothing and mud covered their boots. Darcy slipped and went down on one knee. Toni rushed to her.

"I'm okay," Darcy yelled over the wind. "Go ahead."

Toni picked up Darcy's large suitcase and started once more into the wind.

Finally, they reached the porch. Completely out of breath, they leaned against the wall gasping for air.

Darcy pounded on the door. "Aunt Mae, Aunt Mae." she yelled.

A branch broke loose from a nearby tree and crashed to the ground, just missing the porch. This caused Mae to look out the window. She was clearly shocked to see Darcy and Toni standing there. As quickly as she could, she opened her door.

The wind and rain followed them in. Once inside, Toni dropped the suitcases and fought to close the door against the storm. She put all her weight against it. Darcy did the same. Reluctantly, the heavy oak door closed.

ee of them stood looking at each other, not
saying a word. Water ran off of Toni and
cy's clothing, dripping onto the oak floor.

"My God Darcy, how did you make it through this
horrible storm?" Mae finally blurted out. She wrapped her
arms around Darcy, holding her tight.

"Mrs. Harmon, we've had quite a trip." Toni replied.

Mae looked at Toni with a blank expression.

"Oh, Aunt Mae, this is my friend Toni Underwood;
remember, from California." Darcy realized her aunt was
confused. "You do remember me telling you about her last
night, don't you Aunt Mae?"

"Oh, oh yes, of course I remember. I'm not senile yet,
young lady," Mae said smiling. "I've just had a lot on my
mind, and with this gale and all . . . well . . . I'm sure you
understand why I had a momentary lapse of memory.
Welcome to my home, Ms Underwood. I'm sorry your visit
couldn't be under better circumstances."

"Don't worry about it, Mrs. Harmon. Everything's
fine now, and please, call me Toni."

"It's a deal Toni, as long as you call me Mae." Mae
held out her hand.

"Nice to meet you Mae," Toni responded, taking
Mae's hand in hers.

"Come now, lets get you two into some dry clothes."
Mae led them to the kitchen. "Here, hang those wet jackets
right in there." She pointed to the laundry room.

Toni and Darcy removed their jackets and boots. Mae
brought towels for their hair, and two pair of heavy wool
socks. Mae put on a pot of coffee. Then she took them into
the living room, and sat them in front of the fireplace. Soon
she was back with mugs of hot coffee. Darcy and Toni held
their hands around the mugs and sipped the steaming brew.

"You girls must be starving," Mae said.

"Well, not too long ago, I thought I'd never want to eat again, but I am kind of hungry." Toni replied. Darcy laughed. Toni shot her a dirty look.

"Have I missed something?" Mae asked with a puzzled look on her face.

"It's a long story Aunt Mae. I'll tell you all about it tomorrow." Darcy still had a wide grin on her face.

Mae shrugged her shoulders and toddled off to the kitchen.

"Do you have storms like this often in Washington?" Toni asked as she took another sip of coffee.

"At this time of year, we usually get several full blown gales. We expect rain most everyday until summer. We do the best we can when these types of storms hit. We're a hardy bunch up here in Washington, so we just take it all in stride, as much as possible." Darcy answered.

Suddenly, the lights flickered just as Mae came out of the kitchen with a plate of sandwiches.

"Looks like we might just lose the electricity," she said matter-of-factly. "But don't worry, I have plenty of candles and hurricane lamps. And tomorrow I'll see to getting the generator going."

Another flicker, and the lights went out. It was four in the afternoon, and yet it was almost dark. Mae bustled about placing candles in various spots around the house.

She went to the hall closet and pulled out two feather comforters. "You'll probably need these on your beds tonight," she said, laying them down next to the stairs.

After eating, the threesome sat quietly drinking more coffee and staring into the fire. It was dark now, so Mae and Darcy got up and went about the room lighting the candles.

The glow from the fireplace and candles danced on

the walls and ceiling. The howling of the wind was steady and showed no sign of letting up.

A growing knot began forming in the pit of Toni's stomach. Mae's body language and strained expression gave Toni the sense it was more than the storm causing this woman to be on edge.

"Would you girls like to play cards?" Mae said, breaking the silence.

Toni stretched, "Not me, thanks, but there is something I've been dying to ask you ever since I heard about it." As usual, Toni wasn't going to pussyfoot around.

"Oh, and what's that?" Mae responded, raising her eyebrows.

Darcy held her breath. She knew what was coming next.

"Well Mae, Darcy's been telling me about some nightmares she's had lately. She remembers having them as a child, but just recently they've returned. Being her friend, I told her I'd help in anyway I could to find out why." Toni paused to shift her position on the couch.

"She also told me about an old house you have here on your property. From her story, I have a feeling this house has some connection with the dreams. We thought maybe, just maybe, you could shed some light on this for us. These nightmares are beginning to interfere with Darcy's well-being, and I knew you'd do anything you could to help." Toni's eyes never left Mae's.

Mae's eyes grew wide. She sat staring at Toni, not saying a word, her mouth slightly open. Then, she looked at Darcy. Toni knew she'd hit a nerve.

"Aunt Mae, you do know something about my dreams, don't you?"

Mae didn't respond, but sat frozen. Then, she put her face in her hands and began sobbing. Her whole body shook.

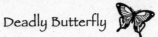

"Go in the kitchen Darcy, and see if she has some whiskey." Toni said hurriedly. "And bring back three glasses, I think we're going to need them." Moving close to Mae, she put her arm around the small woman's shoulder.

Darcy returned. "Here," she said, handing the bottle of whiskey to Toni.

Toni poured a drink for Mae. "Drink some of this," Toni said softly, holding the glass to Mae's lips.

Mae coughed as she swallowed the whiskey. She put her head back and sighed. She looked completely deflated and lost. Slowly, she brought her gaze even with Darcy, who was now sitting at Mae's feet, and looked into her eyes.

"My sweet child, I'm so sorry." She placed her hand gently on Darcy's cheek.

"Aunt Mae, what is it? What happened to me so long ago?"

Mae Harmon suddenly felt very old and tired. Her body seemed to slump and those little flashes of light faded from her eyes. Her throat felt tight and closed. She opened her mouth, but nothing came out.

"Mrs. Harmon," Toni gently urged. "We understand this is something you've held inside for many years, and it's not easy to speak of it after all this time. But for Darcy's sake, you must find the strength to tell her your story. Darcy loves you very much, and nothing you say will ever change that."

Mae looked at Toni. "Why do you care about this? You hardly know me. I know you're Darcy's friend, but this is a family matter. How and why would you go out of your way to help?"

"Mrs. Harmon, I realize I'm not part of your family, and it's hard to understand that I'm only here to do what I can to ease your pain, but your niece believes it, and I give you my word I only want to help. I lost someone I loved very deeply and I was filled with anger and hate for a long time. It almost destroyed me." Toni took Mae's hand and held it tightly.

"I didn't care about anyone, or anything, during that time. I finally realized the person I loved so much wouldn't want my life to be wasted on hate and self-pity. I've vowed to do whatever I can to help people who are living in fear and pain through no fault of their own.

"Now, Darcy is the one who needs her life back and that's why I'm here." Toni looked directly into Mae's eyes as she spoke.

Somehow, Mae knew Toni was telling the truth and squeezed her hand firmly. After a sip of whiskey, she cleared her throat and began the long painful journey that would take them all back some twenty-five years. Darcy was five years old once again.

Chapter Eight

"Hi, sweetheart," Darcy's father called out.

Jumping off her tricycle she ran into her father's outstretched arms.

"How's my beautiful girl today?" Paul Bennett said smiling. He hugged Darcy and kissed her pink cheek.

"Are you home for good, daddy?" Darcy asked, hugging his neck.

"I'm home for awhile honey, and I promise I won't go away again until after your birthday, okay?" He kissed Darcy and put her down.

She put her tiny hand in his, and he walked toward the house, with Darcy skipping along beside him.

Nancy Bennett's beautiful long red hair blew gently in the breeze as she stepped out onto the porch. She waved and smiled at Paul. He took the steps two at a time and swooped her up into his arms. Darcy giggled as they kissed each other. She was very happy.

Because of his work at the Jansen Lumber Company, Paul was away from home for two to three weeks at a time.

He was the foreman at one of the Jansen logging operations in Washington.

After Paul got the job as foreman, Darcy's parents moved to Whidbey Island and lived with Mae and Fred Harmon. Mae was Nancy's older sister, and she and Fred insisted the Bennetts stay with them.

Mae would not hear of Nancy living alone while Paul was away. The house was big, and since Mae and Fred had no children, they loved being surrounded by the warmth and love of Paul, Nancy, and Darcy.

One day soon after Darcy's father had returned home, a letter came in the mail addressed to Fred. Fred's face was serious as he read the letter.

"Fred," Mae said. "What is it? You're as white as a sheet. What's wrong?"

As Fred sat down at the kitchen table, he was trembling and looked as if he'd just been slapped in the face.

"My mother and step-father have been killed in a fire. Their house burned down and they were trapped inside."

"Oh, my god Fred." Mae sat down and put her arm around him. Fred handed the letter to her.

"I can't believe this." Mae whispered. "Why didn't someone call us?"

Fred wiped the tears from his eyes. "No one called because there was no one around who knew us except my half brother Aaron. He has been taken in by the youth authority. All they could get from him was our name and that we lived in Washington. I haven't seen my mother in sixteen years, and I've only seen Aaron once right after he was born. God, I feel so guilty now."

"My dear sweet Fred," Mae said gently as she patted his pale cheek. "There's no reason for you to feel guilty about

anything. Your mother knew how you felt when she married Lenny Blake. That was her choice. She knew you loved her, but you couldn't stay. We always kept in touch through phone calls and letters. You begged her to come live with us. She knew she was always welcome here." She kissed Fred, and held him close.

There was a long silence. Then Fred took a deep breath and said, "We're going to have to take care of Aaron. He has no one else."

"Of course we will sweetheart. He's your half brother and we're all the family he has now. Poor thing must be scared to death. We have to call the youth authority right away and get him out of there as soon as possible."

Slowly, Fred rose to his feet, picked up the phone and dialed the number at the bottom of the paper. After speaking to a Mr. Larson at the Hayward California Youth Authority, he hung up and turned to Mae.

"Mr. Larson said I could come down and pick Aaron up at the end of this week." A deep frown cut across his forehead. "Something's not right here, I can feel it."

"Everything is going to be all right Fred. You're just in shock right now. Once we get used to the idea, I'm sure Aaron will fit in just fine with all of us." Mae took his hand in hers to reassure him that everything would be all right.

Later that afternoon they told Paul and Nancy what had happened. Although they had never met Fred's mother, Nancy and Paul understood the pain he must have been going through and offered any help they could.

"How did the fire start, and why couldn't your mother and her husband get out?" Paul asked Fred in a concerned voice.

"I don't really know any details yet," Fred answered. "But you can bet I'm going to try my damndest to find out."

"We'll move Darcy in with us, and Aaron can have her room until the new house is ready." Nancy said.

"The new house should be finished soon," Mae replied. "So then Aaron will move with us, and you and Paul will have this place to yourselves."

"Everything will work out. We'll all do the best we can to make Aaron feel at home," Paul responded.

"Come on Nancy, let's make some coffee. I think we could all use a cup. There seems to be a chill in the house and a nice cup of hot coffee sounds good," Mae said as she got up from the sofa.

Fred walked over to the fireplace and stared into the blazing fire. Even though it was early June, the afternoons were cold, and a misty fog hung and floated close to the ground. A sudden shiver ran through Fred's long thin body.

"You know Fred, you've never mentioned the reason why you stopped seeing or visiting your mother after you left and got out on your own," Paul said as he joined Fred. "Does it have something to do with Aaron? I don't mean to pry, but maybe it would help to talk about it."

"I don't know Paul. I just never wanted to burden anyone with my problems. Mae knows the whole story, and anyway the whole thing is over now that mom's gone."

"Look Fred, you and I aren't just brothers in-law, we're friends and anything that affects you concerns me. I know you're hurting right now and I'd like to help if I can." Paul placed his hand on Fred's shoulder.

There was a long silence. Then Fred spoke in a low, flat tone. "After my father passed away my mom and Phil and me had a rough time of it. Phil and I were both pretty young and couldn't be of much help to her. We didn't have much to begin with and dad left us no insurance or savings." He sighed and took a deep breath.

"Mom got work cleaning houses and Phil and I mowed lawns and did odd jobs. The money we all brought in barely kept a roof over our heads."

After a painful pause Fred returned to the sofa and sat down. Then he continued his story. "About two years after my father's death, mom met Lenny Blake at a church social. He was a brute of a man and ugly as sin, but he was kind to my mother and he had a good job in construction.

"I knew mom didn't love him, but she needed someone, and Lenny was willing and ready to marry her and take care of us. She explained to us boys that Lenny could never take our father's place in her heart, but she felt this would be good for all of us in the long run." Fred closed his eyes for a moment.

"Within a short time we found out who the real Lenny Blake was. He kept my mother a virtual prisoner in the house. He didn't allow her old friends to visit. He isolated her from all those who really cared about us. My brother and I didn't find out until later the reason she put up with this was because of his threats to do us harm if she tried to leave. My brother Phil left first. He was only seventeen, but he couldn't take the abuse any longer. I stayed, because of my concern for mom."

A sad smile crossed Fred's lips. "You know, my father used to say mom was like a beautiful butterfly that was never set free to fly. She loved all of us so much she sacrificed her own place in the sun to take care of our needs. But dad vowed someday he would make his fortune and then we would see her spread her glorious wings and reveal her beauty to the whole world. My mother was a talented musician. When she played the piano it sounded like the music of heaven. Now her day in the sun will never come." Fred's body sagged, as his voice trailed off.

"Jesus Christ Fred, why didn't you just take her out of there?" Paul asked.

"I tried Paul, but she wouldn't leave. He had her convinced no matter where we went he would find us and kill us both. Then she found out she was pregnant." Fred swallowed hard.

"She was thirty nine and that son of a bitch insisted she have his child. After Aaron was born I couldn't stand by and watch her slowly fade away. Maybe I was a coward, but I left. I tried over the years to get her to come live with Mae and me, but because of Aaron she stayed. Now she's dead and I blame myself for not being there." Fred's shoulders shook as he broke down in tears.

"God Fred, that's really rough. You know people can always say what they'd do in your situation, but until you live it yourself, it's not fair to judge someone else. Don't blame yourself my friend. You were a young man and your mother did what she thought she had to do. Wrong or right, that's what she believed." Paul patted him on the shoulder. "All you could do was let her know you were there if she needed you. That's all any of us can do." Paul urged him to his feet.

"Come on Fred, let's go have some coffee. We all love and respect you, and now you're willing to take her son in. That's probably the best thing you could have done for her."

"Thanks Paul. Telling you really helped, but in my heart I'll never forgive myself. But maybe I can make up for a few things by taking care of Aaron, and seeing to it he has everything he needs."

Two days later, Fred packed the car, kissed Mae, and left to bring Aaron home. He promised to be home in five days, which would be Sunday, Darcy's fifth birthday.

Mae and Nancy were busy setting up the picnic table. They had strung balloons on the clothesline and covered the poles with bright red and blue and yellow crepe paper. Nancy had baked a beautiful cake and all Darcy's presents were wrapped, except for the very special one Paul had gone to pick up.

Four neighbor children were invited to share in the birthday fun. They arrived at noon and Darcy was already busy shaking and feeling all her gifts. Her face was beaming and the children's laughter filled the air.

Mae turned as she heard the car coming up the driveway. "Oh look, it's Fred." She waved and ran toward the car.

Fred stepped out slowly. His face was drawn and he looked very tired. Mae threw her arms around his neck. The shadowed figure sitting on the passenger side of the car hadn't moved.

"Mae, I have to talk to all of you right away," Fred whispered as Mae threw her arms around his neck. He was cold and stiff.

She stepped back and looked into Fred's face. There was something in his eyes she had never seen before. A sadness, a fear, something.

"What is it honey?" Mae asked, frowning.

Before he could respond Nancy and Darcy were hugging him.

"Oh Fred, it's so good to have you home. We all missed you." Nancy kissed his cheek.

"Uncle Fred. Uncle Fred." Darcy was jumping up and down tugging at his shirt sleeve. "Uncle Fred, it's my birthday."

Fred reached down and lifted her up. "Your birthday? Well, my goodness, so it is." He managed a laugh, but his eyes were full of pain.

They all turned as they heard the click of the door handle, the car's passenger door slowly opened. As the emerging figure stepped out and straightened up, Mae's mouth fell open and Darcy held her uncle tighter. Nancy looked stunned.

Aaron Blake turned toward the now silent group. He was at least six foot three inches in height. His build was thick and heavy, not at all like that of a sixteen year old.

Below a protruding forehead and thick eyebrows, his gleaming black eyes cut through them. Unblinking, he stood motionless, not uttering a word. His wild hair and pock marked face only added to the shock that Mae, Nancy, and Darcy felt at the sight of Aaron Blake. A dark unseen foreboding seemed to fill the air surrounding him. No one spoke or moved for what seemed an eternity. Mae slowly took Fred's hand in hers and squeezed it tight.

Finally Fred said, "Mae, Nancy, Darcy. This is Aaron, my half brother."

Still no one moved.

Aaron reached into the car and pulled out a green duffel bag. After straightening up, he stood stone-like staring at the threesome.

"Come with me Aaron," Fred said quietly, "I'll show you your room."

Without a word Aaron walked past Mae, Nancy, and Darcy as he followed Fred into the house. A shudder ran through both women.

"Oh my god, what have we brought into our home?" Mae's voice was a whisper.

"It's all right Mae," Nancy replied half-heartedly. "Maybe it's just us. We need to give this some time." She put her arm around Mae's shoulder. "Come on now, we have a bunch of restless kids to entertain."

Down deep they both knew from this moment on, nothing would really be all right again, as long as Aaron remained here.

Darcy ran back to where her friends were and soon forgot the sight of Aaron Blake. Mae and Nancy rejoined the group and tried to shake off the coldness still running through their bodies.

"Daddy, it's Daddy," Darcy yelled.

Paul got out of the Ford pick-up carrying a large box with a big red ribbon on it. "Hi, birthday girl." He called to Darcy. Then, he sat the box down on the ground.

"Is it for me?" Darcy squealed as she and her friends ran to where he was.

"You bet it is honey," Paul answered, a wide grin on his face. "Go ahead, open it."

Everyone gathered round as Darcy pulled at the lid. She looked inside and found two big brown eyes staring back at her. The next thing she knew, the box tipped over knocking Darcy back onto the lawn.

Before she could regain her feet, four paws and a very wet tongue were all over her. She looked into the happy face of the cutest puppy she had ever seen. Everyone was laughing. The Golden Retriever pup began running in circles tripping itself as it fell over its own clumsy feet.

"Do you like her?" Darcy's father asked. "Your mommy and I picked her out especially for you."

Darcy ran to her mother and father. She kissed and hugged them over and over. "She is the most wonderfulest thing in the whole world," she answered, beaming.

The dark figure stood at the window in the upstairs bedroom silently staring down at the happy scene below. The expressionless face and unblinking black eyes expelled an evil insanity.

That evening Fred gathered everyone together at the new house. Mae, Nancy, and Paul stood in the kitchen watching Fred as he paced back and forth. Darcy played in the big unfinished living room with her new puppy.

Suddenly Fred stopped and turned toward them. "Look everyone, I know what a shock meeting Aaron was to all of you. Believe me, after traveling with him for two days, I'm still not over it myself. He is very strange, even frightening. Right now, I can't think of anything to do with him except let him stay here until we come up with a solution."

"Fred, it's okay," Paul said, patting Fred on the back.

"But, you don't understand," Fred replied, almost pleading. "It *isn't* okay. The police found my mother and Lenny locked in the basement of their home. They had been bound and gagged."

Mae gasped. "Murdered? God, what do they think happened?"

"They don't know for sure, but they found Aaron outside standing on the lawn just staring at the house. The police assumed he was in shock. He never answered any of their questions. In fact, he hasn't said more than two words to me since I picked him up. No one knew what to do with him. The police are still investigating."

"Fred, you're not saying Aaron had something to do with this are you?" Nancy asked. A sudden fear gripped her.

Fred took a deep breath, "I'm not saying that, but there's something about him that turns my heart cold. You've all felt the same thing; I know it."

"What do you want us to do Fred?" Paul asked quietly.

"I promise all of you he won't be here long. Tomorrow I'm going to check into private schools, foster parenting, and anything else I can come up with to get him away from here. In the meantime, I want you all to be very aware of what he's doing, and where he is at all times." Fred's face was taut and pale.

No one said a word as they walked back to the old house. A bond of fear now held them in its grip. A fear Fred prayed would keep them alert and safe.

Aaron kept to himself the first week. He wouldn't come down to dinner with the rest, so Mae would set a plate of food outside his door. She repeated this ritual three times a day. The plates were always cleaned and replaced outside the door.

Early one morning as the sun shone on the pond and the June air was warm and sweet, Mae entered the kitchen.

The smell of the blossoming trees and flowers caught on the soft breeze and filled the house. Mae smiled to herself and hummed softly as she pealed fresh peaches for a cobbler. Then, something drew her attention to the kitchen window and when she looked out, she saw Aaron.

He was standing naked to the waist at the edge of the pond. He wasn't moving. Fred was outside getting ready to head down to the new house and do some painting. The only sounds were of the birds singing and leaves rustling in the morning breeze.

Maybe he's finally coming around. Mae thought as she watched Aaron. Without warning, Aaron's arms suddenly jutted out from his body hurling something through the air into the middle of the pond. She jumped as her heart leapt into her throat.

Fred had turned just in time to see Aaron's motion. The water splashed high into the air as the Golden Retriever puppy hit the pond. Dropping what he was doing he ran toward Aaron. The puppy was fighting to keep its head above water. She was panic stricken and losing ground fast.

Without stopping Fred ran head long into the pond.

As he reached the pup her head was disappearing for the last time. He made a grab for her catching hold of the new leather collar around her neck and pulled the puppy up to him.

Her large brown eyes were filled with panic. Water was running from her nose and mouth. Fred held her close as he made his way back to shore. Aaron was still standing in the same spot. His face was expressionless.

By this time Mae had reached the pond. She helped Fred out of the waist high water. He was coughing and out of breath. The puppy was shaking and whining.

Mae turned to Aaron. "Why did you do this?" She screamed at him.

His coal eyes cut through her as a sneering smile crossed his cruel mouth. He turned, and without a word walked back to the house. The tattoo of a large butterfly glistened on his sweating shoulder as he disappeared through the back door.

Fred and Mae stood staring, openmouthed. The puppy whined once more jolting them back to reality.

"Come on Mae, we have to get the puppy dried off and warmed up." Fred's voice was hoarse.

Nancy met them at the back door. "What happened?" She asked as she grabbed a towel.

While Fred wiped the frightened puppy off, Mae told Nancy what had gone on down at the pond.

"What are we going to do? I'm afraid for Darcy. I've caught Aaron watching her play with the puppy from his bedroom window. We have to do something." Nancy's voice was high pitched.

Fred took Nancy's arm. "I'm going to do something today. I've got a line on a hospital in Seattle that deals with emotionally disturbed teens. I don't care what it takes. Aaron will be in this hospital before the middle of next week. You have my word on it. In the meantime we don't let Darcy or her puppy out of our sight."

When Nancy related the story to Paul, he wanted to confront Aaron. "That son of a bitch. I'll beat the shit out of him," he raged.

"Please Paul, don't do anything. Fred's going to place him in a hospital next week. He's so strong. Even you're no match for Aaron." Nancy said pleading.

Reluctantly Paul agreed to wait, but told Nancy if anything else happened, he wouldn't hold back from taking Aaron on.

The rest of the week no one saw Aaron, but they knew he was somewhere watching and listening. Fred, Mae, Nancy, and Paul remained on edge and nervous.

On Monday, Fred had gone to the hospital and arranged for Aaron's confinement. He was to bring Aaron in Wednesday. It was only on a temporary basis until they could run psychological tests on him and make a determination as to treatment. There was no doubt in Fred's mind that Aaron would not be returning.

Tuesday afternoon was humid and hot. Fred was at the new house making sure everything was ready for the move. Paul was in the driveway working on Nancy's car, which had been stalling on her for about a week. He was leaving again on Friday so he wanted to be sure she'd have no more trouble with the car while he was gone.

Mae was in the new house putting dishes away and cleaning up her new kitchen. Nancy and Darcy were getting ready to fix a snack for Paul. All in all, it was turning out to be a lazy, slow moving summer day.

Nancy stood at the sink washing lettuce, glancing up

now and then to watch Paul. He was bent over the fender of the car. His upper body and head were under the hood. The air was still and heavy. Not even the birds seemed to have energy enough for singing.

Off to her right something suddenly moved through the trees. It drew Nancy's attention. At that same instant Aaron burst through the thick patch of woods like a wild bear, and ran across the open space toward the driveway.

The scene before her seemed to move in slow motion. She was unable to speak or move. Her eyes froze on Aaron Blake as he drew closer to Paul. She opened her mouth to yell at Paul, but nothing came out.

He never had a chance. Aaron's huge hand slammed the hood down. Paul's body stiffened and then went limp. Aaron continued to raise the hood again and again each time, smashing the heavy metal down on Paul's head and shoulders.

Breathing heavily, Aaron turned and looked at the house. He was looking directly into Nancy's eyes. Even though he was too far away to really see her, Nancy knew somehow he knew she was there watching him.

The blood drained from her face; she couldn't move. Her knuckles turned white as she clutched onto the edge of the sink to keep from falling to her knees. Aaron smiled as he began slowly walking toward the house. His bare chest was splattered with blood.

Not really knowing what she was doing, driven only by the instinct to save her child, Nancy turned and grabbed Darcy. She pulled her along dragging her off her feet. Darcy began crying.

Stumbling and fighting to keep her balance, Nancy made her way upstairs and threw her bedroom door open. Quickly, her terror filled eyes scanned the room. Then, her gaze fell on the air duct outlet. Turning to Darcy, she tried to sound calm and reassuring. Gently, she wiped the tears from her small daughter's eyes.

"Honey," Nancy said in a whisper. "Listen to me. Mommy's sorry if she hurt you, but you must do as I say."

Sensing she had very little time left, Nancy pulled the grill from the air duct outlet. Darcy was whimpering quietly.

"You must get in here. You trust mommy don't you?"

Darcy shook her head yes in response.

"This is not a game. I want you to stay here until I come back. Don't make a sound. Mommy loves you." Nancy kissed Darcy and gave her one last hug.

Darcy crawled into the small space and her mother replaced the grill. She heard the door shut and she was alone.

Chapter Nine

A sudden flash of lightning illuminated the living room causing Mae and Toni to jump. Darcy sat frozen as though she were in a trance. The expression on her face was one of total horror her eyes round and glassy like large marbles, mouth hanging open.

Then the room grew dark once more as the lightning flash faded. Only the dancing light of the fireplace and candles remained. It took Toni a moment to clear her head and bring herself back from the unbelievable tale she had just heard.

Finally, she looked at Darcy and Mae. Their faces had taken on a ghostly mask- like appearance as the firelight played on their skin. Carefully, Toni moved closer to Darcy. It was clear she was in shock.

"Get a blanket and hand me that whiskey," Toni said quietly to Mae.

Mae's eyes were riveted on Darcy and the sound of Toni's voice caused her to jump, but her gaze never left Darcy's pale face.

"Did you hear me?" Toni's voice grew firm and demanding. "She's in shock. We have to try and snap her out of it."

Blinking a few times, as if she was waking from a deep sleep, Mae slowly got to her feet and walked to the foot of the stairs, picking up one of the feather quilts she had taken out earlier. Returning to the sofa, she silently offered the quilt to Toni.

Hurriedly, Toni covered Darcy's shaking body. Then, she poured a shot of whiskey and held it to Darcy's lips, forcing some of the liquid into her mouth.

Coughing as the whiskey reached her throat Darcy fought to catch her breath. Toni held her tight while Mae rubbed her hands. They fought hard to bring Darcy back from the edge of the abyss her mind had taken her to. After twenty minutes Darcy finally blinked her eyes, and looked at Toni.

"Was I dreaming? What happened to me?" Her voice was no more than a whisper.

"No Darcy, you weren't dreaming, not this time," Toni answered softly.

"Oh my dear, are you all right?" Mae said, holding Darcy's hands tight.

Tears filled Darcy's eyes as the realization of what had happened so long ago began to take hold of her conscious mind.

"God, god no. How could this be?" she pleaded in a lost, confused voice. Then, Darcy became silent once more.

After a few minutes, without any warning, Darcy attempted, frantically, to get to her feet. Toni held her more tightly. She struggled against Toni's strong grip as she wrenched her hands free from Mae and began pushing them against Toni's chest. Toni knew if she let Darcy go she would run, run into the storm, run to nowhere trying to escape the terror and fear now consuming her.

It seemed an eternity passed before Darcy finally stopped fighting and sagged limply in Toni's arms. Sobs racked her body as she put her arms around Toni's neck. Toni rocked Darcy gently back and forth, as one would a frightened child.

"Sh, everything is all right. You're going to be okay. I won't leave you." Toni kissed her softly on the forehead.

"Darcy, it's me, Aunt Mae." Mae was on her knees in front of her. "I'm so sorry. Please forgive me." Tears streamed down Mae's strained face.

Darcy looked blankly at her aunt for a moment, and then reached out her hand and placed it on Mae's cheek. Sliding off the sofa, she stretched out her arms and pulled Mae to her. They both knelt on the floor holding each other. Tears held back for twenty-five years soaked their faces.

Toni had quietly gotten up and poured three very large shots of whiskey. "Here you two, I think we all need a good stiff one right now," she said as she offered them each a glass.

After taking a long gulp, Toni cleared her throat. "Mae, I don't know if this is asking too much, but I believe it's important you finish this story once and for all. Darcy needs to be done with it forever." Toni paused and looked at Darcy. "Do you think you're strong enough to go on?"

There was a long pause as Darcy tried to sort out some of her thoughts. One part of her wanted to run and hide from knowing anymore, yet, deep inside she knew she must hear the rest if she were ever to be free of her nightmares.

"I don't know if we should subject Darcy to anymore of this tonight," Mae said as she grabbed Darcy's cold hand.

"It's all right, Aunt Mae. Toni's right, I need to end

this now. As long as I have the two of you here with me, I'll make it." She managed a warm smile to her aunt.

Toni took Darcy's other hand and held it tight. "We're with you every step of the way on this Darcy. Don't ever doubt that." Her voice was gentle and caring.

"Go ahead, please finish," Darcy said giving Toni's hand a firm squeeze.

Mae took a deep breath and another sip of whiskey. "I am not going into details concerning what happened to your mother, except to say, along with your father, they were both killed that day by Aaron Blake."

Darcy's breath caught in her throat. "Oh god."

Mae continued, "About the time this was all happening, your Uncle Fred had started back to the old house for something or other he needed. He had caught sight of your mother running from the old house waving her arms frantically. She was screaming, but Fred couldn't make out what she was yelling.

"Before he completely realized what was happening, Aaron had caught Nancy and was dragging her back into the house.

"Fred turned and ran back to his truck and grabbed his twenty-two rifle. He always carried it on a rack in the back. I saw him from the window. He screamed at me to call the police and then ran toward the old house. I didn't know at this point what was happening, but I did as he said. Then I took off running after him. I was no more then three to four minutes behind him.

"I ran through the open front door. There was no one there. I called out for someone to answer me but no one did. I ran from room to room screaming for someone, anyone to please answer.

"In the kitchen I froze in mid-stride. Blood covered the walls, floor, and table. It was everywhere. My heart almost stopped; my mind couldn't take this all in. The room began spinning and I knew I had to fight with everything in me to keep from passing out."

Mae leaned back against the sofa and closed her eyes. Toni reached over and took hold of her shaking hand.

"Take your time Mae, it's all right."

Swallowing hard, Mae continued, "Then I heard loud noises coming from upstairs. Crashing sounds, something being thrown about. My legs were like jelly, but I managed to get to the staircase, and holding on to the banister for support, I pulled myself up the steps one at a time.

"Suddenly everything was silent; deadly silent. A trail of blood led to your mother's bedroom. The door was partly open and Fred's gun was laying on the floor just outside. Carefully I reached down and picked it up. I knew how to use it because Fred insisted I learn. I was thankful for that now.

"Slowly, I pushed the door open with the barrel of the rifle. That's when I heard a soft moaning. Taking one step inside, I saw Fred lying on the floor. Blood was coming from his mouth and head. Aaron was standing over him. His arms were high over his head and his fist was clenched, poised to crash down on Fred.

"I must have screamed because Aaron turned. He had an insane grin on his hideous face as he stared at me. He stood motionless for a minute and then started toward me. I don't remember pulling the trigger, but I hit him three times. Two bullets ripped into his upper body and the third hit his leg, breaking it.

"The next thing I remembered was kneeling over Fred holding him in my arms and the police rushing into the room. I remember hearing you crying and finding you hidden in the air-outlet. Fred had staggered to his feet and we took you from the room. But before we could reach the door,

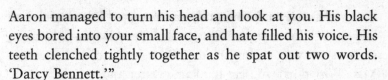

Aaron managed to turn his head and look at you. His black eyes bored into your small face, and hate filled his voice. His teeth clenched tightly together as he spat out two words. 'Darcy Bennett.'"

"Oh my god," Darcy whispered breathlessly.

"After the trial, Aaron was committed to the state asylum for life. We never went back into the old house, not even to clean up or remove our things. Our good neighbors removed our clothing and a few items we needed, and things we couldn't replace."

Mae looked deep into Darcy's tear-filled eyes, "Your uncle Fred never got over the guilt he felt. He never forgave himself for bringing Aaron to the island. The only thing that kept us going through all these years was you, Darcy. You were our salvation and life. We realized you didn't remember anything of that day, except for the disoriented dreams. So right or wrong, we never told you the truth of what happened that dreadful day." Mae sat back and sighed.

Darcy was holding Toni's hand so tight her nails cut into Toni's flesh. Again there was a long silence as they all tried to digest the foul truth of what happened.

"Why didn't you tear down the old house?" Toni asked.

"I pleaded with Fred to burn it to the ground, but he always said no. It was as if the house had to be there so he'd never forget what happened. Maybe it was his way of somehow hanging on to Darcy's family. I really don't know. Sometimes if he had a bit too much to drink, he would tell me he could hear the laughter of the happy times still coming from the house. Then he would cry himself to sleep. When he died, I knew his soul was finally at peace." Mae looked completely spent and frail as she finished the last of her drink.

"Come on." Toni said, standing up. "I think we've all had enough for tonight." She gently helped Darcy to her feet; she was swaying and unsteady. "I'll help Darcy to her room, Mae. Why don't you get her some water and aspirin?"

Mae helped Darcy undress and get into her bed. She held Darcy close, for a very long time. Neither of them saying a word. Finally, she let go and Darcy eased back down against her pillow, falling asleep almost immediately.

Toni had waited in the hall until Darcy was safely tucked into bed. She knew Mae and Darcy needed this quiet time alone, together. Stepping out into the hall, Mae looked up into Toni's blue eyes. "I think she'll be all right for tonight," she whispered.

After showing Toni to her room, Mae kissed her on the cheek and retired to her own room at the end of the hall.

The storm outside raged on as Toni blew out her candle and buried herself under the thick feather comforter. She tossed and turned for almost an hour, fighting to block out the sound of thunder and pounding of the rain and wind. The pictures of death kept flashing across her closed eyes. Toni knew, somehow, this was not the end of the story. The final act had not yet been played out. Finally, she fell into a restless, fitful sleep.

The clap of thunder shook Toni's bed. She bolted upright, her heart pounding. The next flash of lightning outlined the dark figure standing at the foot of her bed. Toni's first instinct was to grab her gun, but it was still in her suitcase.

"Who's there? I said who are you damn it!"

Darcy's voice trembled as she spoke. "It's me, Darcy. The storm woke me. I can't stay asleep. Aaron Blake's face keeps looming up at me when I close my eyes."

Toni could tell she had been crying. "Come here," she said gently, without hesitation. Throwing back her covers she slid over to allow room for Darcy.

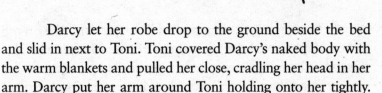

Darcy let her robe drop to the ground beside the bed and slid in next to Toni. Toni covered Darcy's naked body with the warm blankets and pulled her close, cradling her head in her arm. Darcy put her arm around Toni holding onto her tightly. Her shaking began to subside as Toni's breath warmed her neck.

Toni felt the cold tears fall on her arm. With her free hand Toni pushed the soft curls back from Darcy's face.

Darcy looked into Toni's eyes as another flash of lightning lit up the room. As Toni softly kissed the tears away from Darcy's eyes and cheeks, her fingertips caressed the outline of Darcy's lovely face.

Then Toni pulled her close once more. She could feel the firm fullness of Darcy's breasts against her own. Their hearts seemed to beat in rhythm as one.

They lay this way for a long time. Not moving, not speaking, drinking in the warmth between them. Then, slowly Toni raised her head. She cupped Darcy's chin in her hand and pressed her soft full mouth against Darcy's. The kiss became deeper as Darcy rose to meet Toni's lips.

Toni moved her hand down the small of Darcy's back and pulled her thighs tight to her own. A slight moan escaped through Darcy's mouth as Toni wrapped her leg over Darcy's. Toni's tongue traced the contour of her neck, her hand touched Darcy's breast, fingertips teasing the nipples.

Darcy turned over onto her back spreading her legs open wide. Toni's hand moved down Darcy's stomach to the inside of her thighs. Her fingers found Darcy's wetness and rubbed slowly and deliberately against the hard, raising head of Darcy's clit.

Two of Toni's fingers gently entered her. Moving her fingers in and out, slowly, at first, and then more rapidly as Darcy's hips responded. She was riding on a wave of pleasure which was Toni's hand.

Then, gently, Darcy pushed Toni over and slid on top of her. Neither of them wanted this to end too quickly. This unexpected passion, needed to be explored and felt fully.

Straddling Toni, Darcy placed her pulsating succulent flower against Toni and began rubbing back and forth. Toni closed her eyes as she pushed her warm wetness to meet Darcy's. She held Darcy's nipples with her fingertips pinching them gently. The lips of their wet clits met and joined in a dance of delight, their hips moving to a silent rhythm.

Darcy bent over and sucked Toni's extended nipple into her mouth. Toni moaned as a chill ran down her spine. Then, Darcy moved her head down Toni's body, until she was between her legs. Her tongue teased the throbbing core of Toni's flower, while her mouth sucked the hard head in. Toni's stomach twitched as her passion mounted.

Unable to stand it any longer, Toni pulled her up and rolled Darcy back under her body. She kissed Darcy with a passion she had not experienced in a long time.

Turning her body around and straddling Darcy; she lowered her head down between Darcy's quivering thighs. Toni lowered her hips, and once again, Darcy found Toni's full blossoming clit and began sucking it in.

Toni's tongue moved back and forth against Darcy. They could barely breathe as their overpowering passion reached its peak, bursting forth in unison. The sensation was overwhelming as both women moaned and cried out.

Out of breath and weak, Toni crawled back up to Darcy and held her tight. A shudder ran through them as they shared a long sweet kiss. Then, peacefully, they fell asleep in each other's arms, safe for the moment from all the terrible secrets this night had revealed and from the horror to face them in the days to come.

Chapter Ten

Toni opened one eye, and quickly closed it again. The blankets were pulled up over her head so just her eyes nose and mouth were exposed. She was wrapped in a cocoon of comfort and warmth, and was not ready to let go of it. *I think I'll just stay here forever,* she thought lazily.

Smiling sleepily, she slid her arm over the mattress to Darcy's side of the bed. The unexpected empty space next to her was cold. Startled, she turned over, throwing the covers back.

Blinking her heavy eyelids she stared blankly at the mattress. Darcy was gone. *Did I dream last night? Where is she?*

With a great effort, she pulled herself across the feather bed and peered over the edge. Darcy's robe still lay crumpled on the floor. Toni shook her tousled head to clear the cobwebs in her brain. Then she smiled to herself; *she was here, everything that happened last night was real.*

Flopping over onto her back, Toni stretched her long body. A satisfied smile slowly spread across her full mouth. Lying there with her eyes closed, she remembered the feeling of Darcy's eager response to her touch. It felt good to experience, once again, the wonderful excitement that comes from making love to someone she really cared about.

After lying there for a few minutes reveling in the thought of Darcy's touch, the cold fingers of the morning air began jabbing at her naked body, forcing her back to reality. A sudden chill ran through her as she jumped out of bed and headed for the shower.

The hardwood floor was cold against the bottom of her feet as she hurried to the bathroom. Quickly, Toni turned on the shower and as the steam began to rise and the water warmed her, for the first time in almost two years she felt content. Even after the grueling horror story she had heard last night, she felt strong and alive. She was to take on anything.

Dressing in Levis, boots, and a heavy sweatshirt, Toni brushed her short wavy dark hair and headed downstairs. As she hit the last step, she smelled fresh coffee brewing and bacon frying. Her stomach growled and the hunger pains increased with each breath she took.

Darcy's back was to her as she quietly entered the kitchen. Toni slipped up behind her and put her arms around Darcy's small waist. The scent of fresh clean soap filled her nose as she kissed Darcy's neck softly. Darcy rested her head back against Toni's shoulder, a contented sigh escaping from her lips; her eyes closed.

"Good morning." Toni whispered in her ear.

Then, Darcy turned and faced Toni. She slowly slid her arms around Toni's neck and they shared a long full kiss.

"Thank you." Darcy said smiling softly.

Toni returned the smile as she studied the lovely redhead she held tightly in her strong arms. "Thank me? For what?"

"For being here, for last night, for everything." She kissed Toni once more.

Their bodies seemed to have been molded and fit for one another as they held each other tight.

"Where's your aunt?" Toni asked breathlessly.

Darcy suddenly pulled away. "Oh damn, the bacon's burning." She rushed to the stove to pull the pan away from the burner. "Aunt Mae's outside checking on damage from the storm last night," Darcy answered over her shoulder.

"Can I help?" Toni offered as she poured herself a cup of coffee. "I'm a pretty good cook ya know."

Darcy turned and winked "Not this time, sport, but I *will* take you up on that. You can count on it."

"Anytime, Red, anytime. I can sling hash with the best of 'em," Toni joked as she sat down at the kitchen table.

With both elbows resting on the table, she cradled her coffee mug in both hands, as she watched Darcy move about the kitchen. Toni sensed a tension creeping over Darcy as she broke the eggs into the hot skillet.

"Are you okay?" Toni asked, a slight frown covering her forehead.

"I will be, but I still have a lot to digest. What I learned has proven one thing to me, though."

"Oh? And what is that?" Toni asked.

"I'm stronger than I thought I was. I know last night I fell apart, but today, today I know I can make it. You did that for me Toni."

"No one did that for you Darcy. You've always been strong. You just needed someone to help prove it to you that's all." Toni gave her a big wide grin.

"Before my aunt gets back, I have to tell you something." Darcy walked over close to Toni. "She doesn't know I'm a lesbian. I'm not *that* strong, you see. We don't see each other that often and I just don't want to do anything that may hurt her in some way. Do you understand?" An apologetic look covered her face.

Taking Darcy's hand in hers, Toni answered, "That's your choice Darcy. Whatever makes you feel comfortable; that's how it'll be. We're going to have plenty of opportunities to express our feelings to one another. When the time is right, you'll have a long talk with her about your lifestyle. Right now we have more pressing things before us."

Just then, Mae came huffing and puffing through the back door. She stopped on the back porch and took off her mud caked boots. Then she proceeded into the kitchen, where she quickly put on her fur lined slippers.

"Good morning," she grumbled.

"Is everything alright?" Toni asked pouring Mae a cup of coffee.

"Well, half the fence is down, some trees were lost, and my garden is under a foot of water. But all in all, I guess we were lucky. I got the emergency generator going early this morning so at least we have lights and hot water." Mae managed a slight smile. She glanced at the clock over the stove. "Lord, it's only 9:00 a.m. and I feel as if I've done a day's work already."

"It looks pretty clear out there today Aunt Mae. If the weather holds until tomorrow or Thursday, Toni and I will do what we can to help clean up outside." Darcy kissed her aunt's cheek.

Darcy returned to scrambling eggs and fixing toast. Toni and Mae sat silently at the table. The reality of what Mae had related last night was beginning to grip the trio once again.

A deep frown cut across her forehead as Mae sat staring into her coffee cup. Toni could tell Mae was uneasy. She sensed there was more to come from Mae, more about Aaron Blake. Things she had not told them last night.

A coldness fell over the threesome as they ate breakfast in silence. Darcy's face had grown taut and her hand shook slightly as she poured more coffee for everyone. Mae and Darcy picked at their food pushing it around the plates.

After eating a few bites, Toni shoved her plate forward. "We're not finished with this, are we Mae?" Toni said looking directly into Mae's eyes.

Mae looked away as her lower lip began to tremble.

"Aunt Mae, I can take it. Please, what is it?" Darcy took Mae's hand in hers and held it tight. "We've come so far. We can't stop now."

Mae looked at both of them for a moment. Then, in a hoarse voice, she said, "He's loose."

"What?" Toni wasn't sure of what she had just heard.

"He's loose! He escaped!" Mae repeated in a louder voice. Terror was written all over her face.

Darcy's mouth dropped open, her face grew pale as she felt the blood drain from it. She didn't move but seemed to be frozen as she sat staring blankly at her aunt.

"What does this mean?" Darcy finally whispered.

Trying to pull herself together, Mae took several deep breaths. She knew she had to remain strong, now more than ever. She had to be open and honest. There was no turning back.

Toni looked deep into Mae's pale blue eyes and knew the past, once again, had caught up with the two women. It was twenty-five years ago all over again.

Mae picked up the newspaper and laid it in front of Toni. Toni read the article carefully. Then she sat back looking at Mae and Darcy.

Darcy turned the paper around and looked at it. "This is him. This is the man I read about who escaped from the mental institution and killed those people. Oh, my god! He looked familiar to me the first time I saw the newspaper."

"Do you feel he'll come after Darcy after all this time, Mae?" Toni asked with a frown.

"He's insane. Who knows what he'll do. All I know is he's loose, and he never finished what he started here. I'm scared to death for Darcy. I want to take her away until he's caught."

"Look Mae, we can't even get off the island right now. We don't know if he made it over here before us, or if he tried. He may be miles from here, or back where he belongs. We have no way of knowing. Our main objective must be to protect ourselves just in case. You have to get mad and stay that way until we can get out of here. This beast almost killed all of you. Be angry about that, not afraid."

"Toni's right. This insane bastard killed our family. If he *is* here somewhere, we have to get him before he gets us." Suddenly, Darcy's voice was firm and strong. She realized she had to face this head on, or it would beat her.

Toni smiled. "That's it Darcy. What about it Mae. Are you ready to fight?"

Mae hesitated for a moment; then she answered, "I shot the son of a bitch once and almost killed him, maybe this time, I can finish the job."

Darcy laughed. She had never heard her aunt swear before. The three women felt a surge of strength race through their bodies as they clasped hands.

Toni knew fighting and winning against such an evil foe would not be easy, but she needed Darcy and Mae to be strong. She couldn't reveal her own fears to them.

"Okay. Mae you said you had a twenty-two rife around here. I want you to get it, load it, and keep it with you at all times. Make sure you have extra ammo on you too. I always carry my Smith and Wesson." Mae and Darcy listened intently to every word.

"Darcy is never to be left alone. One of us will be with her at all times. In fact, we will all stay within earshot of each other every minute. Lets make sure the locks on all the windows and doors are working and locked from this moment on. If this asshole is going to come after us, he'll have to make noise doing it." Toni smiled. "Are we tough or what?" Down deep she wished she had ten police units surrounding the house.

Squeezing Toni's hand, Mae got up from the table and went in search of her rifle.

"You're really something." Darcy said.

"What do you mean?" Toni asked raising her eyebrows in a surprised expression.

"I think you just created a small, but very angry army."

"That's nothing new, I've always believed women can do anything as good or better than men. I've lived that way all my life. I just passed it on to you and your aunt that's all."

"When this is over, you and I have a lot to talk about. I want to learn more from you . . . about *everything*." Darcy gave Toni a sly smile.

"It will definitely be my pleasure, but after last night, I believe that learning stuff will be a two way street." Toni raised her eyebrow and returned the smile.

"Well, here it is. All loaded and ready to go," Mae said, cradling the twenty-two under her arm as she came back into the kitchen.

Getting to her feet, Toni replied, "Now, let's go take a look at the old house. This will be your last challenge, Darcy." After going to her room and getting her 45 semiautomatic from the suitcase, she met Mae and Darcy outside the back door.

None of them said a word as they made their way up the crumpling driveway to the old house. Brush and mud covered the driveway and the going was hard and slow. The clouds were gathering once again and the wind had intensified. The three women pulled their heavy rain jackets tighter around their bodies and leaned against the wind.

Finally, there it was. The broken windows and loose hanging boards reminded Toni of an old horror movie she had seen long ago. The steps leading up to the porch were rotted and the front door hung by one rusty hinge. A steady rain began to fall as they carefully made their way closer to this dark, lonely place.

Without warning, Mae stopped dead in her tracks. "I haven't been in there since that day. I don't know if I can do this."

"Mae," Toni said quietly. "We *must* go on, for Darcy's sake *and* yours, or this will never end for either of you. The house is not evil. It can't hurt you. Only what's in your mind can. Remembering is painful sometimes, but if you remember the good, as well as the bad, it can free you from your fear of this place."

Hesitantly, Mae took several steps forward, then stopped once again. Toni put her arm around the small woman's waist and gently urged her toward the steps. Darcy had gone on ahead and had disappeared through the front door.

"Be very careful where you step," Toni warned, as she held Mae in a firm grip.

A gust of cold musty air hit them as they walked inside. The wallpaper had long since peeled from the walls exposing the bare wet rotting wood of the structure. Water dripped onto the floor through holes in the ceiling and gathered in dark puddles on the muddy floor. Slowly, they

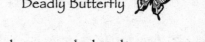

advanced further in. The house creaked as the ever mounting wind slammed against it.

"I don't think it's safe in here." Darcy whispered from the foot of the stairs.

"I'm all right now," Mae said quietly as she pushed Toni's arm away from her waist.

Toni released her grip and stood silently watching as Mae walked unsteadily toward the kitchen door. She stopped in the doorway. Mae's knuckles turned white as she held onto the door jam for support. Toni moved close to her. She knew Mae was flashing back to the day Nancy and Paul Bennett died.

Mae saw the blood covered floor and walls. Her eyes grew wide as she envisioned the large butcher knife stuck in the kitchen table; blood covering the handle and blade.

She began shaking uncontrollably as her mind took its journey back in time. Whirling around, she faced the staircase. Her eyes shut tight as she tried to block out the crashing, thudding sounds coming from the second floor. Mae put her hands over her ears, but nothing stopped the noise.

"Mae. Mae." Toni had grabbed her by the shoulders and was shaking her.

Mae's eyes were wild and filled with fear as she opened them and looked at Toni.

"He's up there," Mae screamed, "don't you understand? He's up there waiting." She was fighting with all her might to break away from Toni.

"Mae, listen to me." Toni said shaking her. "Listen to me. It's over, no one's here but us. The horror is gone. Listen Mae. Listen to the laughter that still lives here. Listen to the joy of the love that filled this house so long ago. We need to put this place to rest. *You* need to put this place to rest. Let it go."

Toni pulled Mae to her breast and held her tightly. The frightened, haunted woman sobbed against Toni's shoulder releasing all the fear and guilt she had nourished for so long. Toni didn't know how long she and Mae had been standing there, but she turned just in time to see Darcy reach the landing at the top of the staircase.

"Darcy. Wait!" Toni called out frantically.

Darcy disappeared through the bedroom door.

Toni looked at Mae. "Go. Go. I'm all right," Mae whispered.

Toni ran to the stairs, hesitating for just a moment to get her bearings. It was getting very dark inside the house and she was forced to pick her way up the steps one at a time. They creaked and sagged as she carefully placed one foot and then the other on the rotten boards.

It seemed an eternity had passed by the time she reached the landing at the top. Breathing heavily, Toni pulled the flashlight out of her jacket pocket and shone the light toward the bedroom door. It was open. A few more steps and she stood in the doorway.

"Darcy. Darcy, where are you?" Toni called out as she shined the light around the room.

The only sound was the howling wind screaming wildly through the old rotting house. Toni strained her ears and called out once more, louder. "Darcy, for Gods sake, answer me, it's Toni."

She stepped cautiously into the room still moving the beam from the flashlight from wall to wall. Finally, the beam caught Darcy pushed up against the wall near the old air duct. Toni rushed to her.

She directed the beam of light on Darcy's face. Darcy was staring across the room at some unseen object.

"The butterfly is so beautiful, so beautiful," Darcy whispered over and over.

"It's all right Darcy. Come with me. You're safe now."

Toni put her arm around her and led her from the bedroom. Darcy leaned against Toni, crying softly. Slowly they made their way down the stairs to where Mae was standing. Mae rushed to them and threw her arms around her niece.

"Darcy my precious child, are you all right?" Mae asked looking into Darcy's eyes.

"I remember Aunt Mae. I remember." Darcy threw her arms around Mae's neck. "My dreams were of that room and what I saw on the day Aaron Blake killed my family. Everything that's haunted me all these years was real. I'm not crazy."

Mae pulled back and looked into Darcy's tear filled eyes. "No, my dear one, you're not crazy." She took her weather worn hand and brushed the hair back from Darcy's face. "Are you all right? Has this been too much for you?"

"I've just lived this nightmare out fully awake, Aunt Mae. I didn't know if I would ever make it back, but I have. I'm going to be all right." She smiled weakly. Then, she turned to Toni. "Hearing your voice pulled me back, thank you." Darcy's fatigue echoed in her voice.

"Come on. We have to get out of here before the weather gets any worse," Toni said taking Darcy by the hand.

Between the long hard walk back and the emotions experienced this day, the three women were exhausted by the time they reached Mae's home. Toni locked the back-door behind them and took off her jacket and boots. Mae started a pot of coffee and Darcy sank into a chair at the kitchen table. Toni moved to the table and sat across from her. Darcy smiled at her, a soft sweet smile. Toni wanted to grab Darcy up in her arms and fill her face with kisses. They had all been through a great battle together, and won. They all knew it.

Mae brought three mugs to the table and poured the coffee. Sitting down, she looked at Darcy and Toni and smiled. She was at peace with herself for the first time in twenty-five years. They sat quietly sipping the hot brew, enjoying the warmth and reflecting on what had just happened to all of them.

After a minute or two Mae cleared her throat and spoke. "Toni, if my niece doesn't fall in love with you after all this, she's crazy."

Darcy coughed and spit her coffee out all over the table. She looked at her aunt in total shock. Toni just smiled.

"Aunt Mae. What are you saying?" Darcy asked as she wiped off her chin.

"My dear Darcy, do you think I'm stupid? I've seen you with your other friends and with Lisa. I felt the love between all of you. I caught the looks and smiles. Why do you think I didn't ask why you never dated men or why you never married? You're a beautiful woman. If you wanted a man, you would have certainly had no problem finding one. I've known you were a lesbian for a long time."

"But . . . but, you didn't say anything or ask any questions." Darcy was completely confused.

"It wasn't my business or place to do so. I knew when you were ready you'd tell me. I love you for who you are, not for what you are. Love isn't something a person should give and then take away because someone doesn't live the same way they do. You're a sincere, honest, loving person who wouldn't hurt a fly. You've brought nothing but joy to me. Why wouldn't I love you no matter how you choose to live your life? I'm proud of you, and always will be. Toni is probably one of the most together people I've ever met. She is caring and tender, yet strong and self-assured. I'd fall for her myself if I wasn't straight." Mae's eyes twinkled as she gave out a snort.

"Then you're all right with this? You're not hurt or angry?" Darcy asked in a quiet voice.

"No dear one, I'm just fine. Everything is just fine now."

"God, what a two days this has been," Darcy said sighing deeply. "I don't think I could ever go through it again, but at least now I can go on with my life without any dark hidden secrets lurking in the background."

"None, except one," Toni stated flatly.

"Aaron Blake," Mae whispered. A pained look shot across her face.

A cold shudder ran through the three women.

"We have to stay alert. I think we should all sleep downstairs in the living room tonight. I've seen no signs of anyone around, but until we can get back to the mainland or use the phone, we have to stay on our toes." Toni rose and headed for the other room.

Mae and Darcy followed close behind.

"Darcy and I'll go upstairs and get blankets and pillows. Mae, if you'll recheck all the doors and windows down here, then when we get back, we can all pitch in and fix something to eat. I don't know about the two of you, but I could eat a horse."

Mae picked up her twenty-two and headed for the back of the house while Darcy and Toni went quickly up the stairs.

Once inside the bedroom, Toni pulled Darcy to her. She kissed Darcy and held her for a moment.

"I've wanted to do that all day."

"I've wanted you too", Darcy whispered. Her heart was pounding and she was short of breath.

They kissed again, a long lingering kiss. Darcy pushed her body against Toni. She could feel every curve of Toni's tall muscular frame melting into her own.

"We better get a move on," Toni finally said softly.

After one last embrace and kiss, Darcy reluctantly loosened her grip around Toni's neck.

After gathering everything they needed, they rejoined Mae in the living room. Dinner consisted of cheeses, fruit, and cold cuts by candlelight. It tasted like a grand feast to the weary threesome. They had brandy after dinner, and then settled down in front of the huge fireplace for the night. Even the storm raging once more outside couldn't keep Mae and Darcy awake.

Toni poured herself another brandy and sat on the floor, leaning her back against the sofa where Mae slept. She looked at Darcy's peaceful face as she slept in the recliner. *She's turned out to be quite a woman,* Toni thought.

Slowly, Toni's eyelids closed and the empty brandy snifter slipped from her hand.

Chapter Eleven

The body of Sue Olsen lay face down in the alley behind Darcy's apartment building. The rain beat against her lifeless body as a torrent of water ran down the street carrying with it Sue Olsen's blood.

The lights of the police cars and ambulance reflected off the wet pavement and buildings, giving the scene an almost carnival look. Two police detective's knelt down over the body.

"Shit. What a mess," the heavyset detective said, shaking his head.

"How long do ya think she's been here?" a uniformed officer asked.

"It's hard to say. We really won't know much until the coroner's report is in. Jesus Christ, this woman's been stabbed multiple times," the bulky detective stated as he heaved his large frame into a standing position.

"Here's her purse." The young officer handed the plastic covered bag to the detective.

Detective Otto Garrison took the purse and headed for his car. "I'm gonna take this to the lab, and get it dusted

so I can check it out. I'll meet ya at headquarters," Garrison
called to his partner.

Steve Garcia waved and returned to his notes. The
crime investigation unit had just arrived, and Garcia stayed
to coordinate the on scene proceedings.

*Shit, I hope this doesn't have some connection with
that nut who escaped from the loony bin,* Garrison thought
as he turned onto 3rd street and headed downtown.

Arriving at the station at 11:00 p.m., Garrison
dropped Sue's purse off at the lab. Then he returned to the
squad room. After removing his rain soaked coat, he walked
to the file cabinet. Pulling the file on Aaron Blake. He quickly read through the pile of paperwork.

Goddamn, this guy's a real piece of work, he thought
as he turned to the last page. He said aloud, "Lets see . . .
only known living relative is a Mrs. Mae Harmon living on
Whidbey Island. I'll get with the guys handling the Blake case
. . . better cover all the bases on this."

"Here's *your* purse." Carol McDonald from the lab
handed the bag to Garrison, giving him a sly smile.

"Very funny. Thanks Carol, that was quick."

Sitting down at his desk, Otto carefully opened the
water soaked leather bag, and dumped the contents out. A
black cowhide wallet fell open revealing the smiling picture
of a young dark haired man. Garrison picked the wallet up.

"Okay let's see . . . driver's license, Sue Olsen, 1053
Daley Street, Edmonds, Washington." Garrison shook his
head. "Only twenty-eight years old. God, what a shame."

He continued through the wallet . . . Thirty-one dollars.
Not robbery, he thought . . . Check book, Thomas Olsen and
Sue Olsen, phone 579-8036. Garrison picked up his phone and
dialed the number.

"Hello." Tom Olsen answered sleepily.

"Yes, hello. Is this Thomas Olsen?" Garrison asked.

"Yes. Who's this?"

"Mr. Olsen, may I speak with Mrs. Olsen?"

"She isn't here right now. Who is this?" Tom Olsen was becoming annoyed.

"Mr. Olsen, this is Detective Otto Garrison of the Seattle Police Department. How long has your wife been gone?"

There was a long silence. "About four hours. Why? What's going on? Where's Sue?"

"Mr. Olsen, we need you to come to the downtown station right away."

"What's the matter? Where's my wife?" Tom was yelling into the mouthpiece.

"Please, Mr. Olsen. I can't say anything over the phone. When you get here ask for Detective Garrison . . . did you get that?"

Tom had already hung up.

Poor bastard, Garrison thought as he continued checking the remaining items from the purse.

Forty-five minutes later Tom Olsen rushed into the police station. Otto Garrison was waiting for him. Tom was pale and shaking.

"Have a seat Mr. Olsen," Garrison said before Tom could say a word. Otto motioned to the chair next to his desk.

"Mr. Olsen, is this your wife's wallet and purse?" Garrison handed the items to Tom.

"Yes, but . . ." Tom Olsen looked dazed and confused as he studied the wallet and purse.

Otto Garrison took a deep breath, "Mr. Olsen, I don't know how to say this to you."

Tears filled Tom Olsen's eyes. All at once he knew. He knew Sue was dead. Garrison got up and poured him a cup of coffee.

Tom didn't move. His head was in his hands as sobs rocked his body. Garrison sat silently as Tom's grief filled the room.

Several minutes passed before Tom Olsen looked up. "What happened?" His voice cracked as he spoke. "Was she killed in an accident?"

Garrison took another deep breath, "Your wife was murdered, Mr. Olsen."

Tom looked as through he'd been hit in the face. He sagged against the desk as if he might pass out.

Otto jumped to his feet and grabbed him by the shoulders, steadying him. "Mr. Olsen, is there someone I can call?" Someone who can come down here and pick you up?" he asked.

"Yes." Tom answered weakly. "My brother Carl, 538-2251."

After talking with Carl Olsen, Otto Garrison turned back to Tom.

"Mr. Olsen, I'm not going to ask you any questions tonight, but I must speak with you tomorrow. Will you be staying with your brother?"

Tom shook his head yes.

Carl Olsen arrived within thirty minutes. Garrison filled him in on what had happened. Carl gently took his brother by the arm and helped him to his feet, and they sadly left the police station.

It was 12:30 a.m. A cold dark Wednesday had just begun, and Otto Garrison would not leave the station tonight.

At 9:30 a.m. Otto Garrison knocked on Carl Olsen's door. A slight drizzling rain was falling. Off in the distance,

dark thick clouds were gathering and another storm was imminent.

Carl Olsen slowly opened his front door and motioned to Otto and Steve Garcia to come in. The house was dark and cold.

"I'll get Tom," Carl said in a flat voice.

Within a few minutes he reappeared with Tom Olsen. Tom was still in a robe. His hair was messed and he needed a shave. His eyes were swollen and red. Unsteadily he made his way to a chair, passing the two detectives as though they weren't there.

"Do you want me to leave?" Carl asked quietly, looking at Otto.

"No, you can stay Mr. Olsen. You may be of some help," Otto responded.

Steve Garcia pulled out his notebook and took a seat on the couch.

Otto cleared his throat as he approached Tom. "Mr. Olsen, I know how difficult this must be for you, but there are some questions we *must* ask. I hope you understand."

Tom looked up at Otto and nodded his head.

"About what time did your wife leave the house last night?" Otto began.

"Around 8:00 p.m.," Tom answered with a shaking voice.

"Did she say where she was going?"

"To see Darcy Bennett."

"Darcy Bennett? Was she a close friend of your wife?"

"They worked together, and I guess you could say they were friends."

"I'll need her address and phone number, if you have them Mr. Olsen."

"That information is probably in Sue's address book. It was in her purse. I don't know the number."

"That's all right Mr. Olsen. We'll check it out when we get back to the station. It's no problem." Otto Garrison pressed on, "There was a bad storm last night. Why do you think your wife found it necessary to drive all the way into Seattle to visit Darcy Bennett? Couldn't she have talked with her on the phone or at work?"

Tom hesitated for a moment trying to gather his thoughts. "Sue had been on edge for the last few weeks. She wouldn't talk to me about what was bothering her. She said it was just work stuff, nothing important. Last night she said she had to see Darcy. There was something she needed to discuss with her; get her opinion on. I tried to talk her out of leaving because of the storm, but she insisted she just had to go." He stopped talking and closed his eyes.

A few minutes passed before Tom Olsen could continue. Then, with tears streaming down his face, he blurted out, "I should have tied her down if I had to, if that's what it took to keep her home." The sound of his voice grew with each tortured word.

"Mr. Olsen. Please, this is not your fault. No one could know this was going to happen." Otto laid his hand on Tom's shoulder, giving it an understanding squeeze.

"Here Tom, drink this." Carl handed Tom a glass of water.

He took a couple of sips, wiped his eyes and looked at Otto, "We have to get the monster that did this," he said in a pleading whisper.

"We will Mr. Olsen. Anything you can tell us can be of great help. So, if you feel up to it, may we go on?"

"I'll do the best I can," Tom answered.

"Did your wife say she would call you when she reached Ms Bennett's place?"

"No, she just put her coat on, picked up her briefcase and purse, kissed me and left."

"Briefcase? She had a briefcase with her? Wasn't that odd that she would take her briefcase when she was going to visit with a friend?"

"I never thought about it." Tom sighed.

"Well, Mr. Olsen, I think that'll be all for now. Try and get some rest. I'll be in touch with you."

Carl Olsen showed Otto and Steve to the door.

"Keep an eye on him Mr. Olsen. He's going to need all the help he can get to pull out of this," Otto whispered to Carl.

"Thank you for your concern, Detective Garrison. I've called Sue's parents and notified the rest of our family. They're all on their way here. We'll make it, but please get this cleared up as soon as you can." Carl shook Otto's hand and closed the door.

Otto and Steve got back to the station around 11:00 a.m.

Otto flopped wearily down behind his desk. The old desk chair squeaked as his weight sagged suddenly against it. A frown covered his broad bald forehead.

"Well, whatta you think so far Steve?"

"I don't know Otto. We have a brutally murdered woman found in the alley behind her friend's apartment building. I'd say she never got to talk to Darcy Bennett. No money missing from the wallet, no rape, and a missing briefcase. There's something strange here, very strange." Steve Garcia tapped his pencil on the desktop as he perched on the corner of Otto's old desk.

"I think we need ta talk to this Darcy Bennett as soon as possible." Garrison picked up Sue's purse and opened it. He checked under the B's. Finding nothing for Bennett, he checked the D's. "Ah, here it is, Darcy." Quickly, he dialed the number.

"Hi, this is Darcy. I can't come to the phone right now, but if you leave your name and number, I'll get back to you as soon as I can. Please wait for the beep."

"Ms Bennett, this is Detective Otto Garrison of the Seattle police. I need to talk with you as soon as possible. Please call me at 673-4927, extension 49. Thank you."

"Not home huh?" Steve stated as he stood up.

"Nope. Maybe she doesn't even know about this yet. Maybe she's at work. Didn't Mr. Olsen say she worked for The Great Northwestern Bank downtown?" Otto began thumbing through the phone book. "Ah, here it is, The Great Northwestern Bank of Washington, Seattle Branch." Again Otto dialed his phone.

"Great Northwestern Bank, this is Sherry. May I help you?"

"Yes, I'd like to speak with Darcy Bennett please."

"Darcy is gone this week; can someone else help you?" The cheery voice responded.

"May I speak with the manager please?"

"Why yes. May I say who's calling?"

"Detective Garrison, Seattle police." Otto heard the buzzing of the extension.

"Hello, Mark Rebal here. What can I do for you?"

"Mr. Rebal. This is Detective Garrison, Seattle police. I'm trying to locate Darcy Bennett. Would you have any idea where she might be at this time?"

"Why, no detective, I'm sorry but I don't. She needed some time off; a week to be exact, and I gave it to her. I don't expect her back until next Monday. Has this got something to do with the death of poor Sue Olsen?"

"You know about that do you, Mr. Rebal?"

"Yes detective. It was all over the morning paper. Haven't you seen it?"

"No Mr. Rebal. I guess I've been too busy."

"Terrible, just terrible. Such a lovely young woman. All the employees of Great Northwestern have been deeply affected by this."

"Yes, yes, Mr. Rebal I'm sure they have. Please, if you hear from Ms. Bennett ask her to call me. Thank you for your time. Good-bye." Otto let out a big sigh and leaned back in his chair.

Steve handed him a cup of coffee. "Here, I think you might need this, and about twelve hours sleep," he said with a smile.

"Is there a newspaper around this dump anywhere?" Otto called out across the squad room, ignoring Steve's comment.

One of the other detectives waved a paper in the air. Steve walked over and got it and threw it down in front of Otto.

Garrison picked it up and began to read. "Goddamn idiots," he yelled angrily.

Everyone looked up.

"What is it Otto?" Steve asked leaning over the desk.

"The bastards are suggesting it might be Aaron Blake who killed Sue Olsen. They really wanna start a panic around here, don't they? We wouldn't give 'em all the details they wanted, so it looks like they made up a few of their own. They've connected the deaths at the hospital and the killings in Olympia with that of Sue Olsen."

"Shit. We're really going to get the pressure from the top brass now," Steve responded disgustedly.

"I'm gonna go home and get some sleep. You don't know where I am, understood? When the shit hits the fan I wanna be alert. I'll call ya in about five hours," Otto huffed getting up from his desk.

"I'll see ya later. While you're catching some *Zee's* I'm gonna check out what progress the guys assigned to the Blake case are making. Maybe it'll come in handy, you never know." Steve gave Otto a wave and picked up the newspaper. Steve Garcia had been Otto's partner for five years.

Steve was thirty-five. He had learned quickly to handle most of the detail work. Otto hated filling out reports and taking notes. The match-up had been perfect; Otto bullying his way forward, and the detail-orientated Garcia making sure everything was done by the book.

Otto Garrison lay on his back in his undershirt and boxer shorts covered only by a sheet. He took in deep breaths and then expelled them with such force that the sheet across his face rose. The snores echoed through his small apartment.

The incessant ringing of the phone finally reached him as Otto twitched a couple of times, coughed, and then picked up the receiver.

"Yeah." His voice was husky with sleep.

"Otto. Otto, wake up. It's me, Steve. You have to get back here now."

"What the fuck? What time is it?" Otto scratched his head.

"Never mind that. Are you awake enough to understand me?" Steve was yelling into the receiver.

"Yes, I'm awake goddamn it! Now, what's so important?" Otto scratched his head and sat on the edge of the bed.

"I checked the Blake case. I was reading the guy's history, you know, the reason they put him away?"

"Yeah. So?"

"Otto, the family he almost wiped out was named Bennett. They had a daughter named Darcy. She survived. *Bennett*, Otto *Darcy Bennett*."

Otto blinked his eyes. "Shit Steve, I can't believe it.

My god, I flipped through that file last night. Guess I should have read it more carefully."

"That's not all. Her aunt's name is Mae Harmon and she lives on Whidbey Island."

Otto didn't answer.

"Otto are you still there?"

"Yeah, I'm still here. I'll be there in half an hour." Otto hung up and hurried to the bathroom. Quickly showering, he threw on an old pair of jeans, heavy knit sweater, and boots. He didn't bother to shave or comb what hair he had left.

It was 5:30 p.m. and already dark. The rain pelted against his head as he ran to his 89' Buick. Even the weight of his car was no match for the pounding wind. It rocked back and forth as each gust hit the side. Otto held the wheel tightly in his ham-like fingers as he slowly worked his way through the rush hour traffic.

Chapter Twelve

The three women had spent a restless night. The storm had blown itself out, but the sky remained dark and cloudy. A steady mist was falling, and the fog drifted in and out of the trees and meadows.

Toni rubbed her eyes as she got up slowly and stretched. Her body was stiff and sore. *Man, am I out of condition,* she thought. Mae and Darcy still slept. Quietly, she went to the kitchen and put on the coffee. Then, leaning against the kitchen sink, she peered through the window.

God what a mess, she thought. Tree branches covered the ground, and bits of wood from the fence lay all over the lawn. Water dripped from the roof, adding to the already deep puddles around the house.

After pouring a mug of coffee, Toni slipped on her jacket and stepped out the back door. Taking a few deep breaths, she attempted to get her bearings and clear her head. As she sipped the hot coffee she explored the area with her eyes.

"Where are you Aaron Blake, you son of a bitch," she whispered.

"See anything?"

Toni jumped at the sound of Darcy's voice. "Jesus Christ. That's a good way to give a person a heart attack."

"I'm sorry. I thought you heard me come out." Darcy kissed her cheek.

"Let's go back inside. It's pretty cold out here," Toni grumbled, opening the backdoor.

Darcy shivered a bit as she poured herself a mug of coffee. Billows of steam floated into the air as the hot brew collided with the coldness of the kitchen. Pulling her heavy jacket tighter around her, she sat down at the kitchen table, cupping her hands around the mug to warm them.

Toni refilled her mug and joined Darcy. Quietly, they sipped their coffee, both trying to expel the feeling of fatigue weighing them down.

"We've got to get off this island today, if we can. You and your Aunt Mae need to be on the mainland until they find Aaron Blake. We should get in touch with the police as soon as we get back, and let them know where the two of you are," Toni stated suddenly, with a deadpan expression.

"Do you really think they want to talk to us?"

"Well if it was my case, I'd want to keep an eye on the two people Aaron Blake might head for."

A chill ran down Darcy's back. "I can't believe all this has happened. There's a maniac on the loose out there somewhere that could be looking to kill my aunt and me. It boggles the mind."

"Yes, it *is* a horrible idea isn't it?" Aunt Mae said from the doorway.

"Oh Aunt Mae, you startled us. How are you this morning?"

"Let's put it this way honey, I'm glad to still be alive."

"Mae, I was just telling Darcy we need to get off the

island today if we can. It'll be much safer for the two of you in Seattle."

"I don't want to leave my home," Mae said stubbornly.

"Look, Mae you have no choice right now. Not until Blake's caught. Darcy and I won't leave you here alone so that's that."

"There's no discussion on this Aunt Mae. You're going with us," Darcy added in a firm voice.

Mae looked at both of them. "Well I can see I'm over-powered here. I just don't want to be a bother to the two of you, that's all."

"Now, *you're* acting crazy," Toni responded. "Don't you think Darcy loves you more than anything in her life? You're the mother she never had. If anything happened to you it would kill her, and I might just miss you a little myself."

"Okay. I give up." Mae threw her hands up in sur-render. "Darcy and I will pack up and make sure the house is secure. I'm sure the ferry is running today."

"I'm going to see if I can get the car out of the ditch," Toni said getting to her feet.

"If you can't get it out, we can use my Bronco. I'll talk to Art down at the garage in town. He'll come out here and take care of it; and when we get back you can pick it up from him," Mae replied.

Toni stood shaking her head in disgust. During the storms on Tuesday and Wednesday, the car had sunk deep-er into the mud. It was imbedded up to the inside of the back bumper.

"Fuck. It's gonna take a tank to pull this thing outta here," she mumbled to herself.

Slowly, she walked back to the house. She was not happy about leaving the Mercedes, but she had no other choice. Darcy and Mae had almost finished packing by the time she opened the door.

"Well?" Darcy questioned.

"It's a no go," Toni answered in a frustrated tone.

"Don't worry Toni, Art's a good guy. He'll take care of it for you, and he won't charge you an arm and a leg for the job either." Mae smiled and gave her a pat on the back.

Mae's four wheel drive Ford Bronco bumped and slid along the road leading to the main highway. The private road had been heavily damaged, but the Bronco seemed to take the new potholes in stride.

Hell, that overpriced Mercedes of mine wouldn't have made it out anyway, Toni thought as they turned onto the main road to town.

After a quick stop at Art's garage, Mae headed for the ferry boat landing. Toni stared at the dark, choppy water, and felt sick already.

The last of the cars had disembarked from the ferry and were moving down the dock. The ferry would be ready to leave again shortly.

Suddenly, appearing from no where, a blue Toyota truck, tires squealing, sped off the deck and headed out the main road. *Fucking idiot,* Toni thought. She took a deep breath as Mae pulled the Bronco onboard the swaying ferry.

The deck moaned and creaked as the huge ferryboat began slowly pulling away from the dock. Toni sat still, staring straight ahead.

"What's wrong with her?" Mae whispered to Darcy.

"Toni got sick on the trip over. She's scared it's going to happen again." Darcy whispered back.

Then, they both sat and stared at Toni. None of them moved or said a word as the bow of the boat rose and fell pounding against the oncoming waves. Twenty-five minutes passed; they were halfway across.

Finally, Toni blinked and looked at Mae and Darcy. They were still staring at her with worried looks on their faces.

"It's okay. I'm okay," Toni said with a big grin.

"Hurray! Hurray!" Mae and Darcy cheered in unison.

"Guess I got my sea legs, huh?" Toni said proudly.

It was four o'clock by the time they reached Darcy's apartment. The drive home was slow due to damaged roads, and Darcy had stopped at the market to replenish her food supply.

As Darcy unlocked the front door, Toni touched her arm. "Wait a minute," she said quietly. "Let me take a look around first before we all go in."

Toni reached in and flipped on the light switch near the door. For the first time that afternoon, they all thought about Aaron Blake at the same time. Carefully, gun drawn, Toni went from room to room. Darcy and Mae remained in the hallway waiting silently.

Finally, Toni returned. "It's okay. Come on in," she said.

"Get the heat going, will you Aunt Mae? Toni and I will put the groceries away."

Toni and Darcy fixed soup and sandwiches while Mae got settled into the spare bedroom.

"Are we going to be okay Toni?" Darcy said as she stirred the soup.

"You and your aunt are going to be just fine. I promise I won't let anything happen to either of you." Toni bent down and kissed her.

After dinner they all sat in front of the fireplace and had a brandy. No one spoke. It had been a long day. The heat from the fire and warmth of the brandy had slowed down the emotional roller coaster the three women had been on for the past three days.

At this moment, the threat of Aaron Blake seemed far away and almost unreal. The sudden pounding on the door caused them all to jump, jolting them back from their brief relaxation. Toni looked at her watch. It was 9:46 p.m. Darcy started for the door.

"Wait a minute," Toni said jumping to her feet. Gently pushing Darcy aside, she stood to one side of the doorway.

"Who is it?" Toni demanded in a loud voice.

"Police," the deep voice responded.

"How do we know you're who you say you are?" Toni asked.

"Open the door and I'll show you my I.D."

The chain lock was on. Toni opened the door just far enough for the hand to reach through. She studied the badge and picture I.D.; Detective Stephen Garcia, Seattle Police Department. She peered through the crack and compared the picture with the man standing there. Then she undid the chain and opened the door.

"Are you Ms. Darcy Bennett?" Steve Garcia asked, looking at Toni.

"No. This is Ms. Bennett," Toni answered motioning toward Darcy.

Then another voice spoke. "May we come in Ms. Bennett? We have some questions to ask you."

Toni stepped back, allowing the two detectives to enter.

Toni's eyes grew wide in surprise. "Well I'll be damned. Garrison. Otto Garrison." She smiled broadly.

"That's correct, how . . . Jesus Christ, Toni? Toni Underwood, is it really you?"

Garrison and Toni hugged each other. Steve, Mae, and Darcy looked completely confused.

"How the hell have ya been? And what the hell are ya doing here in Seattle?" Otto was grinning from ear to ear.

Toni and Otto Garrison had worked together for four years at the Riverside, California police department before he moved to Washington because of a better job offer. Toni had always liked Otto.

He was a big man and his clothes never seemed to fit his bulky frame. His pants were a little too short and his jacket never quite reached around him far enough to be buttoned. His balding head always seemed to have a shine on it. Toni would kid him about how the light reflecting from his *dome* blinded her.

Otto moved slowly, but he was a great detective. Like a bulldog, he didn't let go until he had all the facts and answers. He was straightforward and honest, and made no bones about not understanding gay life. However, straight or gay made no difference to Otto as long as the job got done. He accepted the fact that Toni was a lesbian and it never interfered with their working relationship. *"Live and let live, what people do in their private life is none a my business. As long as they do their job, and cover my ass when I need 'em."* Was Otto's motto.

"It's a long story Otto. Let's just say I'm here visiting friends. Now, what brings your lazy ass here this late at night?" Toni said, slapping him hard on the back.

Otto's expression became suddenly serious as Toni offered the two men a seat on the couch next to Mae. Steve took out his notebook. Darcy sat down in the recliner and Toni seated herself in the chair near the table lamp.

"Steve, look at her." Otto pointed at Darcy. "What do you see?"

"I see Sue Olsen." Steve answered, glancing up briefly from his notebook.

"Sue Olsen? What about Sue?" Darcy asked. A frown shot across Darcy's forehead.

"Ms. Bennett, do you realize how much you and Mrs. Olsen look alike?" Otto questioned.

"Yes detective. It's been brought to our attention many times. But what does that have to do with why you're here?" Darcy responded, looking more confused with each passing moment.

"I've been trying to reach you since night before last, Ms. Bennett. Have you been away?" Garrison ignored Darcy's questions about Sue.

"I've been at my aunt's house on Whidbey Island for the past three days." Darcy said.

"Is this your aunt?" Garrison asked looking at Mae.

"Yes. This my aunt, Mrs. Mae Harmon."

"We've *all* been at the island Otto. What's going on?" Toni interrupted.

"There was a murder in the alley behind Ms. Bennett's apartment building night before last. The victim was Sue Olsen." Otto replied flatly, looking at Toni.

"Oh God, no!" Darcy screamed.

Mae jumped up and hurried to her side. Darcy began crying. Toni stood up, and motioned to Otto to follow her into the kitchen.

"What's this got to do with Darcy, and who is Sue Olsen?" Toni asked quietly.

Otto filled Toni in on the details of the last two days.

"We're beginning to believe Aaron Blake mistook Sue for Darcy and killed her by mistake. And now that I've seen Ms Bennett, I can understand how that could happen."

"Look Otto, these two women have been through hell the last three days, so try and go easy, if you can." Toni patted him on the back and they returned to the living room.

Darcy had composed herself by the time they returned.

"Ms. Bennett, Mrs. Harmon, you're both aware of Aaron Blake's escape and you know how dangerous he is. That's why we're here." Otto proceeded to explained the facts as the police knew them.

"I'm going to fix us all some coffee," Toni said, getting up.

"Thanks Toni, Steve and I could sure use some." Otto said.

"Detective Garrison, do you have any clues as to where Aaron Blake is now?" Mae asked.

"No ma'am. We were hoping perhaps you and Ms. Bennett could give us some help with that," Otto answered with a sigh.

"I don't know how we can help. My niece and I have been terrified since we learned of Aaron's escape. We thought he might even come to the island after us."

"Why would you think that, Mrs. Harmon?" Otto asked looking curiously at Mae.

"Darcy and I are all that's left of the family now, except for my husband's other brother. He lives in Oregon. No one seems to know if Aaron remembers what he did twenty-five years ago, but I know he's evil enough to try and finish the job if he does remember." Mae answered.

"Ms. Bennett, would you have any idea why Mrs. Olsen would drive all the way from her home on a very stormy night to see you?" Otto asked turning toward Darcy.

There was a brief pause in the questioning as Toni returned from the kitchen and handed Steve and Otto their coffee.

Darcy waited until Otto had taken a couple of sips. Then she answered, "I don't know why she had to see me, but if she had called first, she would have known I wasn't home. It would have saved her life."

"Her husband didn't have an answer for that either. He told us she had been on edge lately; something concerning work he thought." Otto rubbed his chin.

"That's right. I do remember. Last week I had lunch with Sue. She seemed ill at ease and a little tense. When I asked her what was wrong, she said it was nothing and she'd tell me about it later. I wasn't sure if it had something to do with her and Tom or with work, though. She and Tom were so happy, I guess it must have been about her work."

"Well, Ms. Bennett, I think that'll be all for now." Otto said as he got to his feet. "If you or your aunt think of anything else, please call me. Here's my card. Please feel free to call at any time, night or day. I'm going to have a watch put on your apartment for awhile, just in case. And Toni, I'd like it if you'd come down tomorrow and see me."

Toni walked to the door with the two detectives. She shook their hands firmly and thanked Otto for being brief with his questioning. After closing the door, Toni turned to Darcy.

"I'm truly sorry about your friend. But I know Otto Garrison. He seems laid back, but believe me he's one smart cookie. With him on the case we can rest easier."

"I can't believe Sue's dead. I just saw her last week. She just got married and moved into a new home. She had everything to live for. God, Tom must be devastated. I have to call him tomorrow. Is there no end to all of this?" Darcy's voice was a whisper.

"Mae, lets get her to bed. I think we've all had it," Toni said quietly.

Gently slipping her arm around Darcy's slim waist, Toni helped her into the bedroom. Mae turned down the bed, gave her distraught niece a kiss and a hug and left the room. Lingering for a moment, Toni pulled the covers up under Darcy's chin and patted her cheek.

"Now close those beautiful eye's and get some rest. Give this time. We're all gonna be okay." Toni kissed her softly. "I'll leave the door open a bit."

Mae was sitting in front of the fireplace watching the fire when Toni entered the living room. She picked up her brandy and sat next to her. Neither of them spoke. Twenty minutes passed as the two women sat lost in their own thoughts. Finally, Mae turned and looked at Toni.

"I feel as though I've been living a nightmare the past three days," Mae said, with a deep sigh.

"I know Mae. This has really been hard on you. A secret kept so long. A secret you believed would die away with time has now come back to life with a vengeance. The same fears and terror you felt so long ago have come back to haunt your life again. I can only promise you I'll do everything in my power to be there for you and Darcy. If Aaron Blake killed Sue Olsen, by mistake, thinking it was Darcy, we know it's more than likely he'll be back. I know he's insane, but I also know he's not stupid. People sometimes confuse the two things and think they go hand in hand. We must never underestimate him."

Mae stood up and sighed. "I'm going to bed Toni; will you check the doors and windows?"

"Sure thing Mae. Try and get some rest. I'll be out here on the couch." Toni patted Mae on the shoulder and kissed her forehead.

Alone now, Toni picked up the poker and jabbed at the dying fire. Something wasn't fitting together right. That all too familiar tightness in the pit of her stomach told her so.

Tomorrow I'm going to have a long talk with Otto. Maybe he can clear up some things for me. Toni settled her long frame down onto the couch and closed her eyes. Her forty-five lay cocked and locked on the coffee table next to her.

Chapter Thirteen

Toni was up early. She had slept fairly well considering she had one eye open all night. She was just finishing her second cup of coffee when Darcy wandered in still half asleep.

Darcy gave Toni a weak smile and headed for the coffee pot. Toni smiled to herself. *She looks like a little kid,* she thought.

Shuffling over to Toni, Darcy gave her a quick peck on the cheek and flopped down onto the kitchen chair.

"Is that all I get?" Toni kidded.

"That's all you can take. My mouth tastes like the bottom of a bird cage. You'd probably pass out if I got any closer."

"How did you sleep?" Toni asked, her forehead wrinkling.

"I didn't sleep I passed out," Darcy answered hoarsely.

Toni laughed. "Good. You needed that."

Staring hazily into her coffee cup, Darcy whispered, "It's all real isn't it?" She didn't look up.

"I'm afraid so, red," Toni answered.

"Are they ever going to catch him?" Darcy looked up pleadingly.

"Don't forget what I told you on the island. We're pissed at this monster. We're fighting mad, and yes, we will get him." Toni took Darcy's hand and held it tight.

Standing up she took Darcy by the shoulders, pulling her to her feet. Toni held her close. The strength and sureness of Toni seemed to melt into her own body as Darcy put her arms around Toni. Toni kissed Darcy's full lips as she drew her even closer.

"That bird cage tastes great to me," Toni whispered smiling.

Darcy couldn't help but return the smile.

"As soon as I get out of the shower I'm going down to the station and see Otto Garrison," Toni said as she finally released her embrace.

"How long will you be gone?"

"Not long. I have a few questions, and I know Otto will let me in on what's happening. They have police watching your apartment, and I'll make sure they know you and your aunt are here alone.

"If it's important then get going. We'll be all right." Darcy attempted to put on a brave front knowing it would make Toni feel better about leaving.

Toni walked into Otto's office at 9:30 a.m. "Hi, you old war horse," she stated, offering her hand to him.

"Toni. Glad to see ya. Want some coffee?" Garrison replied shaking her hand warmly.

"No thanks Otto. I'm here to get the lowdown on this case. Can you tell me anything I don't all ready know?" Toni answered as she removed her gloves and parka.

"Toni, you know anything I tell ya has to be between

you and me. I'm not supposed to discuss this with anyone outside the department. You know the rules." Otto lowered his bulky frame into the worn leather chair and motioned for Toni to take a seat.

"Fuck the rules, Otto. These people are friends of mine, and I'm deeply involved in this. You know I won't do anything to get your wide ass in trouble. Now, how about letting me take a look at the file you got so far?"

Otto looked at her for a long time before responding. "I know you're a good cop Toni, but I also know you don't always go about things the way it's written in the manual. If I do trust you on this, ya better not fuck up or my ass is grass."

"I give you my word Otto. If I find anything you don't already know, I'll tell you. And that's *ex-cop,* by the way."

"That's just great. Now I really am gonna be in big shit." Otto shook his head.

Silently, he got to his feet and headed for the door. Toni followed him to an empty office. Then, he left without a word leaving Toni to wait. Ten minutes later, he returned and handed her the Aaron Blake file and the one on Sue Olsen.

"Remember, it's my ass you're holding in your hands," he stated with a deadpan expression on his face.

"I know old friend, I won't let ya down," Toni replied as she sat down at the long table in the center of the room.

Reading and rereading the files for over an hour, she finally sat back rubbing her eyes. *God damn, what a mess,* she thought. Toni jumped as the door opened and Otto stepped into the room.

"Well Sherlock, have you solved the case?"

Toni shook her head. "Damn Otto, how are we going to catch this maniac? If he did kill Sue Olsen, then he's not far from Darcy. If he can read or watches TV, he'll know he got the wrong woman."

"This is how we figure it so far Toni." Otto began pacing about the room. "*If* Blake did this, he must have gotten Darcy's address from the phone book. He knows she was a redhead, and what age she would be today. Blake must have been hanging around Darcy's apartment building and when Sue Olsen showed up, he mistook her for Darcy. I'm sure the bastard didn't ask for I.D. He just killed the person he thought was Darcy and left.

"These details should fall into place when we get the crazy son of a bitch. Somewhere in that warped mind, he remembers her and is being driven to finish the massacre he started twenty-five years ago. Her aunt's in danger too. After all, she's the one who shot him."

"But what about Sue's missing briefcase, and her rushing through a raging storm to see Darcy? That just doesn't fit somehow. Why would he take her briefcase and not her money?"

"Maybe she had money in the case. We just don't know right now. Sue Olsen was the head auditor for The Great Northwestern Bank. We're going to check out what she was working on just before she died. I have a list of all the people she had close contact with during the last month. Maybe you could have Ms. Bennett look it over. She might come up with more names for us."

"Darcy had a party last week, and I know at least three of the women who attended work at the same bank. Let me do some digging on them, Otto. Knowing I'm close to Darcy may open them up more then being questioned by a *big bad cop* like you." Toni smiled.

Otto was silent for a moment.

"It's against my better judgement, but I'll back off questioning for twenty-four hours. What are their names?" Otto sat down across from Toni and took out an old worn notebook.

"Lets see," Toni paused, running the women's faces through her mind. "Beth Webber, Carol Masters, and . . ." Toni snapped her fingers and closed her eyes, trying to recall the last name. "Oh yeah, Mary Ann Clayton . . . are any of them on your list?"

"All of them," Otto answered.

"I'll get right on this Otto. You won't be sorry. I give you my word."

Toni shook his hand and promised to get in touch as soon as possible. Otto frowned as the door shut behind Toni.

"I'm already sorry," he mumbled to himself.

Toni returned to the apartment and began working out a plan with Darcy to get all three women on Otto's list back to her place that evening.

"We have to be very careful about how we approach these women regarding Sue Olsen," Toni commented as she paced back and forth in front of the fireplace.

"Once we get them here I'll make them all comfortable, and then just back you up on any details you might not understand concerning the bank procedures." Darcy paused for a moment in thought. "But right now our biggest problem is coming up with an idea that will get them over here tonight," she continued.

"I got it." Toni stopped in mid-stride. "We'll tell them you had the feeling Sue wanted to ask your opinion on something very important, and you thought maybe she had already told one of them what it was."

"Good idea, I know these gals well enough to pick-up on questions they might attempt to avoid answering. If Sue told any of them about this, working together, you and

I can get it out of them." Darcy answered in a strong, sure voice.

"Keep your fingers crossed," Toni answered.

Toni was thankful it was Friday and not the weekend. It would have been much harder to get the women all together on a Saturday on such short notice.

Darcy picked up the phone and began contacting each woman. They all agreed to meet at Darcy's at 7:30 p.m.

"Toni, if Aaron Blake killed Sue because he mistook her for me, then why do we have to question Beth, Carol, and Mary Ann?"

"In police work you never assume, Darcy. I want to know more about Sue's state of mind when she came here that night. According to her husband and you, something was bothering her. It might be important to find out what it was, if we can. Right now, the odds are Blake is the one who murdered her, but wouldn't you be interested in discovering why she was coming to see you?"

"You're right Toni. I know it would ease Tom's mind too. He still feels responsible in some way for her death."

They were all silent through dinner. Darcy and Mae were lost in their own thoughts. Toni plotted out her strategy for approaching the three women.

The first few drops of heavy rain had begun to fall as the tow truck slowly sank deeper into the muddy lake bottom. Art Wardlow's face was nearly covered now by the ever creeping mud and water. His broken body lay across the seat. A terrible fear still reflected from his dead, staring eyes.

Aaron Blake stood watching motionless. His black-coal like eyes fixed on the tow truck. An evil, sneering smile

crossed his lips as the front end of the truck and cab disappeared under the dark water. His hands clenched and
unclenched as the bubbles danced to the surface and burst just
as the roof of the tow truck disappeared into its murky grave.

When the ripples ceased, he turned and walked away.
Fingers of fog caught and swirled around his long muscular
legs as they carried him back to the house.

The broken front door lay on the carpet in the
entrance way. Aaron stepped over it and stood in the middle
of the living room.

In his rage at not finding Darcy, Aaron had torn
Mae's house apart. The furniture was broken and the stuff-
ing ripped out of the cushions. Every picture was knocked
from the walls and lay torn on the floor. The mantel over the
fireplace hung loose and splintered. He had ripped every
door from its hinges and stomped them into bits and pieces.
Aaron had smashed holes in the walls with his huge fists. A
madman had come to visit Mae and Darcy, and this was his
calling card.

At 6:30 p.m. Toni asked Mae if it was too late to call
Art Wardlow and see if her car was okay.

"I have Art's home number. His wife Sarah and I are
friends. Let me give her a buzz; I'm sure the phones must be
working again by now," Mae answered as she stepped to the
phone.

"Hello, Wardlow residence," Sarah Wardlow
answered, in a pleasant voice.

"Sarah. This is Mae. Can I speak with Art?"

"I'm sorry Mae, but Art isn't here. Can I do something for you?"

"My he's out late isn't he? Doesn't he close up shop around five?"

"He's gone Mae."

"Gone? Where is he?"

"Oh you know Art. He bought an old '61 VW from someone in Roseburg, Oregon. He went to get it. Of course it's not running, so he has to tow it home. I expect he'll be gone a couple of days or so."

"Oh, I see. Well I was calling about Ms. Underwood's car. It slid into a ditch at my house and Art was going over and pull it out for her. I thought he was going to bring it back to the shop and keep it there until we got back. I'm at Darcy's for a few days."

"I remember. He did say something about going to your place. Maybe he just pulled it out and parked it there. Sometimes I wonder about that man's brain."

"It's all right Sarah," Mae answered laughingly. "I guess nothing was wrong with the car so he figured he'd just leave it. I'll see him when I get back. Let's you and I have lunch one day soon."

"I'd like that Mae. Say hello to Darcy for me; see you soon. Bye now." Sarah hung up.

"Judging from your conversation, it sounds like everything's all right with the car," Toni said.

"I'm sure it is, or Art would have towed it to his shop," Mae answered, in an unconcerned voice.

At precisely 7:30 p.m. the door bell rang.

"I'll get it," Darcy said as she came in from the kitchen.

"Hi Darcy. We're all here," Beth said in her usual flamboyant manner.

"Come in everyone. You all remember Toni, and this is my Aunt Mae." Darcy gestured toward Toni and Mae as she stepped aside, allowing all the women to enter.

Everyone shook hands with Mae and Toni. Then they stood uneasily in the middle of the living room, unsure as to exactly why they were all here. The atmosphere in the room was tense and apprehensive.

"I have coffee or tea in the kitchen if anyone wants any, and you all know where I keep the booze," Darcy stated casually, trying to make everyone feel at ease. "Please help yourselves."

No one moved. They all continued to stand in the center of the room.

"Please, sit down and relax," Toni said motioning to the chairs and couch.

"What's this all about Darcy? Why was it so important we come here tonight? Poor Sue is gone. What can we do now, but hope they catch that madman Aaron Blake," Beth asked, frowning.

"I agree," Carol added.

"Wait a minute everybody," Mary Ann broke in. "Darcy said Sue wanted to tell her something, and it might be important if we can figure out what it was. I'd like to know why she tried to see Darcy that night. One of us might have the answer and not even know it. It could be something that can help the police find this Blake and put him back where he belongs before he kills more innocent people."

"That's right," Toni said picking up Mary Ann's lead. "You never know when one little piece of information will help in an investigation. I know you all worked with and knew Sue on a personal level. Besides, it might do you all some good to talk about it. Sometimes it eases the pain and shock of something like this."

"Well, when you put it that way, maybe you're right," Beth replied as she sat down.

"I'm glad you all brought your other halves with you.

They may know something too. After all, I'm sure you've talked about Sue from time to time with each other." Toni felt she had momentum going now, and she wanted to encourage everyone to participate.

"How are you going to start this *shin-dig?*" Frankie asked looking at Toni.

"Well, we didn't really have a set plan, but maybe I can start off by asking some simple questions. And then just let everyone say what they feel. Does everybody feel all right with that?" Toni asked looking to each woman.

They all nodded yes.

"Okay. Lets get started. Beth, were you close to Sue on a personal basis outside of the office?"

"No," Beth replied.

"How about you Carol?"

"Well, not as a regular routine. I think I had dinner with her twice. Darcy was there, but we were never really good friends outside of work functions. You know, luncheons, the company picnic, that sort of thing," Carol answered.

"I saw a lot of Sue before she got married," Mary Ann said. "She used to go shopping with Darcy and me. She was really a nice person."

"In the last month did Sue speak with any of you regarding a problem at work or at home?" Toni asked.

"I never really saw that much of her," Beth answered. "She was never around the office unless she was working on a audit of some kind. And even then she never had much to say to me."

"I spoke with her the week before she died," Mary Ann broke in. "She seemed okay. But then it was hard to tell with Sue. When she was working she was very serious. I guess . . . well maybe she *was* more absorbed in her work then usual."

"What makes you say that Mary Ann?" Toni questioned with a spurt of excitement.

"I don't know. I really can't put my finger on it, but she was tense, a little nervous perhaps. I didn't pay much attention. I've been pretty busy myself. I just figured it was P.M.S. or something."

"Okay. What about you Carol, anything?" Toni asked.

"As I said before, Sue and I dealt mainly on a business level. When we saw each other, it was usually to go over reports and discuss questions she might have regarding an audit."

"And she didn't bring up anything to you about a problem with work, and you didn't notice her manner as being tense or nervous in anyway? Is that correct?"

"Yes, that's right," Carol replied. "I just . . ."

"Oh, I did notice one thing," Mary Ann interrupted. "She held on to that briefcase of hers as if it was filled with gold."

"What do you mean?" Toni frowned.

"Well, she wouldn't even go to the bathroom without taking it with her. Isn't that strange? I never thought about it again, until tonight."

"Toni, what makes you and Darcy feel Sue was upset about something to do with work? Couldn't it have been a personal thing?" Taylor asked.

"Yes, it could have been. But from what Mary Ann just told us, and from Sue's attitude at work and at lunch with Darcy, I believe the work theory is still the best bet," Toni answered as Darcy got to her feet.

"Lets all have some coffee," Darcy broke in. "It's time to take a break from questions and give everyone a chance to relax for a minute."

"Good idea," Frankie agreed with a smile.

Everyone got up and stretched. Frankie and Darcy went into the kitchen for cups while the rest of the women talked about the murder and how horrible it all was.

"God," Jo said, "Do you think they'll ever catch the insane son of a bitch?"

"I don't know," Taylor answered shaking her head, "but believe me, Carol and I keep our gun handy now, just in case. We don't go anywhere at night without each other. What kind of monster stabs a women twenty-seven times for no reason? Really makes you wonder how many more are out there just like Aaron Blake, especially when it hits so close to home. I just wish I could get one good shot off at the bastard." Taylor was visibly angry.

"Yeah. Beth and I feel the same way," Frankie snorted as she re-entered the living room. "I can barely get her to go to the bathroom alone."

"You all have the right idea about protecting yourselves. Someone like Aaron Blake could be anywhere, and this kind of maniac doesn't need a reason to kill," Toni said as she helped hand out the cups of coffee.

"Maybe if the police could find Sue's briefcase, it might lead them to him in some way. Why would he kill an innocent woman and take only her briefcase? He truly is insane." Carol shivered and sat down.

"You know, that briefcase Carol mentioned may just hold the answer to all your questions Toni," Frankie added as she took a sip of her coffee.

"It's probably out in the middle of Puget Sound by now," Mary Ann stated flatly.

"Well, you never know what Blake might want with something like that. Maybe he considers it a trophy. Who knows?" Darcy replied as she stared into the fireplace.

The room suddenly become conspicuously silent.

Each woman seemed to be lost in her own thoughts and fears. Unnoticed, Toni studied each solemn face. Finally, Frankie yawned and stretched.

"I think we've talked about this all we can for tonight. I know you're all tired and drained. Just keep thinking and digging into your memory. Anything odd or out of the ordinary concerning Sue could be very important. Maybe one of you will remember some little thing that might help," Toni requested as the women got to their feet and began putting on their jackets and coats.

"Thanks a lot for coming and trying to help," Darcy said warmly to her friends.

After all the goodnights were said, the exhausted women left. Darcy closed the door behind them and turned to Toni.

"Well, did we find out anything?" she asked raising her eyebrows questioningly.

"I don't know yet, red. I have to let everything digest in my wee brain. It doesn't sound like your friends knew much about Sue's activities of late, but maybe, just maybe, one of them will eventually hit on something. So far they're unaware of your connection with Blake, and I want to keep it that way for now."

"They seem like such nice people," Mae said. "I'm sure if they can help find Aaron Blake, because of what he did to Sue, they will." She kissed Darcy, wished Toni a good night, and went off wearily to her room.

Once Mae's door was shut, Darcy put her arms around Toni's neck and smiled.

"Are you going to sleep out here on that hard ole couch again tonight?" she said with a sly pout.

"I don't know? Your aunt wished me a good night, and I can only think of one way to have one."

Darcy laughed and took Toni by the hand.

"Come with me, said the spider to the fly," Darcy responded as she led Toni to her bedroom. Slowly, she opened the door. Toni blinked as a surprised expression crossed her face.

"What's this?"

A variety of candles were placed around the room. The light from their flames danced against the walls. The slight scent of Wild Raspberry drifted through the air. The soft sensual voice of Jane Oliver filled Toni's ears. A bottle of Ameretta sat on the nightstand next to a bucket of ice.

"Don't say anything," Darcy whispered huskily. She led Toni to the bed.

She had arranged the surprise while Toni was busy talking with everyone in the living room. No one had paid any attention while she carefully made her secret trips in and out of the bedroom.

Looking at Darcy, Toni felt the beating of her heart beginning to pound in her temples. A sudden flush rushed to her cheeks as she stared into Darcy's green eyes. She was beautiful. Bits of fire from the candles danced in Darcy's eyes and glowed against her red hair, giving it the hue of polished copper. They were standing very close. Gently, Toni ran her fingers through Darcy's soft, curly hair. It felt like fine silk.

Slowly Darcy began unbuttoning Toni's shirt. Her hot mouth and tongue touched Toni's bare skin, as one by one the buttons were undone. Toni's head was back, her eyes closed as she concentrated on each movement of Darcy's lips against her flesh. A shiver ran through Toni as Darcy's mouth sucked in the nipple of her firm breast.

Toni let the shirt slide down her arms until it fell to the floor. Darcy looked into her face, bringing her mouth close to Toni's. They shared a deep, passionate kiss, sucking in the ever growing fever on their hot lips. Pulling away slightly, Toni unzipped Darcy's jeans and placed her hands inside. Then holding Darcy tightly to her once more, Toni caressed Darcy's buttocks, squeezing them as she pushed her own hips forward. They stood together slowly rubbing against each other.

Then, Toni lowered her onto the bed and gently slipped Darcy's pants off. Pulling her sweater off, Darcy threw it across the room. Toni stood up and removed the rest of her clothes. Her heart was beating so hard she could barely catch her breath.

Eyes gleaming with passion, Toni filled the two glasses which sat next to the bed. Leaving one on the nightstand, she kneeled down on the floor in front of Darcy, holding the glass in her hand. Darcy was sitting on the edge of the bed; her eyes never leaving Toni's. Toni took a sip of the liqueur and placed her mouth on Darcy's. They shared the thick liquid as it flowed from mouth to mouth.

Darcy laid back as Toni poured a thin line of Amaretta on Darcy and around her nipples. It ran down her stomach and between her legs. Tracing the line with her mouth and tongue, Toni slowly slid down Darcy's body drinking in the sweet sticky liqueur. Darcy opened her legs as Toni began licking and sucking the liquid from Darcy's thigh's. Her stomach twitched as Toni's mouth found her clit. Toni's tongue danced and played against it until the head throbbed and became hard. Darcy moaned with each tantalizing touch. The Amaretta and Darcy's own wetness mingled into a sweet luscious dessert which Toni ate with a great hunger. She lingered, exploring the beauty of Darcy until she felt Darcy could take no more. Then, she gently backed off and slowly worked her way back up to Darcy's waiting lips.

Shaking and breathing heavily, Darcy pushed Toni over onto her back. She picked an ice cube out of the bucket, and placed the edge against Toni's hot, sweating flesh. Toni gasped as the ice hit her skin and began to melt.

Darcy drew a straight line down between Toni's breast to her stomach, caressing Toni with her mouth as she went. Toni's muscles contracted as the ice touched each part of her body. Darcy continued until she reached Toni's feet. Then, her tongue moved up the inside of Toni's thigh until it reached the warm wetness between her legs. As she took Toni in, Darcy's hand continued to trace Toni's stomach and breasts with the remains of the ice cube. Each tingling touch brought Toni closer to the peak of passion.

Knowing she wouldn't be able to hold back her climax much longer if Darcy continued, Toni pulled Darcy up onto the bed next to her. She gently brushed the hair away from Darcy's face with her fingertips. She stared into Darcy's face for a moment. Darcy was flushed and her lips were slightly parted. Her eyes were half open.

"I want us to come together," Toni whispered in a husky voice.

Easing herself into a scissor like position, she pulled Darcy up between her legs. As their throbbing heads met, they moaned. The lips opened and pressed together, their hardness touching, they began moving back and forth against one another, slowly, deliberately. Their dance of passion grew as they both gasped for breath.

Darcy's fingers grabbed and pulled at the sheet, gathering it into her hands. Her breathing became heavy and deep as Toni pressed into her.

"Harder baby. Harder," Darcy pleaded.

The hot wetness between them mingled and became one. Beads of sweat ran between Toni's breasts as the mounting passion consumed her. The increasing rhythm of their bodies became a dance of complete ecstasy.

Just as they both reached the peak of their passion Toni stopped and laid down next to Darcy. She pulled Darcy close. Each reached across to the other and began massaging the extended head of their clit's. Until it brought them to the long explosive climax they both hungered for. Moaning with delight, they shared a deep kiss.

Exhausted, they lay in each others arms wondering what was happening between them. This was all so fast; so unexpected.

Neither of them had expected the overwhelmingly deep emotion they had just experienced. The candles had burned themselves out and the music had long since ended. The only sound was the rain beating against the window. They fell asleep still holding one another.

Aaron Blake lay in Darcy's old bedroom; in Darcy's bed. His mouth twitched as his eyes stared into the empty darkness.

"Darcy Bennett," his hissing voice repeated over and over again. Whidbey Island lay silent and dark as the storm beat against its shore like a wild beast trying to devourer it. But the wild beast had already landed and had begun his feast of death.

Chapter Fourteen

Toni was dressed and out of the apartment before Darcy or Mae was awake. She needed to be alone and think. It was drizzling and a frigid wind swept through the streets of Seattle. She pulled Darcy's Ford Mustang into the parking lot of the Cozy Nook Cafe. After parking, she jumped from the car and made a dash for the entrance. Once inside the warm cafe, Toni made her way to a table near the rear of the small diner.

The waitress approached Toni and handed her a menu. "Want some coffee?" she asked.

"Yes please." Toni quickly replied as she rubbed her cold hands together.

The waitress returned shortly and the smell of the freshly brewed coffee filled Toni's nostrils. She smiled as the young woman filled the cup. Toni hadn't had her usual morning coffee and was eager to get some of the hot dark liquid into her body. The first sip burned her lips.

"Damn," she muttered. Dropping two ice cubes from her water into the steaming cup, she took another drink. "Ah that's better," she sighed, satisfied.

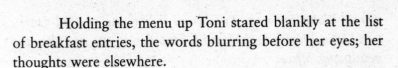

Holding the menu up Toni stared blankly at the list of breakfast entries, the words blurring before her eyes; her thoughts were elsewhere.

"Ready to order?" The waitress' voice startled Toni.

"I'm sorry, I haven't even looked at the menu yet. Tell you what. If you'll just keep that coffee coming I promise I'll order soon."

"You got it honey," the waitress answered. "Just give me a wave when you're ready."

Toni stared out the window as the droplets of water gathered together and ran down the glass in long streaks. The feelings she had for Darcy disturbed her. *What am I doing? She thought. I've come into this woman's life out of the blue. I didn't even know her two weeks ago; yet every time I get near her or look at her, my heart jumps into my throat.*

It's because I want to help her so much, and she's in so much danger. That's got to be the reason why I feel this need to be near her every minute. Toni took a drink of coffee and frowned. *She'd probably laugh in my face if I even mentioned how I'm feeling toward her. She just needs my help, and of course her emotions aren't under control. Yeah, that's it; we're just two people in need of tenderness and warmth in our lives right now. That's all it is.*

Picking up her menu Toni waved to the waitress. "I'll have sausage and eggs basted, sourdough toast, and a glass of milk."

While waiting for her order, Toni forced herself to concentrate on Sue Olsen. *Darcy's friends sure weren't any help last night. I need to read all the newspaper reports on Aaron Blake's escape, and Sue's murder. Between the police records and the newspaper, sometimes a small clue comes out of nowhere and smacks you in the face. The cops have to find*

Aaron Blake soon, or I'm afraid he's going to find Darcy first. After I finish breakfast I'll drop in on Otto and then the newspaper office.

Darcy walked sleepily into the kitchen and saw the note lying on the table. "Dear Red, couldn't sleep. I didn't want to disturb you and your aunt so I sneaked out. There are a couple of things I want to check on. I'll call you later. Toni. P.S. The policeman watching your place knows I'm gone, so don't worry."

Darcy frowned. She felt hurt that Toni would leave without waking her. *Maybe she doesn't have any feelings for me.* Darcy thought. *Maybe she just feels sorry for me. Damn it! Why should she have feelings for me? She doesn't really even know me.*

Darcy slammed the coffee pot down. She was angry with herself. *Where do I get off thinking Toni should have to report her every move to me? The woman's doing everything in the world she can to keep me safe. I'm lucky she hasn't already washed her hands of this whole mess and left. Got to control myself. Everything's happening too fast. Toni probably thinks I fall into bed with every butch I meet.* Flopping down in a kitchen chair, she continued silently berating herself.

"Good morning honey," Mae said as she walked into the kitchen.

"Oh, hi Aunt Mae," Darcy responded flatly.

"You seem to be in a low mood this morning honey. Is there anything I can do?" Mae asked as she poured herself a cup.

"No, I guess I'm just scared that's all. I try not to think about Aaron Blake, but I know he's out there somewhere waiting for us. If it wasn't for Toni, I probably would have lost my mind long ago."

"We're very lucky she came into our lives when she did. She's been like an anchor for both of us. Don't worry honey, she's not going anywhere."

"What do you mean? Do I seem worried Toni is going somewhere?" Darcy suddenly sat straight up in her chair with an air of defiance.

"Honey, I know you pretty well, and I've seen how you look at Toni and how she looks at you. That woman isn't here because she's some kind of saint. She's here because of her feelings for you. You're important to her and she wouldn't, or couldn't even think of leaving."

"We're just friends Aunt Mae. Toni has no feeling toward me other then trying to help a friend. In fact, she probably wouldn't even have stayed in the first place if Frankie wasn't such a close friend of hers," Darcy's attempt to sound business-like fell flat.

"You can say what you like my dear, but these old eyes have never deceived me yet. They see something growing between the two of you, and that's that." Mae smiled warmly, picked up her coffee cup, got to her feet, and left Darcy sitting at the table with her mouth hanging open.

"Hi Otto. What's new?" Toni said standing in the doorway to Garrison's small office.

"Toni. Well you're up bright and early this morning. Have a seat. God, if I didn't know better, I'd think you were still just another poor cop comin' into work at 8:00 a.m. on a Saturday morning." He gave her a sly smile.

Toni took off her parka and sat down, ignoring

Otto's observation. "Anything new Otto?"

"Nothin' yet. We're gonna have a talk with Mr. Rebal, the bank manager, this afternoon. It seems he knew Sue Olsen better than we thought. Her husband played golf with him, and they were in a bowling league together. This morning we're going up to Everett and talk with one of the big mucky-mucks and try and find out what Sue was working on last month."

He paused and smiled. "I just love makin' these big shots come into the office on a Saturday." Otto winked at Toni and then continued, "We wanna look through her desk and files. Do ya wanna tag along?" Otto shoved the last of his sugar donut into his mouth, washing it down with a big gulp of coffee.

"I don't think so," Toni answered. "But I would like to get a copy of those files you were so kind to let me see the other day. I need to get them home where I can really study 'em. Can you do that without getting your ass fried?"

Otto stared at Toni for a moment. "Well, I've gone this far. I guess one more step into the quicksand can't hurt."

"Thanks Otto. We're both working toward the same end on this, ya know. After all, everyone can use a little extra help from time to time. Right?" Toni batted her eyes innocently.

"Okay, okay, don't push your luck. By the way, did Ms. Bennett's friends come up with anything?"

"Afraid not. From what they said, none of 'em has a clue as to what seemed to be bothering Sue Olsen. Maybe when *you* question 'em they'll think of something new."

Picking up his phone Otto pushed the intercom button.

"Hi Alan, will you run me copies of both the Aaron Blake and Sue Olsen files real quick? I need to take them with me this morning. Thanks." Otto hung up and looked at Toni.

"So, Toni, what do you think of our fair city?" Otto asked leaning back in his squeaky chair.

"Well, from what I've been able to see of it, it's very wet. With the shit that's been going down ever since I got here, I really haven't had much of a chance to check it out."

"It rains most of the time during the winter months, but it's unbelievably gorgeous in the spring and summer. The people here are great. The life style is so different from California. Oh, we have our share of crime, but most of the time it's pretty laid back round here."

"You wouldn't be trying to sell me on this place, now would ya Otto?" Toni smiled.

"Why not? You sure to hell don't have any ties anywhere else do you? This would be the perfect place to start a new life. And besides, I'm here. What more could you ask for?"

Toni laughed.

The door opened, and Detective Alan Swensen entered carrying two file folders. "Here they are Otto." Alan handed Otto two manila envelopes.

"Thanks Alan, I owe you one." Otto replied.

As soon as Detective Swensen was well out of view, Otto slipped the folders to Toni.

"Here ya go Toni. Don't let these outta your sight, and don't let anyone see ya leave the building with them."

"I won't Otto, and thanks. I'll see ya later." Toni slipped the folders under her rain parka, shook his hand, and left.

It took her a while to locate the newspaper office. She wasn't familiar with the streets in Seattle, and got lost twice before getting her bearings.

"Too many one way streets in this town. Should have asked Otto for directions." She grumbled as she opened the door to the lobby of The Seattle Times. The lobby was all but empty. There was no receptionist at the desk, only a security guard standing by the elevator doors.

"Good morning. I'm interested in getting some back copies of your paper. Where would I go for that?" Toni stated as she walked up to him.

The older man seemed surprised to see her. "Err," he stammered, "just take the elevator to the top floor, turn left to the end of the hall. But there might not be anyone around. It's Saturday and . . ." His ending comment was not heard by Toni as the elevator doors closed in the guard's face.

Once on the top floor, she hurried down the long hall, her boots echoing against the tile floor. Morgue, the large black lettering printed on the door blared out at her. She opened the door and entered a large room. A long counter stood in front of her. To the right were several electronic viewing machines, each labeled with operating instructions.

Behind the counter were shelves filled with video tapes. A tall thin man in his fifties was busy at a desk. The screen of a computer glowed before him. He hadn't noticed Toni.

"Excuse me," she said quietly.

The clerk jumped. His glasses slid to the bottom of his nose as he whirled around toward her. "Yes. What can I do for you?" He said sounding a bit out of breath.

"I'm looking for several past issues of your paper. I would like to get copies of them if that's possible," Toni answered pleasantly.

"Do you know the dates of the issues you want?" The man replied as he shoved his thick glasses back up to the top of his long nose.

"Yes, I think so. I'd like to see all the stories and information your paper printed regarding the escape of Aaron Blake, and the account of the Sue Olsen murder four days ago. In fact, it would be great if I could get all the papers starting with the Aaron Blake story right on through the Sue Olsen murder. Can I do that?"

The clerk frowned. "You know we're officially closed today?" he answered in an irritated manor. "Have you just arrived in town?"

"Is that important? As long as you're here, is there any reason why I can't get the copies?" Toni was beginning not to like this guy's attitude.

The clerk sighed. "No, there's no problem. I can get them for you, but you'll have to pay for them."

"That's fine. How long will it take?" Toni was all business now.

"Not long. Just have a seat." He disappeared down one of the long aisles.

Returning twenty minutes later he was carrying a load of newspapers wrapped with twine to hold the stack together.

"Lucky we keep copies of these on hand. If we'd been out, I would have had to run the whole bunch off, and that would cost you extra."

"How much?" Toni asked.

"Lets see. Ten newspapers at a dollar apiece, that's . . ."
Toni shoved a ten dollar bill at him.

"Do you need a receipt?"

Toni had grabbed up the papers and was halfway out the door. "No," she called back over her shoulder as the door closed behind her.

By 10:30 a.m. Toni was knocking on Darcy's apartment door. Darcy peered through the small peephole. "Oh Toni. Hold on a minute."

Toni heard the chain rattle and then the door opened.

Darcy was standing there in a forest green jump suit. Her red curly hair framed her face; her eyes were emerald green from the reflection of the jump suit. She took Toni's breath away.

"Toni, are you all right?" Darcy asked placing her hand on Toni's arm.

"Oh, yeah I'm fine," Toni replied, trying to sound casual.

"What all have you got there?" Darcy's gaze fell on the bundle of newspapers in Toni's arm.

"Well, I've got police reports, newspapers, paste, and a scrapbook," Toni answered heading for the kitchen.

"Hi Toni," Mae greeted her, as she closed the dishwasher.

"How's it going Mae?"

"Other than being on the verge of a nervous breakdown, I guess I'm okay," she replied.

"I know how hard this is on you and Darcy, but you have to believe me when I tell you things will be coming to a head soon. We just have to hang in there a little longer." Toni patted Mae on the back.

"We're trying Toni, but that maniac is still out there looking for us, and until he's caught there's no way Aunt Mae and I can forget that," Darcy said frowning.

"I may have found a way to keep our minds busy for awhile," Toni responded, as she laid the papers down on the kitchen table.

"Oh, and what's that?" Mae asked as she dried her hands on the dish towel.

"We're going to go through all these newspapers, and cut out every article and report concerning Aaron Blake and the murder of Sue Olsen. Then, we're going to make a scrapbook, and when we're through, we're going to read each and

every word over and over again until we can't see anymore," Toni stated matter-of-factly.

"What's the point? What are we looking for?" Mae asked, confused.

"I'm not sure, but when we find it, I'll know. In police work details are very important, and even the smallest of these can solve a case. There may be something here that will help us zero in on Aaron Blake so we can get ahead of him and be ready when he shows up the next time. I'm going to go over the police reports until I know them by heart, while you two begin our scrapbook." Toni picked up the files.

"Okay Aunt Mae, lets get started. I've got two pair of scissors around here someplace. You clear off the table while I go look," Darcy said eagerly.

"I'm going to work in the living room at the desk," Toni said. Once in the living room, she sat down at the roll top desk and laid the folders out in front of her.

"Toni, is something wrong?" Darcy questioned quietly as she walked up to the desk.

"Wrong?" Toni looked puzzled.

"You know what I mean, and I'm not talking about Aaron Blake. You haven't looked me straight in the eye since you got back. Have I done something to upset you?"

Getting to her feet, she turned to face Darcy. She took Darcy's hands in hers. "You couldn't do anything wrong or upset me even if you tried. It's me, I've got some things on my mind that shouldn't be there right now, and I'm doing my best to shake them off. It's important I keep myself focused, and that's what I'm trying to do."

"You just seem sad and withdrawn, that's all. Are you sure I can't help?" Darcy put her hand on Toni's cheek.

"I promise, when this nightmare is over we'll sit down and have a long talk about things I need to know. But until then, if I seem distant or cold, please remember that's just the way I am when I work on a case. If I don't throw my whole mind and soul into it I can't find the answers. So bear with me for now, okay?"

"Okay," Darcy responded softly; understandingly.

Toni kissed her gently, and then sat down once again. Darcy turned and continued looking for the scissors. The apartment grew silent as the three women lost themselves in the tasks at hand.

It was three o'clock when Darcy came in with a sandwich and coffee for Toni. She had just begun her second reading of the police files.

"I thought you might be hungry." Darcy bent down kissing Toni's cheek.

"Oh man, you're right, I need a break." Toni stood up, stretched and rubbed her bloodshot blue eyes.

Darcy sat the food down on the coffee table.

"How's it going in the kitchen?" Toni asked walking over to join Darcy on the couch.

"We're just about through pasting everything in the book. Should we let you know when we're done, or should we start reading?"

"Why don't you two start reading, and when I'm done in here I'll join you.

Toni finished her lunch quickly, returned to the desk, and began pouring over the files once more. By 4:30 p.m., she felt she knew Aaron Blake as well as any *sane* person could. The report on Sue Olsen was etched into her mind. *Now,* she thought, *let's see what the newspapers have to say.*

"Hi you two," Toni said smiling as she walked into the kitchen.

Mae and Darcy both jumped. "Toni, you just gave me a heart attack." Mae said holding her hand over her heart.

"Sorry," Toni responded sheepishly. "Boy, you two were really absorbed in your work weren't you?"

"We don't ask questions, we just follow orders," Darcy said with a mock salute.

"Reading all this again really gives me the creeps," Mae stated with a shiver.

"I know it's not easy, Mae. Why don't you take a break and give it a rest for awhile? Darcy and I can take over for now."

"Well, I hate to poop out on you kids, but these old eyes and neck could stand a rest," Mae conceded as she slowly got up.

"Why don't you go in, lay down on the couch, turn on the TV and relax? Toni and I will call you if we need you." Darcy kissed her aunt.

Mae didn't argue. She poured a cup of coffee and went into the living room.

"This is really hard for her," Darcy said looking at Toni.

"It's hard for both of you," Toni answered. Then she turned the scrapbook around toward herself.

"Hey. What am I supposed to do now?" Darcy said pulling at the book.

"Okay, okay, pull your chair up next to me and we'll read together."

"But I was further ahead than you in reading."

"Where did you stop?"

Darcy flipped through the pages. "Here." She pointed to the headline reporting the murder of Sue Olsen.

"Okay, we'll start there, I can go back and read the first half myself, later."

Toni and Darcy settled into a slow deliberate reading of the story of Sue Olsen. When they finished, they turned the pages back and began once more.

After another hour of reading, Toni turned over the last page and leaned back. Her eyes were closed. Darcy stared at her, not saying a word.

"Something's wrong here. Something I can't quite put my finger on. It's there; why can't I see it?" Toni sounded frustrated.

"You're tired . . . we both are. Maybe it would help if we sat back and thought of something else for awhile. You know, it's like when you can't remember the name of a song. If you don't try so hard and go about your business, all of a sudden it comes to you."

"I think ya might just have something Red," Toni said smiling.

"Listen, why don't we call Frankie and invite her and Beth over. It would do us good to see Frankie's smiling face. We've been like prisoners here. Let's back off for tonight, and just relax. They don't have to know anything. How about it?" Darcy asked in a pleading tone.

"Well . . ." Toni frowned.

"Oh come on, what harm can it do? We can fix a nice dinner, have some drinks, maybe play cards. Anything, anything to get our minds off of Aaron Blake and poor Sue for a few hours. I know Aunt Mae will go to bed early. She's exhausted."

Darcy was standing now. Toni got up and pulled her close. "How can I say no to you?" she whispered.

Darcy put her arms around Toni's neck and looked into her eyes. There was a long silence.

"I . . . I," Darcy started to speak.

Toni placed her fingers on Darcy's mouth. "Sh, don't say anything. I already know."

Toni brushed Darcy's eyelids with her lips. Darcy raised her mouth to meet Toni's. Their kiss was passionate.

Toni felt the beat of her heart pounding against Darcy. Darcy pushed her body against Toni. They stood holding and kissing each other for a long time. Finally, Toni spoke.

"If we don't stop this, I'm afraid we *will* give your aunt a heart attack when she comes in here and finds us on the floor together."

Darcy laughed, kissed Toni once more, and headed for the phone.

Chapter Fifteen

The sky was slate gray as Aaron Blake lumbered up the road toward the old house. Art Wardlow's dried blood looked like rust against Aaron's jacket. As he approached the broken steps leading to the porch, he stopped suddenly, and turned around.

His eyes gleamed as his mind drifted back in time. It was twenty-five years ago once again. The sunlight sparkled on the lake as the soft warm breeze kissed the leaves of the trees.

His breathing quickened as the carefree laughter of Darcy Bennett echoed through the air once again. The sound enraged him.

Aaron's cruel mouth twitched as he felt the hot metal hood of the car against the palm of his hand. His heart pounded as he recalled crushing the life from Paul Bennett.

Then, turning back toward the old house, a crooked smile crossed his lips as he continued up the steps to the front door. He pushed against the rotting wood; it gave way easily under the weight of Aaron's huge hand.

Nancy Bennett froze as their eyes met. A bit of spittle ran from the corner of his mouth as he took a step toward her. Nancy screamed as she ducked under his out- stretched arm and ran past him. It took little effort on his part to catch her and drag the screaming, helpless woman from the front porch and back into the house. His hands opened and closed as his excitement grew, the memory still vivid.

After a moment or two he walked to the kitchen. His eyes darted around the dark damp room.

The horrified woman had broken free momentarily and had grabbed a kitchen knife in a futile effort to protect herself. Sweat began pouring down his face as he recalled how easy it had been to wrestle the knife from her small hand. Aaron's arm rose and fell time after time as he plunged the knife in and out of Nancy Bennett. He stood with his head back and eyes closed as he relived and relished the moment.

Then, as though in a trance, he turned and walked to the bottom of the crumbling staircase.

Nancy Bennett's lifeless body lay across his arms. Her head dangled loosely, like that of a rag doll. Blood spilled from her body leaving a crimson trail behind as he started up the stairs.

He paused in the doorway of the bedroom and then, slowly, he walked to the bed and dropped Nancy Bennett upon it. Bits of drool formed in the corners of his mouth as he bent over her. His coal like eyes studied the once lovely woman. Straightening up, his fingers pulled wildly at the zipper of his pants. Then, suddenly, he froze, cocking his head from one side to the other.

What was the sound? Aaron turned abruptly. His eyes searched the room. The grate covering the air-duct caught his attention. He stood motionless, staring and listening.

Yes. There, she's there. The little bitch is in there.

Taking one slow deliberate step after another he stood in front of the duct opening. The excitement he had felt so long ago filled him once more. He knew he had Darcy within his grasp. His fingers ripped at the metal grill.

Suddenly, Aaron shook his head as he remembered the pain running through the back of his neck. His eyes narrowed as he whirled around toward the center of the room.

Fred Harmon had hit him with the butt of his rifle. Aaron had jerked the gun from Fred's hands. Throwing it across the room it slid out the partially open door into the hallway as it landed. Fred had begun pulling at him, and kicking him.

Aaron smiled, remembering how small and weak Fred had seemed when he grabbed him under both arms and threw him across the room as though he were a feather pillow. Fred's head had smashed against the wall; he lay there stunned.

Walking over to him, Aaron raised his fist. The explosion of the gunshots suddenly filled Aaron's ears. He put his hands over them to block out the sound.

Aaron's teeth were clenched tight together; his eyes filled with hatred. Mae Harmon's face flashed before him. He ran to the doorway smashing his fist against the wall.

"Three left. Three left," he screamed, as he pounded on the rotting wood. Aaron didn't know Fred Harmon was already dead.

As he stumbled out of the house and down the front steps, rage consumed every fiber of his being. He was completely out of control. His body twisted in circles; his arms jabbed at the air. His animal-like screams echoed through the trees and fell on the lake. Aaron went to the ground. His eyes were closed, his breathing deep and labored. His fingers dug into the muddy earth as an insane frenzy overwhelmed him. Turning onto his back, he lay motionless for over half an hour, as though he were dead. The drizzling rain washed over his mask-like face.

Suddenly, his eyes opened and stared unblinking into the gray sky. Slowly he got to his feet, turned and walked back to Mae's house.

Wait here. Wait here. They'll be back. No one escapes the butterfly man. He repeated over and over again to himself. Aaron sat on the front steps staring into the growing storm. His wet, mud covered clothes stuck to his body. Aaron Blake didn't feel the cold.

Frankie and Beth arrived about 6:30 p.m. Darcy opened the door and was greeted by Frankie's round smiling face.

"It's about time you invited us over. Shit, we haven't seen *our* house guest in days," Frankie grumbled jokingly as she kissed Darcy.

"Who in their right mind wants to see you anyway?" Toni said entering the living room.

"Let's see . . . the face looks familiar, but I can't place the name," Frankie kidded, as she walked toward Toni.

"How are ya, you old fart?" Toni shook Frankie's hand warmly.

"It's good to see you both," Beth said.

"Hi Beth. You look as beautiful as ever," Toni remarked, giving her a big hug.

"So what's going on? You two have become hermits lately. Toni just up, and more or less moves in with you, and then we don't hear from either of you again," Frankie questioned as she removed her jacket.

"How about some drinks before dinner?" Toni replied casually, trying to change the subject.

"Yeah, that sounds good, but don't try and avoid the question. What's up?" Frankie persisted as she followed Toni into the kitchen.

Again, Toni ignored Frankie's question. They fixed the drinks in silence and then returned to the living room. Mae and Darcy were busy examining the new diamond bracelet Frankie had given Beth.

"Wow. That's some present. What did ya do Frankie, rob a bank or something?" Toni prodded jokingly.

Frankie laughed. "Didn't ya know, I'm not only handsome and smart, I'm also rich."

They all laughed. It felt good. Toni and Darcy hadn't heard that sound for a long time. After finishing the drinks, they all sat down to a huge spaghetti dinner. Tossed salad, lots of fresh garlic bread, enhanced by a rich red wine to make the meal complete.

Frankie finally sat back holding her stomach. "I'm gonna explode, I just know I'm gonna explode."

Darcy smiled. "Come on Aunt Mae, let's clean up while Toni entertains Beth, and *Miss Piggy*."

"I'll help too," Beth offered, as she picked up her plate.

Toni and Frankie retired to the living room. Toni threw another log on the fire, while Frankie flopped down on the couch and undid the top button on her Levis.

"How about a nice brandy to help digest some of that food you inhaled," Toni said.

"Thanks," Frankie answered, "I'm miserable."

After Toni poured the drinks she sat in the recliner, contentedly staring into the flames roaring in the fireplace.

Frankie finally broke the silence. "Okay Toni, I'm gonna ask ya one more time. What the fuck's goin' on? Don't try and tell me nothin', because I know you too well. The three of you look tired and drained. I'd like ta think it's love keeping ya so near Darcy, but my gut tells me it's more than that. Now level with me." Frankie's voice was quiet but persistent.

Toni continued to stare into the fire for a moment, and then looked at her. "When I tell you I can't say anything right now, you have to let it go at that. I know it's asking a lot, but for now that's the way it has to be. All I can say is it's extremely important for Darcy's safety that you stop asking questions. I swear you'll be one of the first to know what's been happening when I'm free to discuss it. You just have to trust me on this. Don't express these feelings you have to anyone, including Beth. Please Frankie, if you love Darcy, you'll do as I ask."

"This being in the dark doesn't make me happy, but if you say it's that important I believe ya. You have my word, no more questions."

"Thanks Frankie. Now, can we try and have a nice relaxed evening for Darcy's sake?"

The three women had finished in the kitchen and joined Frankie and Toni just as their conversation ended.

"How about some poker? Frankie's got loads of money, and I feel like relieving her of some of it," Darcy said smiling.

"You're on smart ass," Frankie answered.

"I'm going to my room," Mae said. "I'm suddenly very tired. It was good to see you and Beth again, Frankie. Next time, perhaps you'll all come to my home for dinner."

"Thank you Mrs. Harmon, we'd enjoy that," Frankie answered getting to her feet.

Mae hugged everyone and left the room.

"Is your aunt all right? She seems a little down or something," Beth asked in a whisper.

"Oh, she's just fine. Toni and I have kept her pretty busy since she's been here. I guess it finally caught up with her," Darcy answered casually.

They played cards for over two hours, keeping the conversation light. Frankie kidded Darcy about Toni, making her blush on several occasions. Frankie loved to play matchmaker, and she was happy to see the closeness growing between Darcy and Toni. By eleven o'clock they were all yawning.

"Damn, I'm gettin' old, can't even stay up after nine without my eyes closing." Frankie stretched.

"We better call it a night *sweetie*," Beth said looking at Frankie.

After all their good nights were said, and kisses given, Frankie and Beth shuffled wearily down the hall toward the elevator.

"Oh Darcy," Beth called back over her shoulder. "Fifteen of your loans closed, all on the same day. I thought it would make you happy to know that."

"How did you know that?" Darcy asked.

"I was there. Isn't it amazing? Fifteen loans in one day. That must be some kind of record. I was delivering some documents to your branch on Tuesday, and just happened to be there at the same time the news hit. See you soon," Beth said as she disappeared into the elevator.

Toni frowned as she shut the door. "Doesn't Beth work at a different branch than you?"

"Yes, she works in Bellevue," Darcy answered as she began turning off the lights around the apartment.

"But she said she was in your branch in Seattle on that day so she knew exactly how many loans closed. Is that a regular routine for her?"

"Well, not really. But if we're short handed and it's important, they'll have someone deliver documents who normally wouldn't be doing that. Does it mean something to you?"

"Not really," Toni answered. "My brain is just working overtime I guess. I'm beat. Come on, let's go to bed."

They lay next to each other, a strained silence between them. They both seemed uncomfortable; as though they had never slept together before. Both trying to believe what was happening between them didn't exist. Each afraid to let the other know the feelings they had. Afraid to drive the other one away by appearing too eager.

Finally, Toni turned and kissed Darcy. It was a soft sweet kiss. "Goodnight," she whispered gently touching Darcy's cheek with her fingertips. She wanted more, but instead, Toni turned on her side away from Darcy and stared into the darkness. *Don't push her,* she thought. *Give her time.*

Darcy lay on her back. Tears filled her eyes and ran down both sides of her face onto the pillow beneath her head. *God, I want her so bad, but I've got to give her space, can't push.*

It was 3:00 a.m. when Toni sat straight up in bed. Her eyes wide open.

"That's it! By god, that's it!" she shouted.

Darcy jumped. "What's happening. Is Aaron Blake here?" She pulled the covers up around her neck and began shaking. Panic was written all over her face.

Toni slapped her hands together. A wide grin spread across her lips.

"Toni, what is it? Are you sick? Did you hear something?" Darcy was reaching a full stage of panic.

"It *was* there, I knew it was. What time is it? I've got to talk to Otto." Toni turned to Darcy and kissed her. "It's okay, nothing's wrong. Please forgive me if I frightened you." Then she sprang out of bed.

Darcy's heart was still pounding wildly in her chest. She blinked her eyes trying to get herself fully awake. Her mouth fell open as she watched Toni dress.

"What are you doing? You scared me to death." She was angry now.

Getting up as quickly as she could, Darcy followed Toni through the apartment and into the kitchen. Fighting with her robe, she finally managed to get her arm in the sleeve.

It was cold, and Darcy's bare feet were freezing. Her hair, tangled and swirled, stuck out in all directions. The blinding kitchen light was giving her a headache. Toni was ignoring her as she got a pot of coffee going.

Finally, Darcy grabbed Toni by the arm. "What the hell are you doing? It's three o'clock in the morning, are you crazy?"

Toni kissed Darcy again. "I can't tell you anything right now, not until I check with Otto, but I've just solved *one* of our mysteries."

"Toni, I think you've finally snapped. The only mystery I know about is where is Aaron Blake, and when are we going to find him."

"Ah, but you're wrong. There are many mysteries here, and now one of them is solved. Remind me to send Beth a thank you note when this is over." Toni was smiling from ear to ear.

"Beth? What has Beth got to do with anything?" Darcy's voice was filled with frustration and confusion.

Toni didn't respond. She was busy dialing Otto Garrison's home phone number.

By this time Mae was up and awake. She squinted her eyes as she entered the kitchen, trying to shield them from the light.

"What's all the fuss? Did they catch Aaron?" Mae asked.

"Aunt Mae, Toni's lost her mind. I don't know what to do with her. She's raving about mysteries, and how she's solved one. She won't tell me what she's talking about."

"Yeah, that's what I said. Get your lazy ass up and meet me at the station right now. Don't ask questions. I'll see you there in half an hour." Toni hung the phone up.

"See . . . that was Detective Garrison she was talking to. I'm telling you she's gone mad." Darcy waved her arms in the air as she spoke to her aunt.

"Toni. What's happening here? Why can't you answer Darcy?" Mae demanded.

Toni turned to both women. Her face suddenly became deadly serious.

"I only have a couple of minutes, so listen to me. I've solved one of our mysteries. That's all I can say right now. As soon as I get back, I'll explain everything. Trust me."

She filled a large mug with coffee, grabbed Darcy's car keys, and headed for the front door. Darcy followed her. Mae stayed in the kitchen pouring a cup of coffee and trying to grasp what was happening.

Toni opened the door and then turned toward Darcy. She pulled Darcy to her, kissing her deeply.

"I love you," Toni whispered, and then she was gone.

Darcy stood in the doorway totally confused and shocked. She stared at the elevator doors as the arrow slowly moved downward. The words I love you echoed through her mind.

It was 5:00 a.m. before a very sleepy Otto Garrison arrived at the station. Toni had been waiting for almost an hour, and she was stressed and angry.

"Where the hell have you been? I told you I'd be here within half an hour," she yelled at Otto.

"Cool down Toni. My goddamn car wouldn't start. I had ta wake my neighbor and get him ta give me a jump start. Shit, I almost froze my ass off out there . . . this better be damn good."

"Sorry Otto. You know me. Once the game is about to be won I get outta control sometimes," Toni apologized sheepishly, realizing she needed to calm down and think clearly.

"Game? What are you talking about?"

"Let me start by telling you what I did all day yesterday. Now listen carefully. I picked up all the newspapers carrying any articles on Blake's background and escape, and the Sue Olsen murder. I read your reports on Aaron Blake and Olsen over and over again until I knew them by heart.

"Then I went over the accounts written in the newspaper. Especially the ones concerning Sue Olsen. I spent hours reading and rereading those articles." She paused and took a deep breath.

"So? Now your a walking encyclopedia regarding these two people. What does that prove?" Otto leaned across his desk as he watched Toni pace up and down.

"It proves who killed Sue Olsen." Toni stopped in mid-stride, turned and slapped her hand down on Otto's desk.

He jumped slightly and stared at her. "I don't understand."

"The newspapers never mentioned how many times Sue was stabbed. They only said multiple stab wounds. They didn't know anything about her missing briefcase. Your office never gave out that information."

"Yeah, so?"

"So, I've talked to one person who *did* know how many times Sue was stabbed, *and* another who knew her briefcase was with her at the time of her death."

"But the only one who would have that information is the person who was there. The one who killed her."

"You got it Otto. *She knew because she was there!*"

Otto was excited now. "Okay Toni, let's have a name."

"You mean *names*." Toni sat down in the chair on the other side of Otto's desk.

"Okay goddamn it, *names*." Otto was losing patience.

"Taylor Austin and Carol Masters," Toni stated matter-of-factly.

"Sue Olsen worked with them, didn't she?"

"Just with Carol Masters, but you can bet your ass Taylor Austin is in this up to her eyebrows too."

"But why? I talked to both of 'em, and they seemed deeply concerned about what happened to Sue Olsen. What reason would *both* women have for killing her?" Otto pushed his large frame back into his chair and stared thoughtfully at the ceiling for a moment.

Toni leaned over the desk toward him. "That's your department Otto. I just know they did it. And I'm sure if you dig deep enough you'll find out why. I'd take this real slow if I were you so as not to tip them off. It would probably be a good idea if you got some background on 'em. And quietly did some indepth investigation into what Sue Olsen was working on and what she might have found out about Taylor and Carol, regarding the bank."

"But, how did ya figure this out? I still don't understand." Once again, Otto leaned forward. He and Toni were eye to eye.

"The night Darcy had several of the women over who worked with Sue, we were all standing around expressing our concerns and ideas regarding Aaron Blake and why he might have killed Sue. Taylor Austin knew exactly how many times Sue Olsen had been stabbed, and Carol Masters knew Sue had her briefcase with her that night. Then, last night a friend of Darcy's made the statement, *I knew because I was there*. The words stuck in my brain. I didn't realize why it bothered me so much until three o'clock this morning. That's when everything hit me."

"We can't arrest 'em on just that information, but I can really zero in now. Do you think Taylor and Carol knew about Darcy's connection to Aaron Blake?"

Getting to her feet once more, Toni shoved her hands deep into the pockets of her jeans and began pacing around the room.

"No, but I believe they tried to set it up because of Blake's escape. They knew everyone was panicked by the thought of him being loose in the city. They figured if it was a gruesome enough murder, everyone would automatically blame him. Just because Sue and Darcy looked so much alike had nothing to do with it." Toni took a deep breath.

"We assumed Aaron did it because of what we knew about his past concerning Darcy and her family. But it wasn't a case of mistaken identity. The murder of Sue Olsen had nothing to do with Blake. He's still out there trying to find Darcy and her aunt." She stopped walking and stood staring at Otto, waiting for his response.

"Okay Toni, I'm convinced. Steve and I will handle this from here on. We've got lots of work to do so we can nail these two and make it stick. I don't have to tell you not to say a word to anyone."

"You know me better than that Otto. Now what about Aaron Blake? Do you have a line on him yet?"

"Nothing so far Toni, but if he's still in Washington it's just a matter of time before we get him. I'm gonna notify the captain as to what I've found out about Sue Olsen's murder so the detectives working on the Aaron Blake case won't be spinning their wheels trying to connect Sue's case to him."

"How are you going to explain where you got this information?" Toni asked.

"I'll tell them I figured it out through the questioning of Sue's co-workers. God, I'm gonna look brilliant."

Toni laughed. "Now, you owe *me* one."

"Let's you and me go over this one more time, so I'm sure I haven't missed anything."

"Not until you get me some coffee and donuts," Toni answered with a smile. "After all, the least you can do is buy me Sunday breakfast after what I just did for you."

Chapter Sixteen

"When the fuck are you going to sit down? You've been up pacing most of the night." Taylor said, grabbing Carol by the arm.

"I can't help it. Maybe you can sleep like a baby after killing someone, but I can't. I just know somehow Darcy and that Toni Underwood are going to figure this out soon. Darcy's not stupid, you know. She's going to give Toni enough information about banking operations to make her curious," Carol answered, as she jerked her arm away from Taylor.

"Look baby, come over here and sit down. You know I'll protect you. Just give me a chance to figure out how to handle Darcy."

"You'll protect me? If it hadn't been for you and your greed, I wouldn't be in this mess. We had plenty of money; we had it made. God, why did I listen to you?" Carol's voice was shrill and growing louder with each word.

"You know I never planned on killing anyone. If Sue hadn't gotten her nose so far into this she'd still be alive

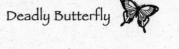

today, and you and I would be long gone. I did what I had to do. I did it for *us*."

Carol fell onto the kitchen chair. Holding her head in her hands she began sobbing. Taylor sat down next to her.

"Listen to me baby. Between the two of us we've managed to stash away over five hundred thousand dollars. That stupid bank you work for wouldn't make the connection for months, and tracing it to you would have taken even longer. All we needed was one more month and we would have been away free and clear. Don't blame me for what happened. Blame that fucking nosy bitch Sue Olsen. She was getting ready to blow the whole thing up in our faces."

"You're really a cold one, aren't you Taylor?" Carol said, as she looked up. "Why do I love you? Am I *that* sick? Was I *that* lonely? I don't even trust you, yet I'm willing to do anything you want just to hang on to you. God, I hate myself."

Taylor wasn't listening. She was already formulating a plan to take care of any threat Darcy might pose.

"We have to get rid of Darcy somehow without throwing suspicion on ourselves. Killing Sue worked perfectly because of that maniac escaping from the state hospital. The whole state of Washington is paranoid right now. He'll get blamed for every murder committed from now until they catch him. That's going to work to our advantage. I can hear it now . . . 'Why yes officer we met with Darcy Bennett today. We had lunch. She and Carol are close friends and they caught up on a lot of gossip and old times. We left her in the restaurant parking lot and assumed she would be heading straight home from there.' . . . It's perfect."

"What do you mean we have to get rid of Darcy?" Carol's voice was a whisper.

"Look, I don't *want* to hurt Darcy, but we don't know what all Sue really told her the day they had lunch. We can't take the chance something Sue said might click in Darcy's mind to connect all of this to us."

"You can't do this. Darcy's my friend. You're out of your mind. I won't be a part to this." Carol's voice grew loud once more.

Taylor's eyes narrowed and became cold and hard. Her face was like a piece of stone. She hissed at Carol. "You *will* be a part of this. You *are* a part of this. You will do what I say, do you understand?" She grabbed Carol's wrist squeezing it hard.

Unable to speak because of the sobs caught in her throat, Carol nodded her head up and down.

"Now, start pulling yourself together. You have a call to make."

At 6:30 a.m. Darcy's phone rang.

"I'll get it Aunt Mae. It might be Toni." Darcy quickly picked up the receiver. "Hello."

"Hi Darcy. It's Carol."

"Oh, hi Carol, what's up?" Darcy answered cheerfully.

"I know it's early, but Taylor and I have been discussing Sue's murder, and we think we might have come up with something that may help in the investigation."

"Oh, that's great Carol. What is it?" Darcy answered excitedly.

"I'd rather not say over the phone. Can you meet us somewhere?"

"Toni's not here right now Carol, and I really don't know when she'll be back. Can we meet you later? Or better yet why not come to my place?"

"We really don't feel this can wait, Darcy. Can't you meet us in Everett? We'll have breakfast and talk."

Suddenly Darcy had a bright idea.

"Tell you what, I haven't been out in days. The weather doesn't look too ominous right now, so maybe we

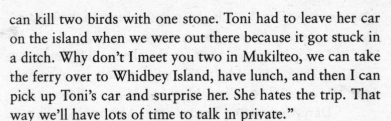

can kill two birds with one stone. Toni had to leave her car on the island when we were out there because it got stuck in a ditch. Why don't I meet you two in Mukilteo, we can take the ferry over to Whidbey Island, have lunch, and then I can pick up Toni's car and surprise her. She hates the trip. That way we'll have lots of time to talk in private."

"That sounds great Darcy. Besides, we don't see enough of each other anyway. We can make a day of it. I understand your aunt has a lovely home on the island."

"Yes she does. You can see it when we get Toni's car."

"Okay Darcy, we'll meet you in Mukilteo at the ferry landing, say in one hour."

"Sounds good," Darcy answered.

"Was that your friend Carol from work on the phone, honey?" Mae asked after Darcy had hung up the phone.

"Yes Aunt Mae. She and Taylor want to talk to me about Sue. It might be important, so I'm going to meet with them. We're going to Whidbey and pick up Toni's car." Darcy smiled.

"Doesn't that seem odd? Why wouldn't they want to wait and include Toni?"

"Carol said it could be really important, and since I don't know when Toni will get back, or where she is, I decided to go ahead and talk with them. Besides, I'm beginning to feel like a prisoner in my own home. I can fill Toni in this afternoon, she'll know if what they have to say is pertinent or not. It makes me feel I'm really being of some help, instead of just walking around shaking in my boots. Remember, Toni told us to be tough."

"She also told us to stick together."

"Oh Aunt Mae. Carol's an old friend of mine. She and Taylor will be with me, so what could happen?"

"I don't like it. I think you should wait for Toni."

Mae was frowning. "What about the policeman downstairs? He's not going to let you go anywhere alone."

Darcy kissed her aunt on the cheek. "I'll simply tell him I'm going to meet Toni at the police station. It's okay Aunt Mae, I promise I'll be careful. Now, would you call me a cab?"

Darcy turned and headed for the bedroom to change clothes.

Mae stood alone in the living room. "I still don't like it," she repeated.

Within ten minutes Darcy was ready to leave.

"Stay near the phone Aunt Mae. I may be calling with some good news soon." Darcy felt good. Maybe she could be of some help to Toni for a change. She had been feeling useless, and wanted Toni to know she wasn't a helpless clinging vine.

Darcy hugged Mae and went downstairs to wait for her taxi. Mae pulled back the drape from the window. The sky was growing black over Puget Sound. A steady rain had begun to fall.

As Darcy's cab pulled to a stop, she noticed Taylor Austin sitting alone in her BMW. Darcy paid the cab driver and walked over to where Taylor was parked. Taylor got out of the car when she saw Darcy approaching, and started toward her.

"Where's Carol?" Darcy asked with a slight frown.

"After she spoke with you, she suddenly began getting stomach cramps. Then she threw up. I knew she was coming down with something yesterday when she complained of an ongoing migraine headache. I think it's the flu." Taylor responded, as they walked to the ticket counter.

"But, why didn't you just call back and cancel for today?" Darcy asked.

"You know Carol. She felt so strongly about this she insisted I go ahead and keep our appointment. I can fill you in on what we came up with regarding Sue's death, and besides, didn't you want to surprise Toni?"

Darcy felt uncomfortable. She didn't know Taylor well, and had always found it difficult to carry on a conversation with her.

"Look Darcy, I know you'd prefer to have Carol here, but there's nothing we can do about the situation. Why not make the best of it? Besides, if we can help the police in any way, that's more important then personal feelings. Don't you agree?" Taylor smiled.

Maybe this will give Taylor and me a chance to get to know each other better. Darcy thought. *After all, she is my friend's other half. I should get to know her better.*

"Okay Taylor, why not? After all, if what you have to say really is important, we better get it out in the open. And I did want to pick up Toni's car. So let's go."

Taylor Austin smiled to herself as the ferry slowly began pulling out. *Darcy is the only one who can fuck us up now. We have no idea what that bitch Sue told her before I got to her. Can't take any chances. This will be a piece of cake. Just another victim of that maniac Aaron Blake.* Taylor watched the bow of the ferry cut through the choppy water.

The sky was black and the wind had picked up. The waves grew in size with each passing moment.

"We could be in for another bad North-Eastern," Darcy said looking toward Whidbey.

"It's going to be all right. Just the usual lovely winter weather here in good old Washington," Taylor answered, sounding casual and sure of herself.

"So, what was it you and Carol think you've come up with, Taylor?"

"Tell you what. Let's wait till we reach the island. We'll have breakfast and discuss it then. I find it hard to concentrate with the boat bouncing around like this."

"I know what you mean." Darcy smiled.

Without warning a gust of gale force wind hit the ferry causing it to dip to one side.

Mae paced up and down. She was still greatly disturbed by Carol's phone call. She couldn't shake the feeling that something wasn't quite right.

Ten minutes after Darcy had left, the front door opened. Toni entered the apartment smiling.

"Hi Mae. What's new?" Toni asked, as she took off her coat.

"Plenty!" Mae responded, sharply.

"What are you talking about? Where's Darcy?"

"She's gone."

"What the hell do you mean she's gone?"

"Her friend Carol called. Something about new information concerning the Olsen murder."

"What?" Toni yelled.

"Carol wanted to talk with her right away. Said it couldn't wait. Darcy left no more then ten minutes ago."

"Where? Where is she?" Toni grabbed Mae by the shoulders.

"Toni, you're frightening me. What's wrong?" Mae's voice was trembling.

Toni tried to speak calmly. "Look, I don't have time to explain. Please, just tell me where she is."

"She's on her way to Whidbey Island with Carol and Taylor."

Toni's face felt cold and frozen; her eyes grew wide.

"Oh my god!" Toni whirled around grabbing her coat.

"Toni what . . . ."

"Call Detective Otto Garrison immediately. Tell him to meet me in Mukilteo at the ferry landing."

Toni quickly checked to make sure her gun was fully loaded and she had extra ammo. Then she ran from the apartment, leaving the door wide open. Mae stood in the middle of the room stunned. She knew now something was desperately wrong. Shaking, she turned to the phone and dialed.

Toni jammed on the brakes, skidded to a stop in front of the ticket booth, and jumped out of Mae's Bronco.

"What time does the next ferry leave?" she shouted to the woman inside.

"There are no more. It's too rough. The last one left fifteen minutes ago. The captain radioed he couldn't make it back."

An overwhelming feeling of hopelessness and despair gripped Toni's gut. She stared out toward Puget Sound. The wind and rain beat against her face.

Fifty yards to her left a thirty-five foot fishing boat was just mooring. The crew was fighting against the rising tide and waves to get the boat tied down.

"I'm not beat yet," Toni said out loud.

She ran to the boat. The captain had just stepped onto the dock when Toni grabbed his arm.

"Please, excuse me, but I need your help desperately," she shouted over the howling wind.

"What the hell do you want?" the captain yelled angrily, as he yanked his arm free.

"This is a matter of life and death. A friend of mine is on the last ferry to Whidbey, and I *must* get to the island or she'll die. I know this sounds crazy, but I'm an ex-cop and I know what I'm talking about."

The captain stared at Toni. "Ex-cop or not, you <u>are</u> crazy if you think I'm going back out in this weather." He turned to leave.

Toni grabbed his arm once more. "I'll give you five hundred dollars if you take me."

"God lady, we could die out there. Do you realize what you're asking?"

"Yes I do." Toni replied. "I'll make it a thousand if we leave now."

He didn't answer. Toni stared into his eyes, pleading with her own.

"All right. Shit, I must be as nuts as you to even try this." He finally said.

"Thank you." Toni answered with a deep sigh. "Here, take my Rolex watch as collateral until I can get the money."

"Hey Pete. I got a job to do here. Do you want in on it?" The captain yelled to his big blond crewman.

"What kinda job?" The blond called back.

"This woman needs to get to Whidbey. It's a matter of life or death. There's three hundred in it if you come along, and give me a hand."

"Jesus Christ Hal, look at it out there. Do ya think we can make it?" The crewman had moved next to Toni and the captain.

"I don't know Pete, all I know is this woman ain't kiddin'. Someone's on that ferry who's in a lot a trouble and if we don't try, she'll die."

The blond looked at Toni. He could tell by the expression on Toni's face that Hal meant what he said.

"What the hell, you only live once, right?" Pete smiled at Toni.

"Come on. The longer we wait the worse it's gonna get." Hal jumped onto the boat.

He grabbed Toni's hand pulling her on board. Pete cast off the lines and leapt on behind Toni. After three tries, the engine roared to a start. Carefully, Hal began easing his boat away from the dock.

"God help us all." Hal whispered.

Toni stared out the window of the control room. She couldn't see past the bow of the ship. The waves crashed onto the deck. Sheets of blinding water hit the windshield. The boat was tossed about like a match stick. The sound of the wind was deafening. Toni held on with every ounce of strength she had to keep herself from being thrown to the deck. She couldn't even tell if they were making any headway.

Otto reached the ferry landing too late. He stood watching as the thirty-five foot fishing boat disappeared into the raging rain and wind. He had no way of telling Toni, because of the storm, radio transmission to Whidbey Island was impossible. The authorities could not be notified as to what was going down. She was on her own.

The Whidbey Island Ferry reached the dock just as the main thrust of the storm hit.

"Listen, Taylor," Darcy said, as they drove off the ferry. "I think it would be best to head for my aunt's house right now. The road is still probably passable, but if we wait, we might not get in or back out. From what I heard on the ferry, they aren't going back until this storm passes. So it looks like we may have to spend the night. My aunt keeps plenty of food on hand, I'm sure we can find something to eat at her place."

"You're right Darcy. I sure didn't think we'd be stuck here like this. I'll bet we can't even call home. Carol will be frantic if she doesn't hear from me."

"My aunt didn't want me to come in the first place, and Toni will probably give me a lecture I'll never forget."

"Well, there's nothing we can do about it, so how do we get to your aunt's house?"

The rain intensified as Taylor's BMW sped down the main road. It was 10:00 a.m. but the darkness covering the sky made it seem more like early evening.

God, I hope we can make it to the house. I don't want to end up like Toni and I did the last time, Darcy thought.

"Slow down; the turn-off is just ahead."

Taylor eased her foot off the gas pedal. *Fuck, I'm going to have to hold off until tomorrow with the plan. Don't want to spend the night with a corpse,* Taylor thought, as she turned off the highway onto the private road.

"Man, this road is really beat up." Taylor remarked as she tightened her grip on the steering wheel.

"We have to take it easy from here to the house. Try and keep as close to the center as you can." Darcy replied.

"What's that up ahead?" Taylor asked, straining her eyes to see.

"Why, that's Toni's car. It's still in the ditch. I don't understand. Art was supposed to have it already pulled out."

Carefully, Taylor eased her car by. Darcy felt nervous inside. Something was not right about all this. She wished Toni was here. She wished she'd listened to her aunt. She felt depressed and alone.

"Here we are," Taylor said jolting Darcy back from her thoughts.

They couldn't see the caved in front door until they reached the porch.

"Jesus Christ," Taylor said. "Damn, a tornado must have hit this place."

Darcy didn't respond. She stepped around the fallen door and stood in the middle of the living room. She couldn't believe the destruction. Slowly, Darcy began moving around the room picking up bits and pieces of broken vases and lamps, then letting them drop once more to the floor.

"What the hell happened here?" Taylor whispered.

"A nightmare," Darcy answered quietly.

Taylor followed Darcy into the kitchen. Taylor shivered as the cold wind whipped through the open doorways and windows. Darcy moved as one would in a dream. Her face was ashen; terror gripped her heart. A clap of thunder rattled the house.

Darcy suddenly turned to Taylor. "We have to get out of here now!"

"What's happening? What's going on?" Taylor replied. She was shouting.

Darcy had already grabbed Taylor by the arm and was pulling her toward the front door. Darcy's heart was pounding through her chest.

"Don't ask any questions. Just run. Run for the car."

Taylor slipped and fell as her foot hit the wet soil. "Come on." Darcy yelled, helping Taylor to her feet.

The two women jumped into the car. Their breath came in deep gulps. They were soaked to the skin and covered with mud.

"Lock the doors." Darcy said in a hoarse voice. "Get us out of this place."

Taylor's hand was shaking so badly she dropped her keys on the floor of the car. Picking them up she tried once again to insert them into the ignition. After several tries, the key slid in. Taylor turned it. The engine made grinding sounds. Taylor tried over and over again to start the car.

"My god, what's wrong? Why won't it start?" Darcy said frantically.

"I don't know. Maybe it's flooded."

"It can't be. Keep trying," Darcy said breathlessly.

Taylor tried again, and again, and then there was nothing.

"Now the battery's worn down. Fuck!" Taylor said hitting the steering wheel with the butt of her hand.

Darcy sat staring straight ahead. Tears filled her eyes.

"You have to tell me what's going on here. I have a right to know." Taylor began shaking Darcy.

"The butterfly man is here," Darcy answered in a small childlike voice.

"The what? What did you say?"

"The butterfly man is here," Darcy screamed.

"Butterfly man? What the hell are you talking about?"

"He's here. He's come for me."

"Darcy listen to me. Who is the butterfly man? Darcy!" Taylor slapped her across the face.

Darcy began sobbing. She covered her face with her hands.

The wind rocked the car and the rain engulfed them.

Taylor took a deep breath then, and spoke softly. "Darcy please, get a hold of yourself. I can't help you if you don't talk to me. Please, look at me."

Slowly Darcy raised her eyes to meet Taylor's. Taylor wiped the tears from Darcy's face.

"Now, take some deep breaths and tell me why you're so frightened."

"Aaron Blake. Aaron Blake is here." Darcy's voice was barely audible. "He's here for me. He's going to kill me."

"Aaron Blake? Why would Aaron Blake be after you?"

Darcy quickly related her history regarding Aaron Blake.

Taylor's mouth dropped open as she listened. Icy fear filled her body.

My god! Taylor thought as she listened. *I've got to get out of here.*

"Don't you see; he's been after me all along," Darcy gasped.

Taylor pulled back and looked at Darcy. Taylor's mind was racing.

"Look Darcy, if what you say is true then we're both in grave danger. I'm going to get out of the car and check under the hood. Maybe I can get this goddamn thing started. When I yell, pop the hood."

"Don't go out there," Darcy pleaded.

"We have to get out of here. I'll be fine. You just keep a look out. This will only take a minute." Taylor opened the door and stepped out into the raging storm.

Darcy couldn't see clearly through the windshield. She rolled down her window. Squinting her eyes, she could only make out blurry forms of the trees and the house.

"Okay," Taylor yelled.

Darcy reached under the dashboard and pulled back the lever. Taylor raised the hood. The minutes dragged by as Darcy waited for a response from Taylor.

Finally, Darcy called out. "Can you fix it?"

No answer.

"Taylor! Will it start?" Darcy yelled at the top of her lungs.

No answer.

She rolled the window up and sat back in the seat. Several more minutes went by. Darcy began breathing hard once more. *Something's wrong, it shouldn't take this long. And why didn't Taylor answer?*

Again, Darcy rolled the window down. "Taylor, answer me. What's wrong? Please. Answer me."

Again, no answer.

Panic took over as Darcy realized she was alone.

Taylor had already fallen twice by the time she reached Toni's car. She was completely out of breath and leaned against the fender, gasping for air. Her dark hair hung in her face and stuck to her skin.

That bitch can fend for herself. Survival of the fittest, that's the way it is, Taylor thought. *Besides, if that maniac finds Darcy, it will give me a chance to get away and I'll be clean as a whistle.* She smiled even though with every breath her lungs ached.

The sudden pain shooting through Taylor's scalp caused her to scream out. Abruptly her head was jerked back, and she was off her feet being drug across the hood of Toni's car. Taylor raised her arms over her head; her fingers ripped at the hand holding her long hair in a vice like grip. Within seconds she was thrown into the ditch, rolling uncontrollably until her body slammed up against the side.

Stunned, she lay there trying to get her bearings. Her head throbbed. She looked up. Standing above her was the massive form of Aaron Blake. His eyes cut through her. Bits of hair hung from his hand. Taylor began sliding backwards through the muddy water which filled the ditch. Rocks cut at her hands and ripped her clothes.

Aaron Blake stood motionless, watching as the figure before him moved away. Taylor's pleas and screams filled his ears. Aaron's lips opened slightly and spread into a leering smile. Taylor tried to gain her footing. She clawed at the sides of the ditch. She fell again and again as her feet slipped out from under her. Aaron began moving toward her.

"Please!" Taylor screamed. "Please, I'll give you anything. You don't want me. Darcy's back there in the car. She's the one you want."

Aaron hesitated for a moment looking back over his shoulder. Then, he turned again to Taylor. He reached down, grabbing Taylor up as though she were a twig, and raised her over his head. Taylor kicked and clawed at the sky. Aaron hurled her through the air. She hit the side of the ditch with a thud. Pain raced through her body. She moaned and fought to open her eyes.

Aaron was on her, pushing her head down into the water. Taylor's hands beat against Aaron's chest and face. Her nails dug deep into his flesh. And then it was done. Taylor lie face up under the ever deepening water. Aaron Blake stood over Taylor's lifeless body as the rain washed the blood from the long wounds on his face. Then he turned back toward the house.

Darcy staggered up the front porch steps. She stood looking out into the rain. *Where is she? What happened to Taylor?* she thought.

The distant figure seemed to emerge from nowhere.

"Taylor?" Darcy screamed into the wind.

The dark figure continued toward her at a slow shuffling pace.

Darcy started to call out once more. She opened her mouth but the words stuck in her throat. Her eyes grew fixed. Her hands covered her mouth.

"Oh my god!" she finally cried out.

She knew; in one horrible instant she knew. It wasn't Taylor walking toward her, it was Aaron Blake! Darcy stood frozen to the spot as the lumbering form approached ever nearer. Slowly, she began taking one hesitant step after the other backwards until she was just inside the doorway.

"NO!" Darcy screamed.

Turning to run, her toe caught the edge of the fallen front door, and she fell hard. Laying there stunned for a moment, she tried to catch her breath. Weakened and shaking, she fought to get to her feet. Once she was standing again, she looked toward the driveway. She could almost make out his features now. Running for the kitchen, she slammed against the doorjam, almost falling again. Making her way out the back door, Darcy pushed her body against the wind and headed for the old house.

I'll be safe there. Mommy and daddy are there; I'll be safe.

Darcy shoved the old door open with her shoulder, and rushed to the center of the living room.

I must get to my hiding place. Mommy told me not to move until she returned.

She ran to the rotting staircase. As she placed her weight on the third step the boards gave way, trapping her foot. Darcy bent down clawing and pulling at the broken wood. She glanced behind her. Through the open front door she could see Aaron Blake. He was almost to the porch. With one last heave she pulled her foot free. Blood ran from the scratches on her ankle and pain ran up her leg.

As she reached the landing she looked down to the entrance way. Aaron was standing there staring up at her. She turned and ran toward her mother's old bedroom. Once inside, she closed the door, and leaned her exhausted body against the moldy, wet wood. Her mouth hung open as she gasped for air.

An old dresser stood against the wall next to her. With her last bit of strength Darcy pulled it up in front of the

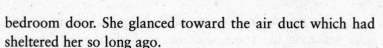

bedroom door. She glanced toward the air duct which had sheltered her so long ago.

Everything came rushing back into her mind; everything that had happened here that sunny summer day when she was a happy carefree five year old. She knew now it wasn't twenty-five years ago. She knew she was a woman, not a helpless five year old waiting in the darkness for her mother. Darcy suddenly knew this was no nightmare, no vision from the past, this was *real* and happening *now*.

She looked around the room for some kind of weapon. Anything, a board, old lamp . . . bed post.

"That's it. The bed post," she said aloud.

The old four poster bed still stood against the far wall. Darcy began pulling and pushing at the long maple post at the end of her mother's bed. It gave way almost immediately. With the four foot long pole in hand, Darcy knelt down behind the bed and waited.

The wind and rain stopped suddenly and everything became deadly calm. Darcy strained her ears. The only sound was the dripping water coming in through a large hole in the roof.

She froze in place for what seemed an eternity. Then, carefully she raised her head and peered across the mattress. A faded rag, which was once a bright yellow curtain, hung motionless from the rusted rod above the broken window. Darcy's gaze was fixed on the bedroom door.

With a sudden flash of lightning, and deafening clap of thunder, the wind and rain began beating once more against the walls and ceiling just as Aaron Blake's fist crashed through the door. It was as though a bomb had exploded.

Darcy's heart stopped as she watched his fists and feet punch through the wooden door until only splinters remained. With one hand he shoved the dresser away from the doorway and was inside the room.

He stood, feet apart, arms hanging loosely by his sides scanning the room with his coal black eyes. He was bare from the waist up. Darcy stared at the terror before her, the terror she had for so long only seen in her haunted dreams. She could feel the evilness of him reaching out to destroy her.

Aaron walked further into the room and turned toward the closet. His back was to Darcy now; he had not seen her. Another flash of lightning illuminated the darkening room, and there it was. The glorious butterfly perched on the shoulder of death himself. The colors, still bright and beautiful, gleamed against Aaron Blake's wet flesh.

Aaron opened the closet door. Seeing it was empty, he turned facing the bed.

"Darcy. Darcy Bennett." His voice came from somewhere deep inside. It hissed out and echoed through the room.

He began walking to the bed. When he was within three feet of her, Darcy jumped up bringing the bed post down cross the side of his head. There was a loud crack as the post broke in two from the force of the blow. Aaron staggered backwards and almost fell.

She tried to run past him but his hand caught her. Pain raced through her arm as his grip tightened. She pulled, trying to free herself.

Aaron laughed as Darcy fought to get away. He watched her as though she were a trapped animal trying to break free from the jaws of the trap. Blood streamed down the side of his face from the deep cut above his left ear. Aaron Blake felt no pain.

He threw Darcy against the wall. The impact knocked the wind out of her. She lay there gasping. Aaron stared down into Darcy's terror filled eyes. He had no face, just two pieces of coal where eyes should be. Pulling her knees up against her chest she tried to become as small as possible. She knew she was going to die!

The first bullet hit Aaron Blake's left shoulder, entering through the center of the butterfly. He whirled around as the second bullet ripped through his broad hairy chest. His expression never changed as he looked down at the gaping wound and watched the blood run down his body. Then, he looked up, and began walking toward Toni.

Toni stood motionless, arms straight out, both hands on her gun. Her legs apart, her eyes staring directly into Aaron Blake's. Her teeth were clenched tightly, the muscle in her jaw twitched.

"Stay where you are you fucking son of a bitch." Toni's voice was strong and steady above the wailing wind.

Aaron stopped. His black eyes never blinked. Blood was running freely from the chest wound, and he seemed to sway a bit. He looked at Toni, tilting his head to one side then the other.

"Darcy. Stay where you are," Toni shouted.

"Darcy Bennett." Aaron screamed and lunged toward Toni.

The sound of three more shots rang out. His huge twisting body fell forward, crashing onto the floor at Toni's feet.

The wind and rain seemed to subside as Toni stood looking down at Aaron. She shuddered, and stepped around him.

"Darcy, are you all right? I can't see you," Toni called out.

Darcy was still sitting with her arms wrapped around her legs rocking back and forth. Tears streamed down her face. Her eyes were wild and staring. Her body shook uncontrollably.

"I'm here. Here by the bed." Darcy's voice was a whisper.

Toni rushed to her. "It's okay. It's okay. He's dead." Toni said as she helped Darcy to her feet.

Toni put her arms around Darcy, holding her tight.

"Sh, now. You're safe. You're safe." Toni whispered over and over in Darcy's ear.

"Is it really over?"

"Yes, it's really over," Toni answered as she kissed away Darcy's tears.

The clouds began breaking up and what was left of daylight streamed in through the broken windows. Toni and Darcy slowly walked toward the bedroom doorway still holding each other. When they reached Aaron's body, Darcy paused, looking down at him.

A lone beam of light fell on Aaron's left shoulder.

"It's gone," Darcy whispered.

"What's gone?" Toni asked gently.

"The beautiful deadly butterfly. The only beautiful thing about Aaron Blake has flown away."

Where once the gloriously beautiful creature sat, there was now an empty, bleeding hole. Toni's bullet had obliterated the delicate rainbow-colored tattoo.

Chapter Seventeen

By the time Toni and Darcy reached the front porch, the storm had finally passed. It was afternoon, and darkness was approaching quickly. The Whidbey Police had just pulled up in front of Mae's house. Toni waved as she and Darcy made their way down the path.

A tall deputy in his early forties walked toward them.

"Hi, I'm Deputy Foster. Hal tells me that nut Aaron Blake is loose somewhere near Mae Harmon's house. Is that right?"

"He's not loose anymore; he's dead," Toni answered.

"Dead? What happened out here, and who are you people?" Foster asked.

"I'm Toni Underwood and this is Darcy Bennett. Ms. Bennett is Mae Harmon's niece. I'm a family friend. Blake tried to kill Ms. Bennett up at the old house, and thank God I reached her in time. I had to shoot him," Toni answered.

Foster called back to his partner. "Bobby, come on up here."

"Look Deputy Foster. Ms. Bennett and I are soaked to the bone, she's got some cuts on her ankle, and she's still suffering from shock. Could we go back to the station and get into some dry clothes? We'll wait there for you. I know you have questions and statements you want taken."

"Well, I guess it's all right. I'll call ahead so they have something for you to change into. Just don't leave."

"Where's Taylor?" Darcy asked wearily.

"Were Taylor and Carol with you at the old house?" Toni asked in a surprised tone.

"No. Just Taylor. She said Carol was ill and couldn't make the trip. When we realized Aaron was here we ran to her car. It wouldn't start and she got out to see if she could fix it. I haven't seen her since," Darcy answered wearily. "And Toni, your car is still in the ditch. Art Wardlow was supposed to have already come here to pull it out."

"I didn't see her when I arrived, and you're right, my car is where we left it," Toni replied. An ominous feeling began filling her.

"Who's Taylor?" Deputy Foster asked.

"She was with me," Darcy answered.

"Look Deputy Foster. It's getting dark fast. I think you should concentrate on Aaron Blake right now, but I have a real strong feeling you're gonna find more than one body out here. If I were you, tomorrow I'd organize a search party and check this area thoroughly. By that time the mainland police will be able to aid in the search."

Toni and Darcy followed the deputy back to his car and waited while he called the station.

"Okay, you two can go now. Do you know where the station is?" Foster asked.

"I do," Darcy answered weakly.

"Thanks Deputy Foster," Toni stated.

"Just stay put until I get there," Foster answered.

Toni helped Darcy into Hal's old truck and began

carefully driving back to town. Darcy was shaking and coughing.

"Sounds like you've got yourself a super bad cold coming on," Toni commented as she turned down the main road back to town.

"I'm glad to be alive to get a cold." Darcy answered. Her face was pale and drawn.

"As soon as we get some warm dry clothes on, I'll make sure you get some hot coffee and rest."

Toni reached over and took Darcy's hand in hers.

"How did you get here? I just realized there were no more ferries after we landed. How did you know I'd be in danger?" Darcy asked frowning.

"I kinda highjacked a fishing boat. This truck belongs to the skipper. I sent him for the police after we landed."

"You did what?"

"It's a long story, and I'll tell you all about it after we get settled and warm. All I'm worried about right now is taking care of you, and making sure you're all right."

Darcy looked at Toni. "You saved my life and sanity. How could I not be all right? My nightmares are ended forever because you made me face my fears. You brought a warmth and caring into my life I've never felt before. God, you even made me toughen up, and I like it. If you don't watch out, I might end up as tough as you, then you'd better watch out!"

Toni didn't answer. She just smiled.

They pulled up in front of the police station. It was dark now. Toni looked up at the sky. The stars twinkled as though they had all been washed clean. The air was fresh and smelled of pine and grass. Toni put her arm around Darcy as they walked inside.

A thin, middle-aged woman sat at the station switchboard. She looked up as they entered.

"Oh my, you must be the two girls Ernie radioed about."

"Yes ma'am, we are the two *girls*." Toni answered with a smile.

"Well, you just follow me and we'll get you out of those wet clothes."

The woman led them to the locker room. Two sets of gray sweats were laid out on a bench.

"The showers are right over there. Probably feel good to have a good hot shower. The towels are stacked on the shelf in front of you. Bandage's are in the cupboard next to the door. I'll make sure none of the boys come back here while you change. When you're done, just come on out front and I'll have some nice hot coffee ready." She smiled and toddled off down the hall.

Toni walked over and turned on the shower. It was a large stall, big enough for three people. Three separate shower heads surrounded the white tile walls. After adjusting the heat Toni and Darcy quickly undressed and stepped inside the steaming enclosure.

The hot water seemed to flow from every direction. It felt good against their cold skin. Toni stood directly under one of the nozzles with her eyes closed allowing the water to beat on her head. She barely felt Darcy's arms slide around her waist.

Toni opened her eyes just as Darcy kissed her. Toni responded. Their kiss was warm and loving. They stood silently holding one another as the steam and water warmed and relaxed their bodies.

"I really hate to say this, but I think we better get out before someone comes looking for us." Toni whispered in Darcy's ear.

"I don't want to move. I want to stay here forever, just like this." Darcy answered. "For the first time, in a long time, I feel safe and secure."

"I promise this won't be the last time we take a shower together. Now come on before we shrivel up like a couple of prunes."

Toni turned off the water and they both stepped out of the shower. They took turns drying each other with the big white fluffy towels. Toni bandaged Darcy's ankle, and then they slipped into the sweats, thick socks and rubber boots. They brushed their hair with the new brush their friend up front had left for them.

"You know, the people around here are really something." Toni said.

"What do you mean?"

"So far everyone I've come in contact with has gone out of their way to be helpful and kind, and they don't even know me."

"Now you understand why I love it here." Darcy smiled.

Toni put her arm around Darcy's shoulder and they walked back down the hall to the office.

"Well, you two girls look a lot better now then when you came in here," the dispatcher commented as they entered the room.

"Thank you so much . . ."

"Oh, my name is Kelly Bunker. But everyone calls me Kel."

"Kel, Ms. Underwood and I are thankful for all your trouble," Darcy said.

"Don't think nothin' of it. Now here, have some nice hot coffee and sit yourselves down and rest. Ernie should be here any time."

Both women felt suddenly exhausted. Neither spoke as they sipped the hot dark brew. Darcy's throat was beginning to hurt and her nose felt stuffy. Her arm ached where Aaron Blake had grabbed it, and her neck and back were stiff. Toni noticed the frown on Darcy's face.

"Are you okay?" Toni asked.

"I think you were right. I am getting a cold and I think the tossing around I got from that bastard is finally beginning to show in my bones."

"That goddamn son of a bitch," Toni said angrily.

"Here girls have some more coffee." Kel smiled. "I ordered you some food. Bet you haven't eaten all day."

"Mrs. Bunker, would you have some aspirin around here?" Toni asked.

"Sure do, I'll get you some. And it's Kel, remember?" Toni smiled. "Thanks Kel."

After taking four aspirins, Darcy turned toward Toni. "Now, tell me how you got here, and how you knew I was in trouble."

Slowly, Toni related what she had discovered concerning Taylor and Carol and the death of Sue Olsen. How she knew Taylor and Carol were going to harm Darcy if she didn't get to her in time.

"Destroying Aaron Blake was an added bonus for me," Toni said as she concluded her story.

"I can't believe Carol could be a part of such a horrible crime."

"Love can cause people to do crazy things, babe. Especially when it's a sick love like that one. In my opinion I think the whole thing was Taylor's idea, and Carol went along because she was afraid of losing Taylor if she didn't. Of course, Otto Garrison has to prove all this and make a case for the D.A., but I don't think he'll have much trouble."

"The irony of this whole thing is, they didn't know my relationship to Aaron Blake, and yet his presence played a big part in catching them." Darcy said with a sigh.

"Oh my god. I have to call Aunt Mae. She must be going crazy not knowing what's happened to us." Darcy jumped to her feet.

"Kelly, are the lines open to Seattle yet?" Toni asked.

"Oh sure. They been working for over an hour now," Kelly answered sweetly.

"Can Ms. Bennett use the phone? She must call her aunt."

"Of course. Just press nine and dial your number. Come on in Ernie's office. He won't mind, and it will give you some privacy."

After her conversation with Mae, and explaining at least a dozen times that she was all right, Darcy hung up.

"I didn't have the heart to tell her about the house," Darcy said sadly.

"We'll tell her when we get home. No need to worry her any more than necessary." Toni answered patting Darcy on the back.

The food arrived and they had no trouble devouring the meal. Finally, Toni sat back satisfied and full. Darcy felt better since taking the aspirin even though her nose was running profusely now.

"Ernie and Bobby are back," Glory called out.

Toni rose and met them at the door. They looked tired and dirty.

"So, how did it go?" Toni asked.

"He's dead all right," Ernie answered. "Pretty messy scene up there. He was a big one, no doubt about that."

"Did you bring the body in?" Toni questioned.

"No, we covered him up and left. Can't get the coroner out there tonight. We barely made it through on the road ourselves; it's just too dark."

"Have you notified the Seattle Police yet?"

"No, and I ain't gonna until Bobby and I have some coffee and relax for a minute. It's not everyday we have a mass murderer killed on Whidbey, and the sight of him took some wind out of our sails."

Ernie got up and poured two large mugs of coffee handing one to Bobby. Then he sat down behind his desk, put his head back and closed his eyes. Bobby sat in a chair with his legs spread apart, his head down. Ernie and Bobby stayed this way for three or four minutes. Toni and Darcy sat silently waiting. Finally, Toni got up and walked toward the desk.

"Look Deputy Foster, I know this has been a rough night, but we have to notify Detective Otto Garrison of the Seattle PD as to what's happened here. He and I have been working on this, and another case that are very much connected. I know he'll want to get out here as soon as possible and besides, he'll want to notify the FBI."

Foster looked at Toni. "You wouldn't be tryin' to tell me what to do now would ya?" His tone was not friendly.

"Not at all sir. I think you and your aide have done a great job so far. But this is a state wide investigation, and the sooner they bring in the other agencies, the sooner you can wash your hands of this mess. You and your office have been extremely kind to Ms. Bennett and myself through this whole experience."

Foster smiled at Toni. "Who did ya say I should call?" He picked up the phone.

"Thanks," Toni replied. "Detective Otto Garrison."

Foster spent half an hour relating what he knew about the events of the day to Otto.

"Yeah, she's right here." Foster handed the phone to Toni.

"Toni what the fuck happened? Are you and Darcy okay?" Otto sounded confused and scared.

"We're okay Otto, but I don't think Taylor Austin or Art Wardlow are. Both of them seem to have disappeared.

I'm going to give my statement to Deputy Foster, and then Darcy and I will get a motel room for the night. Please go by Darcy's apartment and bring us some clothes and shoes before you come. I'll give you a blow by blow tomorrow. Right now we're both dead on our feet and need rest. See ya tomorrow my friend." Toni hung up.

"He sounded pretty glad ta hear you were all right. Must be a good friend huh?" Foster said getting up.

"We worked together some years ago, and yes he is a good friend. Now, deputy, would you like to take our statements?"

"Since I don't have a stenographer here, we'll just tape it for tonight. I don't want to leave anything out, and if we wait till morning you might forget something. Get the details while they're still fresh in the mind. Right?"

"You bet," Toni answered smiling.

After an hour Toni and Darcy had told Ernie Foster everything they could about the events leading up to the shooting of Aaron Blake. They did not reveal the relationship he had to Darcy and her family. Foster shook their hands and instructed them to be back early in the morning.

Outside in the lobby, Hal and Pete were waiting. Toni walked up and shook their hands.

"I can't begin to tell you guys how grateful I am to you. You helped save this woman's life today," Toni said as she motioned toward Darcy.

Hal blushed. "Hell. We're just a couple of useless sailors. We didn't do anything."

"Toni has already told me what you did, and as far as I'm concerned you both should be admirals," Darcy said smiling.

"The lady offered us big money to bring her over here. What else could we do?"

"About the money guys, I can't get it until we get back to Seattle. But I give you my word, you'll get it." Toni promised.

"We don't want your money, we had such a good time sailin' through that storm we may do it again sometime, just for the hell of it. Besides, some things go beyond what money can buy." Hal responded as he handed Toni's watch back to her.

"We'll talk about all this later. Ms. Bennett and I are really beat. But you *will* get your money, a deal's a deal."

Deputy Foster came out. "Bobby will give you a ride to the motel. Can't have our star witnesses walking around the streets." Give me a call in the morning and I'll pick you up."

"Thanks Deputy Foster. You're an all right guy."

"Don't thank me. It's all part of the job. Maybe Bobby should run you by the drug store so you can pick up some cold medicine for Ms. Bennett. Oh, and call me Ernie."

Toni and Darcy waved and got into the patrol car with Bobby. He pulled away heading toward the drug store. Toni laid her head back against the seat and closed her eyes.

I've never known people like this. Rough on the outside and tender on the inside. They're all so open and honest. If they don't like what you say or do, they let you know right up front, and then it's forgotten. Wonder how they'd react if they knew we were lesbians? Toni was deep in thought.

"Here we are." Bobby's high voice startled Toni.

They pulled up in front of the Coupeville Drug Store. Toni looked over at Darcy. Her head was leaning to one side; she was already asleep.

"Thanks Bobby. I'll only be a minute," Toni whispered.

Paying with her charge card, she bought cough syrup, aspirin, cold pills, a hair brush, a couple of tooth brushes, tooth paste, and deodorant. The girl behind the counter was friendly and helpful. As Toni turned to leave, she gave Toni a big *thank you come again.*

It took only five minutes to reach the motel. They waited in the patrol car while Bobby went in and arranged for a room. Then he drove them to the door.

Toni shook Darcy gently. "Wake up babe, we're here."

Darcy blinked, stretched, and gave out a great yawn.

"We'll see you in the morning Bobby. Thanks for everything." Toni said quietly.

Bobby smiled and drove off. Toni helped Darcy to the door and then to bed. *Poor baby, she's really out of it,* Toni thought. Quickly she got a glass of water and woke Darcy enough so she could take two cold tablets. Darcy never opened her eyes. She mumbled something and laid back down.

Toni crawled in next to Darcy, hugging her back. Then she fell into a deep sleep.

Carol Masters was beside herself with worry. She paced back and forth while chewing feverishly on her lower lip. A deep frown cut across her forehead.

"Why haven't I heard from Taylor? She should have been back by now," Carol said out loud.

Carol hadn't slept a wink all night. Between the storm and the vision of Darcy laying dead somewhere, she had been unable to close her eyes for more than a minute or two. The bags were packed and tickets to Rio were stuffed in her purse. She and Taylor had opened a bank account there when they first began embezzling money from the bank. They had hoped to get away with at least a million, but Sue Olsen had put a stop to that plan. At this point, nothing seemed to matter but knowing what had happened on the island and having Taylor walk through the front door.

Carol jumped and froze in place as she heard the thud against the door. Holding her breath, she waited for it to open. After a few moments, she realized no one was there. She carefully approached the door and with a shaking hand turned the knob.

Carol drew the door open a couple of inches. The street was empty. As she turned to go back inside her gaze fell on the newspaper lying at her feet. In bold letters, the words *Special Edition* jumped out at her.

She hurried back inside and to the kitchen table. Laying the paper down, she slowly opened it up. *Woman found murdered on Whidbey Island. Aaron Blake shot and killed by ex-policewoman in life and death struggle.* The headline leapt out at her.

"Darcy. My God they already found her," Carol whispered as she continued to read. Slowly she sank into the kitchen chair.

"Wait a minute, this can't be right!" Carol blinked several times as though something was in her eyes, causing her to misread the print before her.

"*Prominent travel agent, Taylor Austin, found lying in muddy ditch strangled to death. She is presumed to have been murdered by killer Aaron Blake. Escaped victim Darcy Bennett confirms Ms. Austin had accompanied her to the island and that Aaron Blake had tried to murder her as well. Art Wardlow local auto mechanic still missing. More details will follow in tonight's edition.*

Carol read the report over and over until it finally sunk in once and for all Taylor was DEAD! She threw the newspaper across the room. The uncontrollable shaking began in her feet and legs and then spread throughout her entire body. Anguish and rage filled her. Carol cried out like a wild animal, her face twisted into a horrible grimace. A few cold words on a piece of paper had ended her whole world.

"Death to you and yours, Darcy," she hissed, "You'll die for sure this time, bitch!"

The ringing of the phone caused Toni to jump. Quickly she grabbed the receiver.

"Hello." Toni's voice was deep and husky with sleep.

"This is Kelly with your wake up call," the cheery voice replied.

"What time is it?" Toni asked.

"It's 7:30 a.m. Ernie would like you girls here by eight thirty, or sooner."

"Okay Kelly we'll be there." Toni hung up.

"Darcy honey, wake up. It's time to get up." Toni urged.

Darcy moaned and pulled the covers higher over her head.

Toni laughed. "Come on now. If you're a good *girl* I'll take you out for a nice breakfast."

Darcy pulled the covers down past her nose and glared at Toni.

"Can't you see I'm dying of pneumonia? Don't you even care?" Darcy whined, and with that burst into a gale of coughing and sniffing.

"Here take a swig of this." Toni pushed the bottle of cough syrup under Darcy nose.

Darcy tipped the bottle and took two gulps, making a horrible face as she did. Then she blew her nose, and looked at Toni again. Darcy's eyes were puffy and watery.

"Yep, you got a doozer of a cold, all right. We've got to get you home to bed as soon as possible."

With more prodding and pushing, Toni finally got Darcy up and into the bathroom. She heard the shower running. *A good hot shower will help,* Toni thought. After ten minutes Darcy emerged from the bathroom.

"It's your turn. Please hurry. I need some coffee real bad."

Toni kissed Darcy on the cheek. "I will, and then we'll go to the motel coffee shop and get a bite to eat. I know that'll make you feel better."

Darcy smiled weakly and sat down on the bed.

Toni quickly showered and dressed. She packed up the few items she had and picked up the phone, ignoring the slightly raw scratchy feeling in the back of her throat.

"Hi Kelly. It's Toni Underwood. Will you ask Bobby to pick us up at the coffee shop in about forty-five minutes? We need something to eat before we come in."

As they stepped out the door a blast of cold air hit them in the face. Darcy shivered.

"Damn, we don't need this," Toni grumbled as she pulled Darcy along toward the coffee shop.

Bobby drove up just as Darcy was finishing the last of her orange juice. She was feeling better and was a bit more alert.

Darcy smiled at Toni. "I think I just may live after all."

"Good morning," Bobby said as they got in the patrol car. "Feeling better?"

"One of us is," Toni answered, pointing at Darcy.

Otto greeted Toni and Darcy at the police station door.

"God damn, I've never been so happy to see two people in my life."

"How ya doin' Otto?" Toni smiled warmly.

"Just fine now, Toni. Just fine."

They followed him into Ernie's office.

"Have a seat ladies," Ernie said as he gestured to two chairs.

"So tell me again what happened out at Mae Harmon's place yesterday. I need all the details. I brought Allison Perry with me to take your statements," Otto said motioning to the tall woman sitting at a small table next to Ernie's desk.

"Before we get started Otto, what's happening with the investigation of Carol and Taylor? Have you wrapped that up?" Toni asked as she leaned forward in her chair.

"Just about Toni. We put another auditor on it. She's retracing Sue Olsen's steps, and she's on to something. It has to do with large personal loans approved by Carol Masters. We're auditing phone calls to her office from various banks around Washington, Oregon, and California. It's beginning to look like she and her friend had quite a scam going for some time, and Sue Olsen stumbled onto it. I'll have more details this afternoon."

"Have you arrested Carol Masters yet?" Toni asked.

"No. We want to be sure we've got a good, tight case first."

"When you do get her Otto, please let me go with you. I got a couple of things that need to be said to that witch."

"The only way I'll let you go Toni, is if you give me your word you won't start any shit."

"You have my word Otto. I'm a changed person, haven't you noticed?" Toni replied with a sly smile.

"I'll believe that one when cows fly," Otto answered. "Now, lets hear your story."

First Darcy and then Toni retold their experiences. They were careful not to leave out any details. When they were through, Otto Garrison sat back, giving out a long low whistle.

"This whole thing is unbelievable. Whatta nightmare. Thank god Aaron Blake is finally out of the picture. I was beginning to feel he was unstoppable."

"Have you got men searching Mae's property?" Toni asked.

"Yeah, I brought a half dozen with me, and Ernie has ten volunteers working out there. In fact, we're going there now. Do you and Darcy want to tag along?"

Toni looked at Darcy. "I don't think so Otto, unless we have to, that is. Darcy isn't feeling well and I know she wants to get home to her aunt."

"Toni, why don't you go ahead. I know you're curious and want to follow through with this to the end. Besides, you can take a damage report on my aunt's home. Maybe it isn't as bad as we thought," Darcy said sniffing.

"You need me to help tell Mae the news, and I won't leave you when you're sick," Toni answered.

Darcy smiled at her. "I'm fine. I've had worse colds then this, and I think maybe it would be best if I speak with my aunt alone first. It will give me a chance to break it gently. And I know you're dying to go with Otto."

"Come on Toni. I can use ya out there. It will help us to retrace your steps." Otto pleaded.

Toni looked at both of them. "Okay, I'll go with you Otto. Give us a couple of minutes to change our clothes and then I'm all yours."

Toni and Darcy changed quickly.

"I want you to rest. Do you understand?" Toni said with a frown.

"I will. I have to call work and get some more time off. Mr. Rebal probably thinks I've dropped off the end of the earth."

Toni kissed Darcy and held her close. "I'll see you soon."

Otto had a car take Darcy to the ferry landing. Toni told her where the car was parked and gave Darcy the keys.

"You and that lady got something goin'?" Otto asked.

"I think so Otto. I think so," Toni answered as they watched the patrol car drive off.

As they approached Mae's house, Toni and Otto could see several men gathered near Toni's ditched car. Otto pulled over.

"What's goin' on? You guys find somethin'?" Otto called out.

"Yeah, and it ain't pretty," an officer called back. "Come see for yourself."

Otto and Toni walked to the water filled ditch. The officers on the scene had already pulled Taylor's body from the muddy water. She lay there, her eyes filled with mud, her mouth open.

"God, what a mess." Otto whispered. "Cover her up. The coroner should be here anytime now. Two of you guys stay here."

Toni didn't say a word. She had seen many dead bodies, and it had always distressed her, but this time she felt nothing. All she saw was poor Sue Olsen lying dead in the alley behind Darcy's apartment building. She could feel no pity for Taylor Austin.

They returned to the car and continued driving toward the house. The sky was gray and a slight mist had begun to fall. Toni pulled her jacket tighter around her body as a chill ran through her. She hadn't realized how hard it would be to see Aaron Blake again, and relive what had happened in the old house the day before. Even in death, Aaron Blake remained a monster.

Otto stopped the car in front of the old house. "Are ya ready for this?" He looked at Toni questionly.

"I'm never ready for this kinda shit. Let's just do it," Toni answered, tightening her jaw muscles.

Silently they walked up the front steps and entered the house. Toni hesitated at the bottom of the staircase. Then she took a deep breath and started up. They tested each step before putting any weight on it, inching their way along until they reached the landing. An icy wind hit Toni in the back of the neck. It was very quiet. As chilled as she was, Toni felt beads of sweat breaking out on her upper lip.

Otto stopped outside the bedroom doorway. "I can handle this alone, if you wanna stay out here."

"I've come this far, a few more steps aren't going to kill me," Toni answered. Her mouth felt dry and it was hard to swallow.

As they stepped inside, Toni suddenly froze in place. Otto's mouth dropped open as he scanned the bedroom with his eyes. Where Aaron's body had fallen, only a large puddle of blood remained.

Neither of them spoke. Otto drew his gun. Toni still stood motionless, stunned. Otto took her arm and slowly began backing out of the room. He looked over his shoulder, making sure no one was behind them.

In the hall Otto paused. He shook Toni.

"Where the fuck is he? I thought you shot him five times."

Toni blinked. "I did shoot him five times. There's no way he could have lived through it. He was dead. Even Ernie and Bobby said he was dead." Her breath came out in short pants', her heart was pounding in her temples.

"Toni, get a hold of yourself. Use your brain. He has to be dead. We're both logical people. We don't believe in nightmares, or any other weird shit. There has to be an explanation for this."

Toni shook her head as if to clear her mind. "You're right Otto. I know you're right, but you never saw this guy. He was different, like something not of this world . . . like a demon."

"Demon or not, he has to be here somewhere. Everyone just made a mistake. He wasn't dead, that's all. Come on, we're going to search this place from top to bottom. Are you with me?"

Toni looked at Otto. She didn't respond for a few seconds. Her mind was racing now. What if he *is* alive? What if somehow he got back to the mainland? *Darcy!*

"We have to find him." Suddenly panic filled her heart as she grabbed Otto's arm.

They slowly began moving from room to room. Finding nothing on the second floor, they carefully descended the staircase. Again they went from room to room, making a sweep of the whole lower level of the house. There was nothing.

"We have to get the men together and find the bastard," Otto said breathlessly.

"He's gone for Darcy." Toni said. Her voice was trembling.

"Detective Garrison. Detective Garrison."

The loud voice startled Otto and Toni. They whirled around. Running toward them was a young officer from Otto's office.

"Detective Garrison. Come with me. We've found another body."

"Where?" Otto responded.

"Follow me." The officer turned and began running toward the back of the old house. Toni and Otto followed, their hearts pounding.

Laying face down next to the blue Toyota truck was the body of Aaron Blake. His arms were outstretched above his head, and both his fists were clenched.

"Turn him over," Otto said cautiously.

It took all the young officer's strength to pull the body onto its back. They all gasped as they looked into the face of Aaron Blake. No one said a word. Aaron lay there a wide grin frozen on his dead lips. His black eyes stared up into theirs.

Finally, Otto whispered, "God, he was a demon."

"He has something in his hands," The officer said.

Toni bent down. Aaron's eyes seemed to follow her every move. She hesitated, and then, with shaking hands she pried his right hand open. Crumpled inside was a picture of Darcy taken on her fifth birthday.

Must have gotten this from Mae's house. Toni thought. She removed the photo from Aaron's cold hand.

Handing the picture to Otto she began working on opening Aaron's left hand. This time, she couldn't straighten the curled up fingers. They were like iron. Finally, Toni stood up.

"We'll have to wait until they get him to the morgue to find out what else the bastard took," Otto said in a disgusted voice.

"He was still trying to get to Darcy," Toni gasped. "He was dead, and still trying to reach her."

"Look!" The young officer suddenly cried out.

As they looked down at Aaron's body, the fingers of his left hand slowly opened, and then lay still.

A butterfly sat in the palm of his huge hand. Its beautiful wings slowly unfolded as though it was waking from a long sleep. The wings began to flutter as it rose into the gray sky. Its glorious colors looked out of place in this dark scene of death.

No one moved. It circled once. Then, suddenly dipping down, it brushed Aaron Blake's lips with its wings.

The beautiful creature rose and flew off into the woods. When they looked back at Aaron Blake his mouth and eyes were closed. For the first time since his birth, Aaron looked calm and serene.

"Don't say a word Toni. His hand opened and eyes closed due to muscle contractions connected with rigormortis that's all." Otto said.

"If you say so Otto, but how the hell did he get here, and where did a butterfly come from at this time of year?"

"I don't know, and I don't want to know," Otto grunted as he turned and walked away.

Toni took one last look at Aaron Blake. "Nightmares *do* die after all, don't they Aaron," she whispered.

Chapter Eighteen

Darcy opened the door to her apartment at 12:30 p.m. Her head felt as if it weighed fifty pounds. Her eyes burned and her nose was so stuffed she had to breathe through her mouth. She knew, no matter how bad she felt she was going to have to explain things to her Aunt Mae.

"Hello. I'm home," Darcy called out.

"Oh my god, Darcy, you're home. Oh, thank god," Mae cried out as she rushed to her.

Mae held Darcy, kissing her face and crying at the same time.

"It's okay Aunt Mae, I'm all right." Darcy patted her gently.

"You don't know how worried I was. I couldn't find out anything. You were trapped on the island and I couldn't get to you. And I see you're sick too."

"I have a very bad cold Aunt Mae, that's all. I'm sure with you doctoring me I'll be well before I know it."

"You sit down and I'll get you some hot tea." Mae was flustered. She was running in all directions at one time.

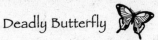

"Aunt Mae, please calm down. I need to tell you some things. Come on, we'll both make that tea. I think you need some too."

They went into the kitchen. Mae tried to fill the teapot but her hands were shaking so badly she dropped it.

"Oh my lord." Mae began crying once more.

"You sit down and let me get the tea started okay?"

Darcy put the pot on the stove. She got two cups and tea bags from the cupboard. Then she sat next to her aunt.

"Aunt Mae, it's over. I'm all right; Toni's all right. Be happy. The nightmare is over." Darcy put her arm around Mae's shoulder.

"I'm trying honey, but for awhile I was so afraid I would never see you again. If anything had happened to you, I don't know what I'd do."

Darcy got up and filled the two cups with boiling water. Returning to the table, she placed the tea bags in the cups. The rising steam felt good on Darcy's nose, and even seemed to clear it for the moment. She reached in her jacket and pulled out two cold tablets. After taking them she sat back and smiled at Mae.

"Aunt Mae, it's so good to see you again, and be home."

"I can't even begin to tell you how good it feels to have you here safe and sound," Mae responded. She was calmer and managed a weak smile.

"If you're up to it, I'm going to tell you everything that's happened. Please, just listen and when I'm finished you can ask me anything you like. Okay?"

"Oh I'm up to it all right. I've waited to hear this for an eternity."

Darcy filled Mae in on all the events of the past two days. She started with how and why Carol and Taylor had lured her to the island and ended her story with the death of Aaron Blake.

"Toni will be here later and fill us both in on any new information I may have missed. Now, there *is* one part of the story I've saved for last, because I know how it's going to affect *you*."

"After all you've told me, I can't imagine anything that would shock or affect me. What is it?"

Darcy took Mae's hand in hers, holding it tight. "Aunt Mae, Aaron Blake completely destroyed your home."

Mae didn't respond. She just stared at Darcy.

"He evidently became enraged when he didn't find us there. He tore the house to shreds. The windows are broken, the doors are all busted, the pictures, lamps, knicknacks, . . . all gone. It literally looks like a bomb exploded inside."

Mae still didn't respond.

"Aunt Mae, did you understand what I said? You're house is ruined. Please aunt Mae, say something."

"That dirty son of a bitch." Mae hissed through her teeth.

"What? What did you say?" Darcy asked leaning closer.

"That dirty son of a bitch!" Mae screamed.

Darcy jumped, almost falling from her chair.

"If he thought that would ruin my life, or stop me from living and going on, well that bastard has another thing coming."

Mae's eyes were flashing, her face was red, and she was fighting mad. Darcy was shocked. She had prepared herself for a crying whimpering woman ready to give up her home and move out. Instead, Darcy was sitting across the table from a firecracker exploding all over the room.

"Tomorrow, I'm going over to the island and get Harvey Iversen. We'll take a look at the place, he'll give me an estimate on repairs, which I'll accept, and we'll make it better than new by the time we're through. It needed some upgrading done anyway. Then we're going to burn that old rotten house down to the ground. No more sad memories for us."

Darcy laughed. "I can't believe you. I thought you'd be falling apart right now, and here you are already making plans for restorations. I haven't seen you this worked up and excited in years."

"Maybe that's been my problem for too long. I've been in a rut. Nothing new going on. Well Aaron Blake, thank you, you crawling piece of slime. I hope you can hear me down in Hell. You didn't beat us."

Darcy got up and hugged Mae. "That's the Aunt I know and love so much."

"Come on now honey, I want you to lay down and rest. I'll wake you as soon as Toni gets home."

"Okay Aunt Mae. I guess I really am beat."

Mae pulled the covers down and fluffed Darcy's pillows. Darcy put on her long flannel nightgown and crawled into bed. She was asleep almost before her head hit the pillow.

The room was quite dark, and Darcy had no idea what time it was when her eyelids flew open at the sound of loud angry voices coming from the living room. Still half asleep, she threw the covers off and ran to the bedroom door. The light in the living room blinded her for a moment. She blinked her eyes trying to adjust them to the bright lights. Then she saw her.

Carol Masters was standing in the doorway screaming at Mae.

"I'm telling you, you can't come in here," Mae was yelling back at Carol.

Carol caught sight of Darcy and pushed her way passed Mae, almost knocking her down. In an instant she was in Darcy's face.

"What did you do to my poor Taylor, you bitch," Carol screamed.

Darcy felt dizzy and was still trying to get her bearings.

"I said, what did you do to Taylor," Carol screamed again.

"What are you talking about? I didn't do anything to Taylor. Have you lost your mind?"

"Taylor's dead! Do you understand? She's dead. And you were with her. You killed her!"

Carol grabbed Darcy's arm.

"Let go of me," Darcy said in a low voice as she jerked her arm free.

"Should I call the police?" Mae said.

"That might be a good idea," Darcy answered calmly.

"You aren't calling anyone you fucking old woman," Carol yelled as she jerked the phone out of Mae's hand, and ripped it from the wall.

"Aunt Mae get out of here and go to the neighbors . . . NOW!" Darcy ordered grabbing Carol by the shoulder.

Mae ran out the door. Carol turned back toward Darcy. Her eyes were wild.

"Look Carol, I don't know what you think I've done, but I didn't kill Taylor."

"You're a fucking liar. Taylor was supposed to come back alone. You were the one who had to die. And now here you are, and she's gone."

"Die? What are you talking about?"

"Don't play games with me, bitch. That nosy wimp Sue told you everything before Taylor got to her didn't she? Don't you see? I would have done anything for Taylor to make her happy. She wanted lots of money and I got it for her. She took care of Sue, and she was going to take care of you too. She was strong, how did you do it?"

"I'm telling you I don't know what you're talking about." Darcy was screaming now too. She still had no idea that Aaron had killed Taylor on the island.

Carol lunged toward Darcy. Darcy sidestepped Carol's attack. Carol stumbled and hit the coffee table as she went down to one knee. Grabbing a heavy crystal ashtray from the table, Carol got to her feet and started toward Darcy again.

"It won't do you any good to run. I have nothing to lose now. My life ended when I heard Taylor was dead. I'm going to kill you, and then that fucking *dyke* Toni. How does that sound, bitch?"

"You shouldn't threaten Toni, Carol. I won't let you touch her."

Running wildly at Darcy, Carol raised the ashtray above her head. Again, Darcy stepped to one side, but this time she kicked Carol as hard as she could just above the knee cap. Carol dropped the ashtray as she grabbed her leg. Darcy caught Carol in the side of the jaw with her fist, knocking her down. Then she jumped on top of Carol and began beating Carol's face with her fists.

Darcy paused for a moment and put her face close to Carol's. "You and that piece of shit you called a lover killed one of my friends, and now you come in here looking for revenge because Taylor got what she deserved. You think I'm going to stand by and let you hurt Toni? Think again you fucking cunt!" With that, Darcy started hitting Carol again.

Suddenly two strong arms were around Darcy pulling her away from the helpless Carol Masters. Darcy struggled to free herself.

"Hold it. Hold it." Toni's voice was saying in Darcy's ear.

Darcy stopped struggling, and the grip around her relaxed. She turned, and found herself staring into Toni's face. The police already had Carol on her feet, placing hand-cuffs on her wrists. Darcy was completely confused.

Carol's nose was bleeding, and her right eye had begun swelling. Her hair hung wildly in her face. The once cool sophisticated Carol Masters had been reduced to a blub-bering piece of putty.

Darcy threw her arms around Toni's neck.

"Where did you come from?" Darcy asked, out of breath.

"Otto and I, and two cops were just on our way to your door when Mae came running out. She told us what was going down. Great timing, don't you agree? Although I can see you really didn't need our help." Toni smiled.

"I'm so glad you're here. Carol was crazy. She accused me of killing Taylor. She said she was going to kill you, and . . . wait a minute. If you saw aunt Mae in the hall, then you must have been here all the time." Darcy pulled away from Toni.

"Well, kind of. You see, Otto wanted to hear Carol's confession, so we waited just a couple of minutes before we came in."

"Let me get this straight. You listened to what Carol had to say, and then you watched as my life was being threat-ened, and you just let it go on without trying to save me?"

"Well, not exactly. When Carol ran at you with the ash tray I was going to make my move, but you took care of the situation all by yourself. You seemed to be having such a good time, I just let you have at it for a minute. That's all." Toni smiled again.

"You stood there with my life on the line and didn't do anything?"

Darcy's eyes were like ice. She jerked away from Toni and stomped off to the bedroom, slamming the door behind her.

"Looks like ya got some heavy duty work ahead of you here." Otto said with a smirk on his face.

"Fuck you," Toni answered jokingly.

"I think that's my cue to exit. Be at the station bright and early tomorrow. I think we got this whole thing in the bag. And please, tell Ms. Bennett we need her statement too."

Mae looked a Toni. "Err, I think I'll just go over to Mrs. Newhouse's for awhile. She's very upset about all the commotion. Maybe I can help calm her down." Mae closed the door quietly behind her.

Toni stood alone in the middle of the room and looked around.

"Just like all the other rats, desert the sinking ship," she mumbled, shrugging her shoulders. Her throat was sore and she had a splitting headache.

Toni walked to the bedroom door and rapped. No answer. She knocked harder. No answer.

"Darcy, I have to talk to you. You have to let me explain. You weren't in danger. I was there ready to jump that bitch if I believed she was going to hurt one hair on your head. You are the most important thing in my life. Did you hear me? Please open the door." Toni's nose was beginning to feel as if it were full of cotton.

The door flew open and Darcy stood motionless glaring at Toni.

Darcy opened her mouth slowly, as if to speak. Toni held her breath waiting for a response. With that Darcy sneezed six times. Toni grabbed her, Darcy's arms went around Toni's neck.

"How can I stay mad at you? Look at that *innocent* face." Darcy said with a mocking tone.

"Think they can get used to two *lesbos* wandering around on Whidbey Island?" Toni whispered into Darcy's ear.

"Haven't you noticed anything *funny* about Ernie and Bobby?" Darcy whispered back.

Toni pulled away looking at Darcy.

"Well?" Darcy said raising her eyebrow.

Toni stood motionless staring into Darcy's face for a few moments. "Well, I'll be damned! Ernie and Bobby huh?" she finally replied, raising both eyebrows in surprise.

Suddenly, without warning, tears filled Toni's eyes and they became narrow slits. Her nostrils flared; her lips curled back exposing her teeth and gums. Toni's twisted mouth gaped open while her tongue flicked in and out. Her body became hard and rigid as her head jerked back. Her whole face changed into a distorted monstrous vision. It was as though some uncontrollable force was consuming her very being.

Darcy jumped back gasping in horror. Covering her face with her hands, she jerked away from Toni. She tried to run! To escape! IT WAS TOO LATE!

Toni's sneezes seemed to rattle the windows and rock the walls of the apartment. Two! Five! Seven times. Toni spun around grabbing hold of the door-jam to steady herself. Again, her face twisted as she staggered to the bed. Three more; worse than the first seven.

Darcy began praying, "Please God, help us all. She has a cold!" Then, she turned and ran for the box of Kleenex.

Rising Tide Press brings you the best in lesbian fiction and nonfiction. We publish books to stir the imagination for women who enjoy ideas that are out of the ordinary.

We are committed to our community and welcome your comments.

We can be reached at our website:
www.risingtidepress.com

About the Author

Mind you, I was raised in the '40s and '50s, when lesbians were described as motorcycle-riding Amazons. And although motorcycles had always scared me, I *was* six-feet tall, and I'd loved women all my life. I just wish I'd known sooner that I didn't need to own a motorcycle to get a woman.

I was brought out in the parking lot of the Seattle Zoo, at four in the morning, but that's another story. After two years in Washington, I moved back to Southern California, where I was born.

Writing has always been my secret passion, but being a single parent, I was too busy raising my daughter and myself to do anything but work. I live alone, now-a condition I am learning to enjoy, and have lengthy conversations with my two dogs and cat, because I like the answers they give.

Now available from Rising Tide Press:

<u>By The Sea Shore</u> by Sandra A. Morris

Sydney lurched to a halt at the kitchen door of 'The Shooting Gallery'. She turned off the car and cradled her head on the steering wheel, seemingly in no hurry to leave the sanctuary of the BMW's compact interior. She chastised herself for following Jennifer when she left the airport. She had not been surprised that Jess Shore had been there. Harley had spoken with Meg the other day and knew that Jess and Buster were expected sometime that week. Just Sydney's luck that she had arrived when she did, running smack dab into Jennifer. Did Jennifer and Jess know each other, Sydney wondered. She couldn't imagine how, but one never knew.

To make things even worse, Jennifer had probably heard the honk of warning Sydney had been forced to blast when the dark figure had darted from the bushes outside Jess's place, directly into the path of her car. Had she not veered suddenly, she felt sure, she would have hit the stranger in black. She would call Jess later in the day and alert her to the incident. Strangers, especially this time of year, and dressed like some movie of the week cat burglar, were likely up to no good. Sydney knew that break-ins in the off-season were a problem for Provincetown's summer residents, and hoped that all was well at Jess's place.

Moving laboriously, Sydney crossed the narrow path to the door and entered the hub of the bistro, her home away from home: the kitchen.

The usually comforting sight of the gleaming copper pots and pans, the redolent smells of hundreds of spices and flavorings and the barren quiet of the interior beyond failed to ease the tension between her eyes.

"Damn you Jennifer Eastcott," she seethed aloud. Your timing sucks, she thought.

She swore an oath and whipped herself into a flurry of activity. Sydney didn't like discord and was determined to pull herself out of her current funk. Whatever the special was tonight, it would surely be chopped, pureed, or diced to within an inch of its life.

Sydney showed no mercy, even as she cleaved into an innocent carrot, sending half of it across the floor only to stop dead against a sneakered foot. She squinted at the silhouette in the doorway, recognition dawning sickly on her.

"What are you doing here?" Sydney questioned.
"I have a message for you, Sydney," the voice whispered.
From behind her, too late, Sydney sensed the presence of another body. As she turned, a white-hot pain exploded across the back of her head and all went dark...

More Fiction to Stir the Imagination
From Rising Tide Press

CLOUD NINE AFFAIR Katherine E. Kreuter

Christine Grandy—rebellious, wealthy, twenty-something—has disappeared, along with her lover Monica Ward. Desperate to bring her home, Christine's millionaire father hires Paige Taylor. But the trail to Christine is mined with obstacles, while powerful enemies plot to eliminate her. Eventually, Paige discovers that this mission is far more dangerous than she dreamed. A witty, sophisticated mystery by the best-selling author of Fool Me Once, filled with colorful characters, plot twists, and romance. **$11.99**

THE DEPOSITION Katherine E. Kreuter

It is April in Paris and the Deposition's loopy narrator, G.B. is plotting the caper of capers. This provocative and hilarious novel by the author of the Paige Taylor Mystery Series resonates with gasps and guffaws. **$12.00**

STORM RISING Linda Kay Silva

The excitement continues in this wonderful continuation of TROPICAL STORM. Join Megan and Connie as they set out to find Delta and bring her home. The meaning of friendship and love is explored as Delta, Connie, Megan and friends struggle to stay alive and stop General Zahn. Again the Costa Rican Rain Forest is the setting for another fast-paced action adventure. Storm fans won't want to miss this next installment in the Delta Stevens Mystery Series. **$12.00**

TROPICAL STORM Linda Kay Silva

Another winning, action-packed adventure featuring smart and sassy heroines, an exotic jungle setting, and a plot with more twists and turns than a coiled cobra. Megan has disappeared into the Costa Rican rain forest and it's up to Delta and Connie to find her. Can they reach Megan before it's too late? Will Storm risk everything to save the woman she loves? Fast-paced, full of wonderful characters and surprises. Not to be missed. **$11.99**

CALLED TO KILL Joan Albarella

Nikki Barnes, Reverend, teacher and Vietnam Vet is once again entangled in a complex web of murder and drugs when her past collides with the present. Set in the rainy spring of Buffalo, Dr. Ginni Clayton and her friend Magpie add spice and romance as Nikki tries to solve the mystery that puts her own life in danger. A fun and exciting read. **$12.00**

AGENDA FOR MURDER Joan Albarella

A compelling mystery about the legacies of love and war, set on a sleepy college campus. Though haunted by memories of her tour of duty in Vietnam, Nikki Barnes is finally putting back the pieces of her life, only to collide with murder and betrayal. **$11.99**

ONE SUMMER NIGHT Gerri Hill

Johanna Marshall doesn't usually fall into bed with someone she just met, but Kelly Sambino isn't just anyone. Hurt by love and labeled a womanizer, can these two women learn to trust one another and let love find its way? **$12.00**

BY THE SEA SHORE Sandra Morris (avail 10/00)

A quiet retreat turns into more investigative work for Jess Shore in the summer town of Provincetown, MA. This page-turner mystery will keep you entertained as Jess struggles with her individuality while solving an attempted murder case. **$12.00**

AND LOVE CAME CALLING Beverly Shearer

A beautifully told love story as old as time, steeped in the atmosphere of the Old West. Danger lights the fire of passion between two women whose lives become entwined when Kendra (Kenny), on the run from the law, happily stumbles upon the solitary cabin where Sophie has been hiding from her own past. Together, they learn that love can overcome all obstacles. **$11.99**

SIDE DISH Kim Taylor

A genuinely funny yet tender novel which follows the escapades of Muriel, a twenty-something burned—out waitress with a college degree, who has turned gay slacker living into an art form. Getting by on margaritas and old movies, she seems to have resigned herself to low standards, simple pleasures, and erotic daydreams. But in secret, Muriel is searching for true love. **$11.99**

COMING ATTRACTIONS
Bobbi D. Marolt

Helen Townsend reluctantly admits she's tried of being lonely…and of being closeted. Enter Princess Charming in the form of Cory Chamberlain, a gifted concert pianist. And Helen embraces joy once again. But can two women find happiness when one yearns to break out of the closet and breathe free, while the other fears that it will destroy her career? A delicious blend of humor, heart and passion—a novel that captures the bliss and blundering of love. **$11.99**

ROUGH JUSTICE
Claire Youmans

When Glenn Lowry's sunken fishing boat turns up four years after its disappearance, foul play is suspected. Classy, ambitious Prosecutor Janet Schilling immediately launches a murder investigation, which produces several surprising suspects-one of them, her own former lover Catherine Adams, now living a reclusive life on an island. A real page-turner! **$10.99**

NO CORPSE
Nancy Sanra

The third Tally McGinnis mystery is set aboard an Olivia Cruise. Tally and Katie thought they were headed out for some sun and fun. Instead, Tally finds herself drawn into a reunion cruise gone awry. When women start turning up dead, it is up to Tally and Cid to find the murderer and unravel a decades old mystery. Sanra fans new and old, won't be disappointed. **$12.00**

NO ESCAPE
Nancy Sanra

This edgy, fast-paced whodunit set in picturesque San Francisco, will keep you guessing. Lesbian PI Tally McGinnis is called into action when Dr. Rebecca Toliver is charged with the murder of her lover Melinda. Is the red rose left at the scene the crime the signature of a copycat killer, or is the infamous Marcia Cox back, and up to her old, evil tricks again? **$11.99**

NO WITNESSES
Nancy Sanra

This cliffhanger of a mystery set in San Francisco, introduces Detective Tally McGinnis, whose ex-lover Pamela Tresdale is arrested for the grisly murder of a wealthy Texas heiress. Tally rushes to the rescue despite friends' warnings, and is drawn once again into Pamela's web of deception and betrayal as she attempts to clear her and find the real killer. **$9.99**

DEADLY RENDEZVOUS
Diane Davidson

A string of brutal murders in the middle of the desert plunges Lt. Toni Underwood and her lover Megan into a high profile investigation, which uncovers a world of drugs, corruption and murder, as well as the dark side of the human mind. Explosive, fast-paced, & action-packed. **$9.99**

DEADLY GAMBLE
Diane Davidson

Las-Vegas-city of bright lights and dark secrets-is the perfect setting for this intriguing sequel to DEADLY RENDEZVOUS. Former police detective Toni Underwood and her partner Sally Murphy are catapulted back into the world of crime by a letter from Toni's favorite aunt. Now a prominent madam, Vera Valentine fears she is about to me murdered-a distinct possibility. **$11.99**

RETURN TO ISIS
Jean Stewart

It is the year 2093, and Whit, a bold woman warrior from an Amazon nation, rescues Amelia from a dismal world where females are either breeders or drones. During their arduous journey back to the shining all-women's world of Artemis, they are unexpectedly drawn to each other. This engaging first book in the series has it all-romance, mystery, and adventure. **$9.99**

ISIS RISING
Jean Stewart

In this stirring romantic fantasy, the familiar cast of lovable characters begins to rebuild the colony of Isis, burned to the ground ten years earlier by the dread Regulators. But evil forces threaten to destroy their dream. A swashbuckling futuristic adventure and an endearing love story all rolled into one. **$11.99**

WARRIORS OF ISIS
Jean Stewart

The third lusty tale is one of high adventure and passionate romance among the Freeland Warriors. Arinna Sojourner, the evil product of genetic engineering, vows to destroy the fledgling colony of Isis with her incredible psychic powers. Whit, Kali, and other warriors battle to save their world, in this novel bursting with life, love, heroines and villains. *A Lambda Literary Award Finalist* **$11.99**

EMERALD CITY BLUES
Jean Stewart

When comfortable yuppie world of Chris Olson and Jennifer Hart collides with the desperate lives of Reb and Flynn, two lesbian runaways struggling to survive on the streets of Seattle, the forecast is trouble. A gritty, enormously readable novel of contemporary lesbigay life, which raises real questions about the meaning of family and community. This book is an excellent choice for young adults and the more mature reader. **$11.99**

DANGER IN HIGH PLACES
Sharon Gilligan

Set against the backdrop of Washington, D.C., this riveting mystery introduces freelance photographer and amateur sleuth, Alix Nicholson. Alix stumbles on a deadly scheme, and with the help of a lesbian congressional aide, unravels the mystery. **$9.99**

DANGER! CROSS CURRENTS
Sharon Gilligan

The exciting sequel to Danger in High Places brings freelance photographer Alix Nicholson face-to-face with an old love and a murder. When Alix's landlady turns up dead, and her much younger lover, Leah Claire, the prime suspect, Alix launches a frantic campaign to find the real killer. **$9.99**

HEARTSONE AND SABER
Jacqui Singleton

You can almost hear the sabers clash in this rousing tale of good and evil, of passionate love between a bold warrior queen and a beautiful healer with magical powers. **$10.99**

PLAYING FOR KEEPS
Stevie Rios

In this sparkling tale of love and adventure, Lindsay West an oboist, travels to Caracas, where she meets three people who change her life forever: Rob Heron a gay man, who becomes her dearest friend; her lover Mercedes Luego, a lovely cellist, who takes Lindsay on a life-altering adventure down the Amazon; and the mysterious jungle-dwelling woman Arminta, who touches their souls. **$10.99**

LOVESPELL
Karen Williams

A deliciously erotic and humorous love story in which Kate Gallagher, a shy veterinarian, and Allegra, who has magic at her fingertips, fall in love. A masterful blend of fantasy and reality, this beautifully written story will delight your heart and imagination. **$12.00**

NIGHTSHADE
Karen Williams

Alex Spherris finds herself the new owner of a magical bell, which some people would kill for. She is ushered into a strange & wonderful world and meets Orielle, who melts her frozen heart. A heart-warming romance spun in the best tradition of storytelling. **$11.99**

FEATHERING YOUR NEST:
An Interactive Workbook & Guide to a Loving Lesbian Relationship
Gwen Leonhard, M.ED./Jennie Mast, MSW

This fresh, insightful guide and workbook for lesbian couples provides effective ways to build and nourish your relationships. Includes fun exercises & creative ways to spark romance, solve conflict, fight fair, conquer boredom, spice up your sex lives. **$14.99**

SHADOWS AFTER DARK
Ouida Crozier

While wings of death are spreading over her own world, Kyril is sent to earth to find the cure. Here, she meets the beautiful but lonely Kathryn, and they fall deeply in love. But gradually, Kathryn learns that her exotic new lover has been sent to earth with a purpose—to save her own dying vampire world. A tender, finely written story. **$9.95**

SWEET BITTER LOVE
Rita Schiano

Susan Fredrickson is a woman of fire and ice—a successful high-powered executive, she is by turns sexy and aloof. From the moment writer Jenny Ceretti spots her at the Village Coffeehouse, her serene life begins to change. As their friendship explodes into a blazing love affair, Jenny discovers that all is not as it appears, while Susan is haunted by ghosts from a past that won't stay hidden. A roller-coaster romance which vividly captures the rhythm and feel of love's sometimes rocky ride and the beauty of life after recovery. **$10.99**

Also available from Rising Tide Press:

	TITLE	AUTHOR	PRICE
❏	Agenda for Murder	Joan Albarella	11.99
❏	And Love Came Calling	Beverly Shearer	11.99
❏	By The Sea Shore	Sandra A. Morris	12.00
❏	Called to Kill	Joan Albarella	12.00
❏	Cloud Nine Affair	Katherine Kreuter	11.99
❏	Coming Attractions	Katherine Kreuter	11.99
❏	Danger! Cross Currents	Sharon Gilligan	9.99
❏	Danger in High Places	Sharon Gilligan	9.95
❏	Deadly Butterfly	Diane Davidson	12.00
❏	Deadly Gamble	Diane Davidson	11.99
❏	Deadly Rendezvous	Diane Davidson	9.99
❏	Dreamcatcher	Lori Byrd	9.99
❏	Emerald City Blues	Jean Stewart	11.99
❏	Feathering Your Nest	Leonhard/Mast	14.99
❏	Heartstone and Saber	Jaqui Singleton	10.99
❏	Isis Rising	Jean Stewart	11.99
❏	Legacy of the Lake	Judith Hartsock	12.00
❏	Love Spell	Karen Williams	12.00
❏	Nightshade	Karen Williams	11.99
❏	No Escape	Nancy Sanra	11.99
❏	No Witness	Nancy Sanra	11.99
❏	No Corpse	Nancy Sanra	12.00
❏	One Summer Night	Gerri Hill	12.00
❏	Playing for Keeps	Stevie Rios	10.99
❏	Return to Isis	Jean Stewart	9.99
❏	Rough Justice	Claire Youmans	10.99
❏	Shadows After Dark	Ouida Crozier	9.95
❏	Side Dish	Kim Taylor	11.99
❏	Storm Rising	Linda Kay Silva	12.00
❏	Sweet Bitter Love	Rita Schiano	10.99
❏	Taking Risks	Judith McDaniel	12.00
❏	The Deposition	Katherine Kreuter	12.00
❏	Tropical Storm	Linda Kay Silva	11.99
❏	Undercurrents	Laurel Mills	12.00
❏	Warriors of Isis	Jean Stewart	11.99
❏	When It's Love	Beverly Shearer	12.00

Please send me the books I have checked. I have enclosed a check or money order (not cash], plus $4 for the first book and $1 for each additional book to cover shipping and handling.

Name (please print)_____

Address_____

City _____State_____Zip_____

AZ residents, please add 7% tax to total.

RISING TIDE PRESS, PO BOX 30457, TUCSON AZ 85751